breaking spades

HAMDEN SERIES 4

W. Ferraro

Table of Contents

Dedication

For Emma

Never allow anyone to make you forget your dreams. You've brought love and admiration into my life in the smallest and most beautiful of forms. My love for you will never waver. Nor will the sound of my applause.

For Haley, Alexis and Kailey

You are beautiful on the outside but so
much more on the inside, never change.

For Kristin

Thank you for being a beacon in the darkness of my new world. Your friendship and laughter helps me through. It gives me the strength to know just because it isn't the beaten path doesn't mean it is the wrong road.

For Amy

For an amazing new friendship, a newfound sister of my soul, and the connection of similar sarcastic dirty minded spirits.

Special Thanks

To my Hamden Helpers (aka Hamden Beauties)
You all have made this journey amazing. You share and spread the word of Hamden, opening the eyes of so many more people than I could have possibly imagined. You all hold a special place in my heart and I couldn't do this without you. Thank you for all the support and incredible laughs you each give me every day.

My wonderful and incredible BETA Team
Deb, Stacy, Amy, Kristy, Tracey, Kim, Jen and Alice
You are always willing to drop what you are doing to read, give feedback and or humor me. I appreciate all of you and genuinely value your input. I am very well aware the success of Hamden is in large part because of you.

For helping to ensure accuracy with the military scene, I'd like to give a special thanks to Tracey and Jeremiah. As well as Randi and Robert, Ashley and Shaun, and one of my very favorite people on the planet, Henry.

To all the blogs and bloggers that have fallen in love with Hamden and my Hotties, I thank you and hope you know how humbled I am by your support. There are so many to name but some that require a special little shout out; Book Addicts Mumma, It Started with a Book Blog, Reviews by Tammy and Kim, Maria's Book Blog, Three Chicks and Their Books, Stephanie's Book Reports, the Scarlet Siren and Two Sassy Chicks.

To Angela at Fictional Formats for making my words that much prettier.
To Rebecca at Berto Designs for making the most beautiful covers and giving amazing, "first look punch."
To Rae at 77peaches, thank you for understanding my need to keep my voice my own, for knowing when to insist and when to compromise.

A special shout out to Tracey, Heather, Lynetta, Alice, Mary, Mayra, and Shelley, it takes a lot of guts to put yourself out there. I believe in all of you and am humbled by your support but most of all, your amazing friendships. I will continue to root for each and every one of you and please know I am sincerely a genuine fan of all your amazing talents.

Mom, thank you for continuing to wrap me in love and show me the kind of mother I want to be to my babies.

Prologue

I want to be here. This is what I want. Maybe this will be enough. Maybe this will show him I can be what he wants.

"Come on, Kitten, let's get these pants out of the way," Jarod urged, his voice husky, as he turned in the cramped back seat of his 1992 Camaro. As they struggled to contort their bodies into position, CeCe noticed how cool the leather felt against her bare thighs and how sensitive her skin had become as she winced at a scratch from a tear in the seat. Neither sensation bothered her enough to stop, though. She didn't want to stop.

He rested between her thighs, her satin panties the only barrier between her and the point of no return. His lips were warm and the path his tongue trailed along her skin, made a tingle hum to life deep inside her. His strong hands molded to her body, caressing as they went. His hands were everywhere, touching every part of her. Through the haze of incredible sensation, CeCe's mind wandered, *Was this really happening?* Between Jarod's legendary skills as a lover, and the sensations she was currently feeling, CeCe smiled to herself. If you asked her three months ago if she would be in the back of a car, about to do the nasty with someone, she would never have thought it would be this man. However, at the same

1

time, now that she was here, it was almost like it was meant to be. Without a doubt, she was firm in her decision to give Jarod Gates her virginity.

Dylan was going to be pissed, but CeCe couldn't think about her honorary brother, Dylan Cross, right now. Definitely no thinking of Dylan. As if he read her mind, Jarod's fingers ignited a flash of fire, which quickly engulfed her entire bloodstream, burning away all her stray thoughts.

This was it. This was really happening. Panic began to set in. "Jarod. Jarod. Wait!"

"Come on Kitten, don't think. Sex isn't about thinking; it is about feeling," he mumbled, as his soft lips continued their sensual journey around her ear lobe while his fingers confirmed what his well-used line tried to sell.

And what a feeling!

His fingers pressed against the now damp satin, and she could not control the purr that fell from her lips as his fingers flexed and caressed her center in knowing fashion. Soon CeCe was arching to get closer to the pressure he so willingly wanted to share. Just when she was sure her panting escalated to a fevered pitch, Jarod pulled until the satin ripped, exposing her completely.

"You feel ready. Tell me, Kitten, are you?" He asked, as he buried his face in the crook of her neck.

Yes!

Still, rather than answering his question, CeCe found herself asking her own, "This is special, right, Jarod? Tell me I'm not the only one that wants this. I need to know this isn't a mistake."

Instead of words, he answered by pushing into her. He was gentle, but it still hurt. CeCe shut her eyes to the discomfort and pain, focusing on the sounds within the car. She knew he was being gentle for her and soon the discomfort was gone, and his tempo changed—demanding, but still wonderful. No words could describe how she felt. Her body felt reborn to this completely new world of sensations. Every nerve ending was alive and vibrating. Even hitting her head on the side panel to the rhythm of his thrusts didn't detract from the splendor radiating from every cell of her being.

Within a few minutes, Jarod's pace slowed. Lifting his head so she could look at his beautiful face, CeCe watched as his eyes squeezed shut, and his jaw clenched as he found his release. Their panting was synchronized; his body heat was hers, and they shared this amazing moment in time. CeCe ran her hand through his shaggy blonde hair. With one final kiss on her exposed breast, Jarod sat up and leaned back, extending his long legs and closing his pants. She watched his jaw tighten as if he was grinding his teeth to keep from speaking. Suddenly, the wonderful connection from a moment ago was broken by the distant look in his eyes. CeCe watched as he opened the door, pulled himself out and closed it behind him.

Through the fogged over windows she could see the orange glow of a cigarette. He stood a few paces away, with his back to the car, but she could clearly make out his lean, yet powerful build. His stance was not his usual cock-sure posture, but slumped like he was disappointed. CeCe quickly dressed and climbed out of the car, instantly assaulted by the frigid air. Surrounded by the snow covered ground and icicle laden trees, CeCe's blood began to go cold. Something was off. Self-doubt and worse, embarrassment, settled over her.

"Jarod?" she squeaked.

He spoke without turning to face her, "Get back in the car CeCe. I'll take you back to your car in a minute." Even his voice was different, almost angry.

CeCe did as she was told, not knowing what else to do. After a few more minutes, he returned to the car, but as he started the engine, he completely ignored her, as if nothing had happened. He never even glanced at her; instead, his gaze remained focused on the windshield, and they rode in utter silence back to the billiard hall and her car. Still, he said nothing as she climbed out of the Camaro. *Jeez, he could at least say thanks for the tumble.* Barely waiting for her to get settled in her car, he peeled out without a backwards glance. As his taillights disappeared into the dark night, CeCe began to doubt everything she thought was truth. Granted, she wasn't dumb enough to think he loved her; he'd made no declarations of the sort. He'd clearly laid the cards out for her, that he was only looking for a good time, but she thought there was…something. The way he looked at her was softer than how he looked at the other girls. His voice wasn't as hard or sarcastic. He was different with her. At least she thought he was. But, thoughts of before couldn't ease the tightness clawing at her belly.

Three Days Later…

CeCe arrived at *Chase's Billiards* after class. She told herself over and over she was just going to hang out, but the truth was she was going because it was Friday, and that meant Jarod would be there. *Chase's* was a place for the local teenagers and young adults to hangout, and was considered the "cool" place to go if you lived in Appleton, or its surrounding communities. Her stomach held what must be the world population of butterflies. There might as well have been a huge neon sign with a flashing arrow pointing to it saying, "CeCe, he's here! He's here! Look there is even still evidence of what you've done on his back seat!"

Feeling her cheeks redden, CeCe parked and checked her reflection in the rearview mirror before getting out and walking inside. She was greeted by many smiles when someone announced her arrival, but the one person she wanted to see joy on his face, was the one person that didn't even acknowledge her entrance.

After greeting and chatting with her friends, and waiting what she thought was an appropriate amount of time, CeCe walked over to the table Jarod leaned against, holding the cue between his legs talking to a cluster of applicants for his next backseat encounter.

"Hey," she said, knowing she was really grasping at straws. No response. In fact he looked at her as if he didn't even know her. The girls hanging on his every word looked from Jarod to CeCe then rolled their eyes at her. Between their overly small, tight clothes and their big, used-a-whole-can-of-Aquanet hairspray heads, they looked like Barbie dolls, something CeCe would never look like.

"You haven't called," she said with all the strength she had, knowing she was being watched like a hawk.

He looked at her for the first time, and she could have sworn his eyes were such a soft blue before turning hard, "Was I supposed to?" This earned a round of giggles from the Barbie dolls.

That hurt. She knew she was sounding desperate, but couldn't help it. She refused to cry. "What have you been doing?"

"What are you, my mother?" Jarod barked. The Barbie's giggled again and began to add their own monologue. Jarod shushed them with a single look. The same looked he turned on CeCe.

His coldness was like an anvil in her stomach.

"I've been busy. Thinking, okay? Funny thing is, you helped me make some decisions I've been procrastinating on. Suddenly, everything is very clear." The way he said the last part had panic racing through her system.

"What decisions?" she asked, unable to look at him and knowing it was barely audible.

"Doesn't concern you." He turned and made a shot, sinking the nine ball with an angry plop, effectively dismissing her.

Didn't he just say she helped him come to these decisions?

Wringing her hands together, desperate to flee, her feet refused to budge. She wanted to hear a word—any word to give her hope. Instead, he stood to his full 6'3" height, and turned to face his audience before loudly declaring, for all to hear, "Look, Kitten," the word sounded vulgar to her now. "I don't know what you think we had, but you are wrong. Just because we did the deed doesn't mean you are anything more than a wet behind the ear kitten trying to be a tigress in the wild. Run along and play with a ball of yarn, and leave the big game to the ones who know the score." The cruel weight of Jarod's words increased with the loud cackling from the Barbie's.

Her world collapsed.

CeCe turned and ran out of *Chase's* without a word to her stunned friends. Her only thought to escape the horrible nightmare playing out before her. Outside she threw herself in her car and slammed the door before any of her friends could try to console her.

One Week Later...

CeCe parked at Dylan's garage, her new place to go after class since the scene from *Chase's* killed her desire to step foot inside the doors. Near as she could tell, CeCe had been able to keep what happened from Dylan. No doubt if Dylan had found out, he would not have bitten his tongue. At least that was the thought when she asked the question that had been plaguing her, "Where's Jarod?"

Dylan had introduced CeCe to Jarod. The two had met at *Chase's* and formed a friendship over their love of cars. Whenever Dylan wasn't trying to get his new construction business off the ground, you could find the duo at either *Chase's* or *Cal's*, the bar in Hamden, or at the garage tinkering on whichever car or bike they were working on at the time.

"Jarod?" Dylan asked, his head under the open hood of his car.

"Yeah, you know. Tall." *Gorgeous.* "Bad attitude." *Makes me wet just thinking about him.* "Chip on his shoulder." *Took my virginity.* "Jarod, ring a bell?"

"Oh, yeah. He left." Dylan answered, his head still under the hood.

"Left?" she felt a lead ball drop in her stomach.

"Yeah, Boot Camp. Apparently, he wants to be a Marine when he grows up." Finally lifting his head up, Dylan turned and leaned so his butt rested on the front grill as he pulled the rag from his back pocket and began wiping his hands. "Probably a good thing anyways. I heard he went all asshole on some poor girl last week at *Chase's*. A man like that needs to grow up."

Was her skin turning as green as she felt? He left. He was gone. It really was nothing to him. She really was nothing to him—the fantasy of him coming to her and telling her he was wrong; that he didn't mean those horrific words he had said to her—gone.

"Hey, you okay?" Dylan asked furrowing his brow.

"Who me? Oh yeah, peachy. You're right, this town doesn't need a man like that around." CeCe prayed she sold the nonchalance in her voice, and vowed to never again fall for slick lines, gooey feelings and drop-dead looks. She would never be a victim again.

Afghanistan - Eighteen Months Later...

Their routine mission felt anything but routine. Even as Jarod walked in formation with his squad, he felt the hairs on the back of his neck stand up. His gaze shifted just in time to see the explosion behind him and to the left. Jarod's body slammed into the Humvee, pain overtaking his left side as the sickening orange afterglow overtook the quiet black night. He could hear the screams of his team echo across the night; some crying out in pain while others lay stunned, unaware their limbs had been blown off.

"Take Cover! Engage!! Engage!!" Jarod heard his sergeant shouts, followed by the quick *rat-a-tat-tat* of return fire. Falling back, the squad regrouped and began returning fire.

"G-man! G-man, c'mon we need to get under cover. G-man, you with me?" Buffy screamed, as he hooked a huge forearm around Jarod's back, dragging him to the front of the Humvee for cover.

"I'm with you, Buffy," responded Jarod, as he slumped to the ground, his back against the Humvee. As he turned to fire, he noticed the shrapnel sticking out of his shoulder, side and most of his leg.

"Shoot the muthafuckas!" Buffy screamed.

Trying to block out the extreme pain, Jarod emptied the clip of his assault rifle alongside his squad. When the clip emptied, and the vibration stopped coursing through his body, his adrenaline began to level out and Jarod's body quickly grew tired. His hearing began to fade and his vision dimmed as everything began to go dark. He could vaguely hear Buffy screaming, "G-man, stay with me, man. Stay with me. You're gonna be fine, you hear me?" The darkened sand and devastation melted away until all he could see was a petite brunette, with curves that made his mouth water. A sweet smile and full lips begging to be kissed; skin so soft, one touch and he felt like the richest man in the world. The memory of a night almost two years ago is the only thing that kept him sane, and drove away the depression and loneliness of the Godforsaken desert. Feeling his body being moved was enough to jostle her perfect image and pull him from her welcome warmth.

"G-man, do you hear me? God Dammit! Don't you dare die on me, you pussy!"

Stay with me. Don't leave me...CeCe! There was no answer, only her beautiful smile before everything went black.

One

"Feel good, baby?" Derrick asked as he slowly moved between her thighs. God how he loved to make love to her, between her silken skin and the noises she made, he didn't think he could get any more turned on than he already was.

"Faster, Derrick, I need to get off," CeCe demanded, her teeth clamped on her full lower lip as she closed her eyes and arched her back, trying to align his cock just where she needed it.

"What's the rush, Baby? We got all night."

CeCe's phone began to buzz with a vengeance.

"Ignore it," he said as he felt his own body begin to close in on ecstasy.

"I can't." As if their bodies weren't joined, she reached over and pulled her phone from where it lay on the nightstand. It hurt she could come out of the moment so easily. No longer moving, Derrick remained inside her, unable to keep his feelings off his face, but holding onto their physical connection.

"Shit!" CeCe shouted as she tried to extract herself from beneath Derrick.

"What is it? Where are you going?" He hated that she moved away from him. For months he had tried to get her to go out with him. When she finally agreed, he never thought there would be a better high. But, he was wrong; being in bed with CeCe was the ultimate of sensations.

"That was an automatic text message from the security system, my store has been broken into. I have to go." She answered, as if what they were doing meant nothing to her.

"Wait. I'll come with you."

Finally, she needed him.

"No need, you'll probably just be in the way, anyways." That halted him, but he could see the moment she regretted her words. Turning, she pulled his tousled dark head toward her, and leaving a soft kiss on his forehead. Quickly pulling away, she bent over gathered her discarded clothes, hastily pulling them on as she found them; hopping on one foot as she slipped on each of her stilettos. Then she walked out of Derrick's room, and house, without a backwards glance.

The drive from Derrick's house to the store usually only took fifteen minutes, but it might as well have been fifteen hours. Fear and dread coursed through CeCe, but more than anything her blood ran hot with anger. She was pissed off! How dare someone try to wreck what she has worked so hard to create. She had to laugh at herself. *Talk about channeling Dylan.* But the momentary humor quickly died when she pulled up to the plaza where *CeCe's* was located. Parked in front of her store were two cruisers and a third unmarked police car. The lights within the store were shining bright, and from ten yards away, she could see the bowling ball size hole in the glass door. CeCe leapt from the car and effortlessly ran in her heels. Officer Mike Nickles was the first to see her.

"CeCe. Careful before you fall. There is glass everywhere." His beefy hand shot out to stop her momentum.

Ignoring him, she advanced, her eyes racing, taking in the store as the confusion began to build. With the exception of the broken glass, nothing looked disrupted. She could even see the register, closed and unmoved. She didn't trust her vision and needed to check everything herself, but Officer Nickles made sure she couldn't do that. *Oh really!?!*

"Mike, please, I need to check my store," she purred, giving him her coyest look, knowing the power it had on the male psyche.

Mike could feel his ears turning red along with his cheeks. Just hearing Cecille Cervetti say his name, made his manhood twitch to life. He hoped the dark blue of his uniform would hide any evidence of the effect she had on him. Perhaps he could allow her to enter, even though it was against orders; of course, he would have to be with her, and maybe she would grab onto him if anything became too much to deal with…Before he could finish the thought, his partner and the lieutenant made their way out of the back room, across the store's floor, and out the front door.

CeCe was about to demand to know what was going on, but the sound of a very familiar male voice cut her off before she could start.

"Idarraga! What the fuck is going on? Why is anyone breaking into my kid sister's store? What did they take?"

CeCe couldn't help rolling her eyes. *Dylan! Of course, they would call Dylan.* Everyone knew they weren't related, but Dylan tossed the term "kid sister" around any chance he got, especially when speaking to other men about her. Groaning, CeCe turned to face the only man she could completely trust. Given his appearance, it would appear he had been similarly engaged when he got the call. His dark hair hung over his forehead, as always, and fury was evident in his jaw locked and narrowed eyes.

CeCe waited, allowing Dylan to do his visual check before he engulfed her, pulling her tight to him. She was surrounded by warmth and strength that only Dylan could offer. Ever since the nightmarish night, thirteen years ago, Dylan has always been there for her. With Dylan around, she was never alone. She was safe. As irked as she was the police called him, she was grateful he was here with her to get some answers.

"Cees, you okay?"

"Other than the fact someone broke into my store, I'm peachy." CeCe answered, returning his hug.

"That's a girl; keep your sarcasm evident, helps being pissed off, too." Dylan chucked her under the chin and winked as they turned to the lieutenant for answers.

Maximo Idarraga, a handsome younger police lieutenant, looked like he should be investigating the clubs and nightlife of Miami rather than the petty happenings in a rural Vermont town. He didn't pull any punches as he approached the duo to fill them in on the details.

"Ms. Cervetti, do you know anyone that would want to break into your store or would want to harm you?"

"What, this isn't a run of the mill burglary? What did you find, Max?" Dylan asked, his annoyance unmistakable.

Shifting only his gaze to Dylan, Idarraga took a moment to consider the well-known, put-up-with-no-shit Hamden resident. The fact they weren't in Hamden meant very little to Dylan, and he'd made it known to everyone. "Look, Cross, I called you as a courtesy and expect us to be square now. Right now, I am the one asking the questions." Max returned his attention to the very attractive storeowner. He needed to remain professional, but the beautiful woman made anything with a dick take notice. The way she arched her beautifully manicured brow showed her surprise that someone would speak to Dylan that way. "Please, Ms. Cervetti, answer the question."

"No. No one. Did they take anything?" She replied to the handsome Latino-looking man, who spoke with the hint of a sexy accent.

"From what we can see, nothing is disturbed, but you would better be able to tell us. Come, I'll walk you in." She entered the store, hearing the crunch of broken glass beneath her shoes. She felt the warmth of a hand at her back, and knew it was the lieutenant's hand and not Dylan's. Modern society was filled with constant and never-ending cock challenges. In most situations CeCe found it amusing but at the moment it was one more part of the evening that was pissing her off.

Once inside, she quickly scanned the store and confirmed nothing was missing from the floor, and the desk and register were untouched. Suddenly, fear gripped her throat, and CeCe ran to her office in the back; concerned for her design sketches nearly overwhelming her. She chided herself for taking so long to consider her drawings could be the target of the break-in. Ignoring the group of men as they crowded into the office after her, she rushed to her desk and pulled out her sketchbook. Relief flooded her as she saw nothing was missing or damaged. Straightening, she took a deep breath to regain her composure as her gaze fell on her office chair and she noticed the single item out of place in the store. In fact, it wasn't even supposed to be in her store.

Dumbfounded, CeCe turned to the men, "I don't understand. Someone broke in to deliver flowers?" Bewildered, she picked up the dozen long-stem white roses from their perch on the green velvet chair.

"Ms. Cervetti, are you saying the flowers were not there when you left tonight?" Idarraga questioned.

"No, Lieutenant, they weren't. Considering my ass was in the chair, I'd think I'd remember the thorns," sarcasm effortlessly dripping from her tongue.

Unable to hide his smirk, Max continued, "Well, if you weren't sitting on the thorns, then it is safe to say the suspect left them for you. You are sure nothing else is missing? You came back here abruptly and looked through that book," he continued, indicating the black covered spiral pad, now sitting on her desk.

"I thought, perhaps, my sketches would be gone, but no, they are all here. Besides, they are worthless to anyone except me." Implying more than she meant to admit —the umpteenth rejection letter came from designer apprenticeship the day prior —she voiced more than the fear of her store being broken into. Once again, she looked toward the gorgeous and expensive bouquet. Gripping the paper wrapped stems; CeCe brought them to her nose, inhaling the sweet and distinct smell of roses. The beautiful buds were large than your run of the mill white roses and simply amazing.

"When we first arrived, we went to your security feed, but the system was turned off; is that normal?" Idarrago asked, jotting notes down in his small notebook.

Now it was CeCe's turn to blush. Dylan was going to flip, but no helping that now. "Yeah, about that, it hasn't worked in about three months." She glanced at Dylan, not surprised to see the furious look he was giving her, she continued, "Nothing ever happens here, and after the pipes burst back in April, I just never got around to getting it back up and running."

"Cees! What they hell are you thinking not having a working security video? Especially when you are here alone at night."

"Well, jeez, Dylan, if I thought some wacko would break in here, not steal anything, and leave me gorgeous expensive flowers, I would have made sure to get the video feed up and running." CeCe couldn't help the smart-mouthed retort. She was tired and cranky. Not to mention sexually frustrated, considering she missed out on her orgasm earlier. She didn't need to be reprimanded by Dylan.

"Ms. Cervetti, I agree with Dylan, it should be a high priority to get your security system back online."

"I'll take care of it tomorrow morning." CeCe answered, exasperated from Idarraga chastising her, too.

"I'll make the call. It will be working by 10AM," Dylan answered.

"D, you don't need to call, I am perfectly capable of calling myself. After all, I believe it is my name on the sign outside, not yours.

The infamous Cross stare was now hammering down on her.

"Lieutenant, there is a glass replacement company here, asking for the go ahead to replace the front door." Idarraga looked to CeCe, noticing her surprised expression.

"That's my guy; I called on my way here," Dylan explained, looking smug and authoritative.

"Of course it is. Thanks, D." CeCe relented and placed the bouquet on her desk, giving in to his take-over rather than go another couple of rounds.

Idarraga nodded permission for the glass replacement before turning back to CeCe. Closing the short distance, he handed her a card he pulled from his inside breast pocket as he said, "Here is my card, if you have any other problems, or if you think of anything, please don't hesitate to call. With your confirmation that nothing was taken or damaged, there really isn't much we can do. Unfortunately, delivering flowers to a beautiful woman isn't against the law. If you can think of anything, anything at all, please call right away. My cell is listed on the back. It really is prudent for you to get your video feed back up and running. I'll have patrols increased at the plaza for the next few nights. Hopefully this is an isolated incident."

She accepted the card, suddenly mentally and physically drained and just wanting her bed. "Thank you, Lieutenant."

Dylan returned to CeCe's office after escorting the officers out and checking on the glass installation. "Cees, you sure you're okay?"

Even though she knew Dylan wouldn't think less of her, CeCe refused to let the tears fall as she collapsed into her chair. She couldn't help but laugh, "Just my luck, some sick fuck would want to give me flowers and choose to go about it in such an unorthodox and fucked up way."

"Yeah, well I don't like it." Dylan walked around her desk, sitting on the edge next to her chair. "Where were you when you got the call?"

Yeah, like she was going to tell him exactly where she was. "I was at my date's house."

Unable to pass up the chance to tease her, Dylan taunted, "Your date, huh? Anyone I know?"

"Just some guy, no one special." CeCe didn't do special; guys were around for only one reason, to spoil her rotten. She expected them to willingly spend their money on her, buy her things, take her to the finest places, show her a good time, and feed her physical needs, and when she had her fill, they were expected to happily, and quietly, accept her severing ties. It had to be this way; she would accept nothing else.

"You going back there?" Dylan he felt foolish asking, already knowing the answer.

"No. I'm gonna head back to my apartment, there is a bottle of tequila in my freezer that is calling my name." She pulled herself out of her chair, and walked out, shutting the lights off as she went.

"Well, I'm coming with you."

"No, D, really, I'm alright."

"Yeah, well, I can't go home and explain to Natalie I let you go home by yourself, let alone without checking your place out to make sure it was safe. I'm kind of attached to my boys."

The irony of such a thought, made CeCe laugh out loud. Natalie Cross, Dylan's wife, and one of CeCe's best friends, didn't have a mean bone in her body. The fact CeCe knew Natalie was quite fond of Dylan's body parts, only made her laugh that much harder.

Two

At the incessant buzzing of the alarm clock, CeCe came out of her hibernation cocoon and slid her legs over the side of the bed. God how she hated mornings! As far as CeCe was concerned, the only good thing about the morning was coffee, lots and lots of coffee. Padding to the kitchen, CeCe was greeted by the amazing aroma of her coffee maker already brewing a full pot of liquid heaven, well the morning kind anyways. But CeCe didn't set the coffee maker to auto-start. Then she saw the note scrawled on the back of an envelope.

I knew you would need this. Your security system will be back up and running before you get to the store this morning. Regardless of whose name is on the storefront, YOU are my responsibility, so no girly hissy fits, just deal. Call me if anything happens again. I MEAN IT! ~Dylan

The note brought a big smile to her face. Its protectiveness brought back the memory of the night she met Dylan thirteen years ago. When he became her knight in shining armor and showed her real men did exist. She always knew Troy had a temper, but she never thought he would physically assault her. Not Troy. He was the hunky jock while she was the quiet art-

17

focused, mediocre student. Vermont's version of Beauty and the Geek. To everyone's astonishment, they dated all through high school. She was half of the couple everyone wanted to be. But that all changed the winter after they graduated, and CeCe saw Troy's true colors while he was home visiting from UCLA after she accidently spilled her orange soda in his pristine 1999 Monte Carlo.

All these years later, she can't help wondering if he had shaken the soda before handing her the bottle so the carbonation would explode when she twisted the cap.

"You stupid bitch! Always making such a mess with everything. I just had the fucking car detailed!"

The apology was on her tongue when the punch landed, high on her cheekbone. Pain shot through her eye socket and it felt like her cheekbone was cracked. Covering her cheek with her hand, her eyes wide, she was stunned at his actions.

"I've had enough of your bullshit, constantly fucking everything up. All I wanted to do was have a nice night out and you had to fuck it up. I should have never come home...especially to you. Get the fuck out of my car, I'll even make it easy for you!" Troy pulled to the curb and slowed down—he didn't even fully stop—reached across CeCe, pulled the handle, and pushed her shoulder.

She fell out of the car onto the trash—and God only knows what else—covered sidewalk, landing on her hands and knees. The floral mini dress Troy asked her to wear did nothing to save her palms and knees from the impact of the concrete. Troy had driven off before she could even get to her feet, leaving her in a sketchy party of Burlington with only bars open at that time of night.

Not one person that saw what happened asked if she was all right, they only stared and went about their business. Tears ran down her face as the biting wind whipped against her uncovered flesh. The pain in her cheek and extremities were quickly forgotten when the fear settled in as she realized she didn't know what to do. She had no phone, no money, and if she had any chance of avoiding hypothermia, she needed to get inside. Looking up and down the street, none of the bars looked welcoming, but she had no choice. Choosing the closest one, she walked to the heavy wooden door and pulled. She entered the smoke filled bar that smelled of stale lives and hopeless futures. A few of the patrons looked up from their perches at the bar when she entered, but quickly returned to their endless glasses of liquid escapes. Even the bartender didn't address her, as it was apparent she was underage.

Seeing a deserted table over in the corner, CeCe hurried over and sat down on the ripped seat. She began pulling napkin after napkin out of the dented dispenser, attempting to tend her cuts and clean what she could.

"There you are, Charlene. What, that no good dick you been shacking up with finally let you have it?"

The scent coming from the obviously drunk man was enough to make CeCe's stomach roll. Her eyes darted from the bar to the smoke filled back area farther back in the shadows. The stench from this man wafted to her nose; causing her knees to knock. "I'm not Charlene."

"You don't think I'd know you anywhere, you bitch?" he snarled.

"My name is CeCe, you have me mistaken for someone else." Her voice cracked from the fear. His eyes were demonic; it was the only word to describe the loathing disgust aimed towards her.

With a last pull on his beer, he smashed the bottle on the edge of the table, shattering it and sending the remains spewing in every direction, including CeCe's face. Holding the jagged edge just a few inches from her throat, he growled, "Should just kill you right here for stepping out on me and fucking that no good asshole!"

CeCe squeezed her eyes shut blocking out the vision of what was about to occur, when she heard and felt a body hitting the table.

"Yo, asshat. Why don't you leave the girl alone? If you want to fight, then fight a man. Only a pussy would hit a girl with a broken bottle."

"Mind your business, boy, this doesn't concern you."

"Well, fuckwad, that's where you're wrong. I got a problem with a dickhead wanting to hurt a girl. Come on, tough guy, I'll even give you the first swing. But I'm warning you, you better knock me out with the one freebie."

Stunned this guy was defending her, CeCe was also shocked he was baiting the fuckwad—to use his word—to actually fight him. CeCe wanted to jump up and run, but she was frozen in her seat. The old disheveled man struck out at the younger man, connecting with the beer bottle. Instantly, the younger man's jaw was dripping blood, but he didn't even react.

"I warned you, motherfucker."

The sounds of fists connecting with flesh were only muted by the grunts of pain and pleas of surrender. When the older man lay on the ground, partly under the table, CeCe thought for sure she was going to be sick. This was too much for one person to handle.

"Come on out, girl, he won't hurt you." Her rescuer spoke softly to her, and when she was finally able to drag her eyes away from the motionless drunk, CeCe looked into kind brown eyes, but her body was still rooted to the seat.

"I won't hurt you, either. Come on, I'll get you out of here. You can trust me." CeCe didn't know if it was his words, his actions, or his light in this dark place, but she put her shaking hand in his, allowing him to lead her out; somehow knowing he would keep his word and take care of her.

Thirteen years later, Dylan was still taking care of her. She may bitch and moan that he was overbearing, but the truth was, CeCe knew if there was anyone that only wanted what was best for her, it was Dylan Cross.

She poured the glorious brew into her hot pink "That's QUEEN Bitch to you" mug, savoring the first delicious taste with her usual cream and sweetener. After empting half the mug, CeCe ran her fingers through her hair, ready to hit the shower and start her day. She set the mug on the counter, next to Dylan's note, and headed down the hallway to her bedroom. *Well, Cees, no sense in reminiscing about the ugly past, you have a day to start, a store to get to, and a fucker to set straight about the proper way to send a girl flowers. MEN!*

Ninety minutes later, CeCe parked her emerald-green convertible mustang in its usual spot under the pole light and boundary island next to

CeCe's. Travel mug in hand, she slid out of the car, lugging her designer handbag and laptop case behind her. With the distinctive double chirp of her alarm, she strode off to her new glass door.

When she got to the door, Kelleigh, her only full time employee, was already waiting.

"Morning, Kel." CeCe greeted her, expertly juggling everything in her hands and the key, effortlessly unlocking the door.

"Hey. Holy shit, Cees, I'm just reading your text now. Someone broke in last night?"

CeCe held the door open for Kelleigh to enter then carried her things to the counter next to the register.

"Yeah, apparently some moron thought breaking in and leaving beautiful flowers was a fantastic idea."

"Oh my God, did they take anything? Did you check all the shipments? The register? The safe?" Kelleigh asked, still completely stunned. CeCe was amused her friend's eyes looked like they were going to bug out of her head. CeCe thought back to when she first met Kelleigh Constantine, when she'd answered the ad for the open position. At first look, CeCe didn't think the punk, spirited, and younger by ten years, redhead would be a fit, but something told CeCe to give her a chance. Boy was she glad she did. She quickly learned Kelleigh had an amazing ability to see contrasting patterns and pieces as the perfect combinations, as well as win over even the toughest, and most biased, of clients that passed through the doors. Over the years that Kelleigh has worked for CeCe, she learned Kelleigh's had a tough life, but she never looks at the glass as half-empty, always such an optimist, unless it comes to herself. As comfortable as Kelleigh was in her own skin, she still struggled with societal acceptance and personal relationship success.

"I double and triple checked everything. Nothing but the beautiful flowers in the back was different from when I left." CeCe said, as she stepped out from behind the counter and headed back toward her office.

With an enormous "O" shaped mouth, Kelleigh followed behind her boss, quickly finding the tainted bouquet. Still wrapped in their florist paper, the flowers were lying on CeCe's desk. The bouquet was so large and extravagant; Kelleigh couldn't miss them, even with CeCe's bags down on the desk.

"You didn't throw them away?" Kelleigh's usually high-pitched voice was even higher.

CeCe looked at the gorgeous buds and felt a twinge of guilt, but Kelleigh was right, maybe she should have just thrown them in the garbage.

"You're right, I should." CeCe pushed the bundle over the edge into the trashcan. "Okay, time to get back to normal, the shipment of intimates that came in yesterday needs to be censored and arranged in the baskets."

"Sure, I'll get right on that." Kelleigh said, and as she stepped toward the boxes in the delivery corner, she turned to her boss, "Cees, it's going to be okay. Some guys are just really fucked up."

CeCe walked out of the office, leaving Kelleigh to her job. Her eyes took in the store, her haven and all she has worked so hard for. It was devastating to know someone would try to taint it, but she was relieved the attempt failed. CeCe prided herself on her specific taste and the selection she offered. Heavy in modern, but classic designs, CeCe chose more luxurious pieces than were carried in the larger department stores, or all-in-one shopping centers. It was a gamble she took at the time, but it has paid off three fold. Whether it was business, casual, or formal, she carried it. Her clientele developed a high standard of what they wanted and expected, and CeCe was proud to deliver on every aspect. She took extra care to give her clients the impression they were perusing pieces in the comfort of their own walk-in closets rather than a stale retail store. CeCe went above and beyond to add personal touches throughout the store, even choosing to display her items in a unique way. Freestanding display cabinets housed sachet lined drawers and wicker baskets, which held foldable pieces, always by color and size and foregoing the common rack after rack display system.

When racks were used for longer pieces or to display complete outfits it was more eye catching and client friendly. She prided herself on standards that were found on Fifth Avenue, but also found and expected right here in her little chunk of Vermont.

Repeating her private pep talk to herself again, CeCe blocked out the ugliness of last night and easily slid on her megawatt smile and moved to greet the customer who just entered the store. Using her first name, CeCe did what she did best: she sold pieces to women, whether they needed them or not; not in a sleazy kind of way, but because CeCe found immense joy in making every woman feel like a million bucks. After all, a woman could only depend on herself to do so.

The day and evening had gone by in a whirl. CeCe was thrilled with the sales for the day. She was able to negotiate an amazing deal—and honestly, borderline highway robbery—for a shipment of silk blouses she wanted to carry from a-still-unknown designer in Milan. The day was remarkably normal, in the no-stalking-floral-deliveries kind of way, adding to CeCe's delights in the workday. Before CeCe knew it, Kelleigh had left at her normal time around 6pm, and Kimmie, CeCe's part time employee, had arrived and was currently closing up shop with CeCe.

"…So, anywho, and he wonders why I don't want to date him. I mean, really, who thinks a tour of a brewery would be a cool first date idea?" Kimmie spoke, clearly wanting CeCe to agree with her opinion of absurdity.

"Well, you do like beer, maybe he was thinking outside of the box, but keeping your tastes in mind," CeCe answered, thinking a brewery tour sounded kind of cool. Turning the lock and dropping the store's keys in her bag, CeCe dug out her car keys. Enjoying the sunshine at this time of night was one of the best things of summertime. Even as late as eight pm, it still felt like you had time left in the day.

"Maybe. I guess it is kind of sweet for him to think like that. I don't know. There is the whole height thing, too. I mean he is only like, 5'5", I could never wear heels with him."

CeCe listened, inwardly cheering that it was time to go separate ways with Kimmie. She was a good, trustworthy, punctual employee, but honestly, Kimmie drove CeCe nuts with her nonstop babbling. Saying goodbye, and grateful for the easy transition, CeCe watched Kimmie get into her small SUV and head toward the parking lot exit, her phone already in her hand. CeCe walked toward the side of the building where her car was, enjoying the warm sunshine, saying goodbye to other storeowners. When she turned her focus to her car, the air whooshed out of her lungs. Lying on her windshield, tucked under the wiper, was a single long-stemmed white rose.

She whipped around, furiously scanning the parking lot, and gripped her keys tighter in her hand, ready to attack. But there was no dark figure, no lurking menace waiting to pounce. Her breath heaved in her chest, sweat dripped down her back and between her breasts.

"Cecille? Everything okay?" the older man asked, concerned, as he slowly walked toward her.

"Malcolm, did you see anyone here earlier, leaving the flower?" she asked her neighbor in the plaza. Malcolm's smoke shop had been in the Appleton Shopping Center for as long as CeCe could remember. When she was younger, her father would visit Malcolm's shop whenever he was looking for a celebratory stogie. CeCe had always asked to go, she found the smell of his shop intriguing and she enjoyed perusing the other items his shop carried as well, particularly the various chessboards. When she opened *CeCe's*, Malcolm greeted her opening day with the largest fruit basket she had ever seen. Making the gesture even more thoughtful was the four foil-wrapped cigars—the expensive ones she knew he saved for his special customers—among the delicious looking custom cut fruit. CeCe smoked one that very night, and one on the first anniversary of her opening. She still had the other two, holding them for special occasions. One such occasion fell through just the other day.

"No, not at all, dear. I take it, not an admirer of yours?" asked Malcolm, a tall African-American man with salt and pepper hair.

"Oh he's an admirer alright. Just in the creepy kind of way." CeCe explained, filling Malcolm in on the happenings of the previous night.

Having known CeCe since she was the age of his youngest granddaughter, Macolm felt protective of her and offered some fatherly advice, "You can't be too careful, Cecille, especially in this day and age. I'll wait with you while you call the police."

"No, really, it's okay, I'll just..."

"Make the call, young lady." He ordered, tilting his head and giving her the look she didn't dare disobey.

Leaving the rose on her windshield, she set her bags on the hood of her car, dug out Idarraga's card, and dialed her phone. Explaining what occurred, she was instructed to wait and he would be there shortly.

Fifteen minutes later Max pulled beside CeCe's car instantly noticing how gorgeous she was, and men found her charismatic, regardless of their age. Putting the unmarked sedan in park, he quickly exited the car, rolling up his sleeves to combat the heat now that he was out of the comfortable air conditioning.

"Ms. Cervetti."

"Lieutenant. Thanks for coming." CeCe said, turning away from the older gentleman standing with her, dropping her softer, more open expression for a more professional one.

Max greeted the gentleman, "Malcolm, how you doing, sir?"

"Just fine, son. Please tell me you are going to do something about these unwanted advances towards my favorite neighbor."

Unable to hide his smile, feeling it was more of an order than a plea,

"I will certainly try my best." After a few more minutes, CeCe assured Malcolm she was fine and insisted he go home as planned. With a kiss to her cheek, and a handshake to Max, Malcolm headed toward his Cadillac.

Once alone, Max turned to CeCe and asked her to go over what happened from the top. As she went through it again, he took in her appearance. The bright green blouse paired with plain black slacks was quite catching, low and seductive, but still tasteful. It made her eyes come alive, as only hazel ones could. Hazel eyes were always so mysterious, never truly this color or that color, until they were reflected off another, just as they were now. Her go-on-forever dark lashes cast gorgeous shadows on her bronzed cheeks. Her hair was pulled back in some sort of twist, except for a few pieces that escaped, showing the different hues of brown and gold. Her luscious lips, so plump and full, begging to be touched, were lined and painted a shade of light mocha. If her appearance weren't enough to distract the most focused of men, her scent would be. It was spicy and dark, the kind of scent that made you imagine primal actions in darkened places. Knowing he needed to focus on the case, he tried thinking of her in a burlap sack in order to shut the door to his raging imagination.

When she was through giving the run down, including the uneventful occurrences of her day at the store, Max looked around. "Do you always park in this location?"

"Generally, either this spot or that one," indicating the one next to hers now.

Asking her to stay put, he walked to the building managers office. He returned five minutes later, an iPad in hand.

"Ms. Cervetti, unfortunately you picked the one location that can't be seen on the security tapes. Either this guy knows it and your habits religiously, or he's just damn lucky. I moved through the feed, from the time you came out to grab the package out of your trunk earlier, until you closed shop for the day. There is no view of this location on any of the cameras, or any persons loitering in the area. There is too much of a blind spot to speculate how he approached."

"Fucking fabulous!" CeCe huffed exasperatedly.

"I suggest you start changing your routines up a bit. Take a different route to and from the store; vary the time you leave your house, that sort of thing. I'm sorry, but I don't have much to go on."

"No, I understand. I mean it's stupid; it's just some flowers."

"No, don't go there. It was Breaking and Entering, which is a serious offense. And I'm afraid it may be quickly turning into a stalking case." Not liking what his gut was feeling, but still limited by the law, Idarraga offered up something his superiors would not be too pleased with, "I'll have an unmarked cruiser stake out the parking lot the next few days, and if our guy shows up again, we'll get him."

After a few more suggestions on how to change up her routine and strict instructions of where to park given the security feeds, they were interrupted by the ringing of CeCe's cell phone. Knowing the ring she rolled her eyes, "Excuse me."

Pressing accept, CeCe didn't need to put on speaker, the caller could be heard, loud and clear, "You get your ass over here, now! I mean it, CeCe!" Dylan bellowed then quickly hung up.

"I take it that wasn't up for debate?" Max asked with a knowing look.

"You think?" With another thanks, and promise to heed his suggestions for safety, CeCe slid into her mustang. At first, she considered just heading back to her apartment, but then admitted how foolish that really would be. Knowing he would literally come and physically retrieve her, CeCe bit the bullet and pulled out in the direction of Dylan's house.

A short while later, CeCe arrived at the secluded log house on the hill. The view was incredible now, the lush greenery and perfection of Mother Nature everywhere her eyes could see. CeCe always felt a sense of peace when she was here, whether it was the rich beauty of the mountains or the love and companionship of the people inside the walls, she didn't know, but she always valued the effect.

Walking up to the grand front entrance, CeCe paused under the enclosed porch. Even through the thick glass that protected the interior, she could hear the endless giggles and laughter, and silently hoped those wonderful sounds would be enough to keep Dylan's temper from exploding. *Better get this over with.* CeCe pushed open the large wooden door, and walked into the lion's den.

Walking into the open concept home was such a vast change from before. The large sunken room that used to be the epitome of a bachelor pad, with masculine starkness and functional-only décor, was no more. In its place, pinkness and femininity covered every surface. From the floral accented pillows and throws, to the immense piles of toys and everything any little girl could want. Gone were the baby necessities, but in their place was proof that little girls liked the finer things, and in this home, it was times two. The large black granite, floor to ceiling fireplace still remained, but instead of the stark granite, a beautiful family portrait now hung over the mantel. Twin angelic beauties, with large chocolate eyes and dark hair to match their handsome father, happily balance on the knees of Natalie, their beautiful blonde mother, with twin smiles identical to her own, as Dylan enfolds his three ladies in his obvious love and protection. The radiant smiles of the family of four tell of an unbreakable bond and proof of the immense love that actually exists in the world. To CeCe, that photograph was better than any fairytale or Disney adaptation. It was real.

Happy she was able to make it this far into the house without being seen, she admired the two little bodies standing motionless in front of the gigantic television watching a cartoon of a singing flowerpot. One girl leaned against an ottoman with various play dishes on it, while the other held a ragdoll by one of its yarn pigtails. CeCe moved quietly down the two steps and crept closer to the two little girls before kneeling down so she could be eye level with them.

"How are my favorite girls? Auntie has missed you so much!" The toddlers answered with screeches of surprise and squeals of delight. Quickly, she had her hands full of two bouncing and boisterous girls. "I can't believe it, but you two just get more beautiful each time I see you. Give the rest of womankind a chance and slowdown, will you?"

"Tell me about it. Dylan already has plans of putting bars on their windows and locks on their doors."

With a final squeeze to each precious little girl, CeCe stood up to squeeze her best friend, Natalie.

With an equally strong grasp, Natalie engulfed her friend, wanting to confirm for herself CeCe was all right and unharmed.

"I'm good, Natalie. Promise. Not a scratch, just my nerves got jumbled," she hoped the physical contact would help her friend know that she was fine.

Finally letting go, Natalie stepped back, but kept her hands on her friend's arms, doing a final visual sweep.

"So roses, huh? Not only every outgoing available man in Appleton, Hamden, and the rest of Carver County, but now the shy ones, too?" Natalie's infectious smile touched all the way to her warm brown eyes behind her glasses where she enhanced her lighthearted banter with a wink.

"What can I say, they just come out of the woodwork, and literally through glass doors, for a chance with me," CeCe responded, with a cocky flip of her long chestnut hair.

"Glad you can make jokes about your safety," Dylan barked in his signature deep baritone voice.

CeCe turned to see him take the last two steps down from upstairs and joined his family in the main living area. Within moments, each leg became an anchor to two giggling cherubs, obviously enjoying the walking pole game, also known as Daddy.

And as quickly as the classic and intimidating Dylan made his presence known, he morphed into the playful, do anything for a smile from his girls

Dylan. The two women watched as he made his way robotically around the room as a pair of little bodies held on until the belly laughs made doing so impossible. Soon the toddlers weren't the only female laughter in the room.

With his twin's attention elsewhere, Dylan's expression quickly changed to his *I'm pissed* look that's been known to take down the toughest of opponents.

"I don't know what you are expecting to do with that expression, but you can stow it!" CeCe changed her stance, crossing her arms, and jutting out her hip, making it clear she was not going to be intimidated.

Without any acknowledgement of her words, he walked toward her stopping only when he was right in front of her, just shy of breaking the personal space rule, "So tell me why I shouldn't whip your ass for not calling me immediately?" Suddenly, the concept of personal space registered as unnecessary, and Dylan pressed his nose to CeCe's. Keeping his voice low, so as not to alert his girls, he knew his point was effectively made.

Oh Hell No! He will not intimidate her like this!

"Well, I don't think your wife would appreciate it, and I kind of enjoy sitting, thank you very much.

"Just keep making jokes about this," Dylan's face changed, he stepped back, ran his hand through his hair, then placed both hands on his hips before continuing in a more conversational tone, "Obviously, this guy is watching you. I don't like it. I don't like it at all."

Knowing he was just trying to protect her, CeCe felt her façade begin to crack. Being sure to keep her tone low as well, she responded, "Do you think I don't know that, and that it doesn't creep me the hell out? What do you want me to do, hide? I have a life to live, and a business to run." Glancing at the destruction of a suburb block, taking place ten feet away, CeCe turned back to Dylan and said, "I appreciate your concern, but I'm handling it, D, I got this."

Dylan's fury boiled as he looked at the woman that had become an important part of his life, frustrated she just didn't get it. So he thought he would clarify it for her.

"Well, as of right now, your life involves you going upstairs and staying in one of the spare rooms. End of discussion," He commanded. Then scoffed, "*I got this, D.* Yeah, right."

CeCe couldn't help but gawk. Natalie apparently heard, or knew, his solution to this situation and joined them. CeCe looked from one to the other, and when nothing else was said, her only response was, "You cannot be serious."

"You bet your stubborn ass, I am!"

"Dylan." Natalie chose this moment to intervene, "She is an adult. As much as I want her safely here, under lock and key, has the situation really escalated to require such tactics? What if she agreed to consider it if anything else happens? Honestly, you can't make her, Dylan, no matter how intimidating you think that cute adorable look of yours is."

CeCe was grateful for just how smart Natalie was. She knew how to manipulate her husband and just when to do it.

Momentarily oblivious to CeCe's presence, Dylan extended his long powerful arm out, snagging his wife around the waist and pulling where she willingly went. Looking into her eyes he whispered, "I hate it when you are right."

"I'm always right; remember that, and it shouldn't be so hard to accept next time." Natalie sassily answered, then went up on tiptoes and kissed her husband.

When the two lovebirds didn't come up for air a minute later, CeCe noticed the twins were watching their parents and giggling.

"Okay, this is a family show, enough of that. Really!" Truth be told, she was jealous of the love Dylan and Natalie shared, but she knew that kind of love was not in the cards for her. For a chance at that kind of happiness, you have to be willing to let yourself be vulnerable, and that was one thing CeCe vowed she never would do. She was okay with that.

Couldn't get hurt that way.

"It's fine, D. They're just flowers. No note, no malicious intent, just flowers. Idarraga said he would have an unmarked car in the parking lot for the next few days. You got the video feed up and running again. I'm sure he will get tired soon, and everything will go back to normal."

"Yeah, unless you continue to do stupid shit, like park in your usual spot—which just happens to be in a blind spot of the building's cameras. Or take the same road, at the same time, every day."

Suddenly, it dawned on her, "Oh my God, you called the police! Seriously? Isn't there a victim-police confidentiality rule?"

"Not when you're involved, there isn't." Dylan said, plain and simple.

Knowing things were escalating to tempers blowing, Natalie suggested, "Dylan why don't you take Cat and Ria up and put them to bed."

Looking to his wife and seeing the *don't argue with me* look, Dylan conceded, "come on My Princesses, come give Mama and Auntie kisses, it's time for bed."

When smooches and hugs were received happily and in excess, Dylan picked up each wiggling little girl in a strong arm and carried them upstairs, leaving Natalie and CeCe alone.

"You know he's just worried about you. I am too." Natalie said as she scooped down and picked up a deserted stuffed animal.

"I know, Nat, I promise I'm okay, I got this."

Staring down at the pink zebra, Natalie caressed its soft skin, lifting her blonde head she said, "If anything were to happen to you, I don't know…"

CeCe happily finishing the thought for her friend, with an ounce of cocky sass, "…what you would do without me, that is sweet."

"Well that, too, but I was going to say I don't know what *he* would do. You have no idea what you mean to him. Give him a break when it comes to him wanting to protect you, please?" Natalie hoped her words expressed the importance of the sentiment.

CeCe's eyes opened wide in surprise. Natalie's words touched her, and she knew they were from the heart. But rather than get mushy-gushy, she settled for, "I love you guys, I'm lucky to have you." She hugged her friend—and for all intents and purposes, her sister—and knew she was truly blessed to have such a wonderful support system.

With his precious daughters safely tucked into their cribs, Dylan left the nursery and went across the hall to the master bedroom. Pulling out his phone, he found the number he was looking for in his contacts and pressed send. The person on the other end answered with, "Yo."

"Yeah, it's me. I get pretty pissed when I pay someone to do a job and they don't do it. I'm paying you damn good money, asshole, time you start earning it."

Three

"Ms. Cervetti, unfortunately, we have no new leads. Since the first incident four weeks ago, our guy has gotten bolder, but still remains three steps ahead of us. Either you have been under surveillance for months, or he is the luckiest SOB in Vermont," the lieutenant explained through CeCe's phone.

CeCe held the phone to her ear and couldn't help rolling her eyes. She was standing at the desk in her office, looking at two dozen long stem white roses, still in the florist box, that were left outside her store front prior to tonight's closing. Before CeCe even made the call, she knew what Idarraga's response would be: they were no closer to getting this guy than they were the first night. Since that night, a month ago, she has had flowers arrive at her work, her home, and on her car, regardless of where she parks. Both CeCe and Idarraga thought they were onto a lead last week when three single roses were left on her car, but when it came time to view the video feed, the view to CeCe's car was obscured by the plaza's landscaping truck. Idarraga questioned the landscaping company, but they knew nothing about the flowers, except that a worker saw a man in the area, wearing a black hoodie, carrying flowers. But the worker was unable to give any other helpful description, so they had squat. There were still no notes attached, and there hadn't been any more breaking and entering. All the flowers were left in completely legal ways. CeCe was no longer scared, she was one hundred percent pissed off.

"I'm really sorry, CeCe, but my hands are tied. There really isn't anything else we can do other than remind you to be aware of your surroundings, continue with changing your routines, and of course, if anything is off, call 9-1-1 immediately." Idarraga sounded as exasperated as CeCe felt, which didn't make her feel any better.

"Thanks, Lieutenant," CeCe ended the call before adding, "for nothing."

She tossed her phone onto her desk next to the floral box, as Kelleigh popped her head in, "Cees, you want me to stick around?" Turning around, CeCe walked out to the store floor.

"No. I'm good, go on home. I'm going to stay and work for a bit. I need to get my mind off these fucking roses. I swear to God, the next man that sends me roses I'm going to tell him to take the stems and shove them up his ass, thorns and all."

Kelleigh laughed, despite the circumstances. "You sure you don't want me to stay and keep you company? I can unpack the shipment boxes we got in today."

Kelleigh was sweet, but honestly, CeCe just wanted to be by herself. "Thanks doll, but I'm good, really."

God, she was saying that a lot lately!

CeCe walked Kelleigh to the door; locking it behind her and waiting to make sure she got safely into her car and drove off. She was half way to her office when she heard her cell ringing. Quickening her pace, she picked it up on the fourth ring.

"Hello?"

"Hey, beautiful. How does dinner at Giovanni's sound?" Derrick asked.

Oh shit! Derrick! Despite what most people thought of her, CeCe really wasn't a bitch. She knew he was a nice guy, and she should be over the moon for him, but she just couldn't wrap her brain around him long term, she didn't do long term. And with this flower guy on the loose, Derrick made her feel even more suffocated. She knew this one was all on her; he was a good looking guy, loaded, treated her like a queen, and was decent in the sack, but there was just something about him.

"Hey. Dinner? I'd love to, but I have a ton of shit to do at the store tonight. In fact, I'm keeping Kelleigh here late so we can get a jump on unloading shipments." She squinted, clenching her teeth in a painful smile, hoping he wouldn't see through her lie.

Multiple heartbeats passed, but he finally responded, "Oh, okay. Perhaps tomorrow night?"

You are COMPLETELY the bitch everyone accuses you of being!

"Uh, well, uh…maybe. I don't know. How about I call you tomorrow?"

Again, after what felt like five minutes, his voice was quiet when he said, "Sure call me, beautiful. Anytime."

With a quick goodbye, she disconnected the call. Guilt set in, and she was just beginning to feel bad about it, when there was a loud knock at the store's front door. CeCe would be lying if she didn't jump at the sound, and looked around for a weapon before she realized a serial killer, or her deranged flower admirer, probably wouldn't knock. She peeked her head out the door of her office and saw it was Dylan standing at the front door. Relief flooded her. She was halfway to the front door when she noticed someone else was with him, but this guy had his back to the door. All she could see was his military-short blonde hair, and his killer ass, perfectly displayed, in well-worn tight jeans.

Pulling her eyes from the Grade-A ass, she looked at Dylan, facing her with his usual annoyed look. She reached the door and undid the lock, pushing the door open for Dylan and his friend. The humidity in the night air rushed in, warming her skin.

CeCe backpedaled to get out of Dylan's way as he stormed in. When he realized his company didn't follow, he chided, "You coming, or you going to gaze at the stars?" CeCe heard her phone ringing and chose to run back and grab it, leaving Dylan and his friend to figure out how to enter a building.

When she was in the privacy of her office, she noticed it was Derrick calling, again. She just couldn't talk to him, so she declined the call. When she returned to Dylan and company, she stopped dead in her tracks. Standing there, looking at her with those clear blue eyes and the same I-have-no-emotion expression, was the man that wrecked her, all those years ago. *Jarod Gates.* He looked the same, but different. He was still tall and lean, but now he was tall, lean, *and* jacked. Even under his pale blue t-shirt she could easily see the definition of his pecs and abs. His arms were ripped, evidenced by the taut material of his shirtsleeves. She could see a tattoo, only partially visible below the hem of his shirtsleeve. He stood, casual enough, with his hands in his pockets, watching her. Their eyes met, and for a moment, she hoped something would come through, but there was nothing; it was as if she was looking at a photograph. *Asshole!*

"Cees, you remember Jarod, I introduced you two, years ago. Jarod runs a private investigation and security company. I've hired him to figure out who this fucker is," Dylan explained, not caring about the annoyance on CeCe's face. "Honestly, I'm tired of waiting for the police to get their thumbs out of their asses."

What. The. Fuck???

Do not get hysterical. Do not whip off a shoe and throw it at him, like you want to, with visions of the stiletto sticking in his eye.

Be cool.

Fuck that shit!

"Well, you can just as quickly unhire him. I don't need him." *Or want him anywhere near me.*

"Come again?" Dylan asked, straightening to his full height, his arms crossed over his chest.

"You heard me. I am speaking fluent English, after all. When are you going to get it through your thick skull, I am not the naïve young girl you found in the bar that night. I can take care of myself and any somewhat problematic thing that comes my way." Knowing Dylan responded to body language, CeCe shifted into her best *I mean business* stance, hoping the message would be adequately delivered.

"We can have this argument when the asshat is found and arrested. Until then, you will deal with this; I will not allow anything to happen to you." Dylan broke the short distance between them, and in a steely, but quieter tone said, "Don't fight me on this. You will lose." Giving her forehead a quick peck, Dylan walked toward the door and said over his shoulder, "I'll leave you two to discuss strategy," and with that, he walked out the door.

CeCe stared out after Dylan for several moments before turning back to the ocean blue gaze that had yet to waver from her. Even now, under that gaze, she could feel her cheeks redden.

"Look I don't know what he told you, or what he hired you for, but your services are not needed."

"He and I beg to differ."

"Good thing your opinion doesn't matter. If I need a private investigator, I can hire my own. I'm working with the police department, and they are sufficient enough for me."

CeCe watched as Jarod's gaze raked over her from head to toe, and back again, several times. His jaw twitched and he let out a breath she didn't know he'd been holding.

"Is this about him hiring someone without your input, or is this about him hiring me?"

His voice hasn't changed, or what it does to me. "What? I said I can take care of myself."

"From what I hear, you have an unwanted admirer and the cops are no closer to identifying him now than they were the first time he struck, over a month ago." When her blush deepened, Jarod continued, "so, I will ask again, is this about Dylan not getting your approval, or is it about him bring me on board, Kitten?"

At the sound of his endearment, CeCe felt a flood of emotions. Fury and anger barely overrode others she thought she buried deep in side. But she would drop dead before letting him know he had that effect on her. "Don't make this to be more than it is. Yes, you and I have history, but that is exactly what it is: history. As in, over, never happening again. Don't delude yourself, and think I played the broken-hearted girl you left behind. I was well aware I was one of many in a long line of Jarod Gates conquests."

"Whatever you say, Kitten."

Unable to hold her annoyance any longer, "Don't call me that!" When her outburst only earned a smirk on his still handsome face, she let her tongue continue to show her irritation, "you are such a twit-twat!"

Incapable of not reacting to that response, Jarod smiled and said, "I think I'd have to have one to be one."

This only made CeCe want to throw both stilettos at him. Her temper took over, "What do I know, thirteen years is a long time; anything could have happened to your twig and berries."

Something in her words quickly wiped the smile from Jarod's face, his position changing from relaxed to defensive. "You don't know anything about me, or how much I've changed."

Changed? "So you say. I used to know you, or at least I thought I did. But it doesn't matter. I don't want to know anything about you. So again, your services, whatever they are, are not wanted." CeCe walked past him to the door, holding it for him to exit. When he remained unmoved, she cleared her throat. When that didn't get any results, she added, "That's your cue, Slick."

Jarod looked into her eyes, and with a slight quirk of his mouth, he walked to the door, but stopped short and turned to face her. His body was only inches away, and she could smell his cologne. She refused to admit it smelled intoxicating. The jump in her heart rate was at the audacity of Dylan, plain and simple, nothing to do with the man in front of her.

"See you around, Kitten," and Jarod Gates walked out of her store, CeCe happily locking the door behind him.

FUCK! Jarod thought to himself after he climbed in and slammed the door to his beat up pickup truck. Relieved to be sitting, his leg and hip throbbed from the tough guy show he'd put on. He allowed the pain to focus him for a moment, but knew he would need to overcome it before it consumed him. As the pain cleared his mind, he focused on the other twinge. He knew seeing CeCe up close would be interesting, but *that* he didn't expect. From the moment he signed on for this job, he knew he would be walking into an emotional inferno. Not wanting to assess those emotions, Jarod struck the steering wheel, bringing him back to the task at hand. Closing his eyes and taking long cleansing breaths, he put his racing thoughts and doubts into perspective. Efficiently, and expertly, scanning the parking lot, he confirmed nothing had changed since he parked over two hours ago, only the departure of many cars. Jarod had run the plates on all the cars in the lot when he first arrived, and all checked out. From this vantage point, he had a clear view of the store, her car and the entrances and exits of the parking lot.

He shifted in his seat, welcoming the physical discomfort. As he watched *CeCe's* he thought how beautiful she looked up close. She was always a looker, but now, she was beyond gorgeous. Her already amazing, petite body had only improved with time. The changes were subtle, but definitely effective, shifting her from the beautiful college student she used to be, to the sexy, vixen of a woman she was now. She knew it, too. The sleeveless, low-cut tuxedo-style blouse clung to her body in a way that left little to the imagination. The gentle lavender hue set off her silky olive skin, making it glow, even as her deep caramel tresses fell in luscious waves about her shoulders. It was obvious to Jarod just how deliberate her clothing choices were, as every inch of fabric or material showcased her assets perfectly. Her impossibly sexier ass combined with the distinct curve of her hips to be unforgettable in the black satin capris that even managed to improve on her already perfect legs. No doubt intentionally emphasized by the sky-high open-toed sandals. Everything on her fed the images and memories of the feel of his hands on her body. He shuddered at the phantom-like sensation rippling over his hands. But for all the delicate wonders of her body, nothing compared to the masterpiece of her face—a face that had haunted and comforted him in his dreams for so many years. The depths of her striking hazel eyes, which he always knew saw to much, were tinged with a heartbreaking coldness, even as they gleamed with her fury. He would be lying to himself if he thought she would greet him with a warm embrace, as if they were old friends; no, truth be told, he knew it would be anything but warm and fuzzy, but still, he didn't expect the unadulterated loathing from her.

Movement pulled him from his memories of her body and his analysis of their five-minute reunion. Jarod watched a motorcycle enter the lot on the west side, keeping to that end of the building; he did a few laps then exited the way he came. Always too far away for Jarod to read his tags, but from what he could tell, it was a newer model racing bike. The motorcycle gone, Jarod brought his attention back to *CeCe's*, and its owner who could clearly be seen inside. *What was she doing?* Pushing the driver's seat all the way back, he got as comfortable as he could, having a feeling it would be a long night. Refusing to massage the constant throb in his leg, he allowed his mind to wander. The upside to this part of his job was he had a lot of time on his hands to play things over in his mind; the down side was he had a lot of time to play things over in his mind—things he spent a lot of

41

time and energy not thinking about. CeCe Cervetti fit that category. She was a double edge sword; she was his talisman, but also his trigger. She was certainly going to make this job harder than anything before. The question was, would he be willing to face the demons he has avoided for years, and if he did, would he live through the fallout?

Four

CeCe's fingers ached from holding the pencil. Her hands, and most likely her cheeks, were smeared with lead and charcoal. Her back hurt, and her neck had such a kink in it from being hunched over her desk. Her legs had fallen asleep hours ago, crossed underneath her in the green velvet chair, but seven new designs lay spread across her desk. Designs she didn't even know she had floating in her head, but they just appeared when she first held the pencil, flowing out through her fingers onto the pages. She reveled in the quiet, allowing her artistic talent to flow without interruption.

Sketching played such a huge part of CeCe's life. For as long as she could remember, she could handle any situation as long as a pencil and paper were within reach. This was when she was the happiest, when she was able to come out of her shell. She loved to sketch people, and the closer a person was to her, the more sketches she did of them. She tried her hand at patterns and clothes, and she was hooked.

Leaning back and rubbing her neck, she admired the darker than usual designs. Her style of fashion design has changed so much over the last few months. What started as cleaner, enhanced classic designs have transformed into truly original and elegant pieces—pieces she honestly couldn't wait to bring to fruition from the sheets of paper laid out before her. To actually touch and hold the clothes she dreamed would be worn by the masses someday. As much as she loved drawing out the lines and angles, there was something entrancing about selecting, cutting, and stitching the fabric to make the idea a reality.

CeCe knew it was well into the early morning without even looking at her phone for the time. It had been years since she pulled an all-nighter designing, but it seemed her mind was telling her she needed this therapy in the midst of her current adventure. Not to mention, she needed the diversion after seeing Jarod after all these years. Unbidden, her mind was flooded with glimpses and memories, both new and old. With amazing restraint, CeCe shut her mind to Jarod Gates like a vault. Rising to her feet, she stretched and walked through her office door, out to the main floor and was amazed the dark night was beginning to fade to morning light. She continued to stretch to get blood flowing back to her neglected muscles and work out some of the stiffness from being in the chair for so long. Sliding her feet into the flip-flops she kept in her office, she grabbed up her things, sent a quick text to Kelleigh letting her know she would be late coming in this morning, and let herself out the front door, locking it behind her before making her way to her car.

The parking lot was empty except for a truck far off in the secondary parking. When she noticed someone was in the truck, she quickened her pace, keeping in tempo with her beating heart. When she reached her car, she quickly climbed in with all intentions to peel out and head home, but then annoyance got the better of her. Rather than head away from the lone truck, she turned the mustang toward it, deciding that if this was Mr. White Rose, she wanted to know and put an end to this shit.

Quickly her V8 ate up the pavement and reached the truck; but instead of identifying her misguided admirer, she was met with a pair of all too familiar blue eyes. When she continued to just stare at him, he gave a plastic smile, unabashed and mimed for her to roll down the window. Annoyed, she complied as she played out in her head what she wanted to say to him for stalking her.

But he beat her to the punch.

"God, woman, aren't you too old to be out all night? Alone, to boot?"

Old? See, complete asshole! Like she needed any more proof.

"What the fuck are you doing here, Gates?"

"Told you earlier, I'm working."

"And I told you, you were fired."

"Technically, you never said I was fired. You told Dylan he could unhire me—which isn't even a word, by the way—you told me I was not needed, but you never said the words 'you're fired'."

Oh My God! Was there anyone more infuriating than this man!?!

"Well, let me not get caught on such a technicality, again. YOU. ARE. FIRED! As in, axed! Will not get paid! You do not work here! You have nothing to investigate! Oh, and just for good measure, you are an ASSHOLE!" CeCe peeled out, causing quite the sound and leaving heavy tread markings in her wake.

Jarod watched as the emerald-green mustang fishtailed around the corner before coming to a stop at the exit, where she once again put all the Mustang's horsepower to the test. He couldn't help his smile as he pulled out, much slower, and onto the main road.

By the time he reached CeCe's apartment complex, he estimated she had been home for ten minutes. He parked in plain sight on the street, and as he sat there observing the other cars coming and going, he began to wonder if he wanted her to see him so easily. There was something about seeing her so passionate, even if it was in anger. Moments later, she reappeared walking down the steps after exiting the security door from the apartment building. She had just reached her car when she looked over the roof and locked eyes with Jarod. You didn't need binoculars, or even 20/20 vision, to clearly see the obscene gesture she had for him. Foregoing the car, she dropped a bag on her trunk and walked with purpose toward him.

He definitely enjoyed the sight she made coming toward him, in a black sports bra and lime green, off the shoulder shirt that exposed just the right amount of midriff above black yoga pants—talk about bouncing in all the right places. Her face was anything but happy.

"You are like a bad toothache, Gates," she said in a cyanide-laced whisper when she reached the beat up pick-up.

"Oh yeah, how's that?" he asked, happy his mirrored aviation glasses were on so she wouldn't be any more pissed at him when he enjoyed the view of her exposed cleavage, especially when she crossed her arms like she was doing now.

"No matter what I do, I can't shake you." Tapping her toe in annoyance, she looked at the car pulling in and grabbed her composure. When she turned back to face him he could see the gears shifting. He was not wrong when she spoke, "Look, I know you are kind of stuck in the middle, but really, your services are not needed. I will talk to Dylan and make sure you get paid for your time."

"See, I knew you cared."

"Care? Oh no, I don't care anything about you; I just want you gone. And apparently, being a nice human being, and doing as another asks is too advanced for you, so I thought I'd appeal to your wallet instead."

"Why do you think it would only be my wallet you could appeal to?"

Avoiding the question, CeCe swooped in and ripped the aviator's off Jarod's face and put them on her own before asking, "What is it going to take for you to get lost? Or is my annoyance a turn on for you?"

Tell the truth, or not?

"Where you off to dressed like that?"

Cocking her head to one side and pursing her lips, she huffed irritably, "I'd say it's none of your business, but I have this uncanny feeling you're just going to follow me anyway."

"You always were a smart little thing." The fact he already knew she was off to Workout Place was beside the point.

"I mean it, Gates, get lost."

"Can't do that."

"Figure it out, as I recall you were quite good at disappearing when you wanted." CeCe took the aviator's off, threw them in the open window, and walked off without another word.

Jarod enjoyed the view of her departure, and as she backed out and drove toward the gym, he remained parked where he was. Pulling out his phone, he dialed, and when Dylan answered he calmly stated, "We've got a problem. I'm coming to you." He disconnected the phone call and couldn't help smiling from ear to ear.

Five

Jarod arrived at Dylan's office thirty minutes later. When he reached the second floor, his leg and hip were crying in defense. He rubbed his thigh as he walked in the door marked *S&D Construction*. Behind the front desk, a pretty blonde was on the phone, indicating with one finger for Jarod to wait. He stood to the side, leaned against the wall, and rubbed his thigh methodically. He hated being in public and showing weakness, but days like this just couldn't be helped. The blonde finished her call and asked, "May I help you?" refusing to hide her appreciation of the fine male specimen she thought Jarod was.

"Looking for Dylan. He's expecting me." Jarod did not return her over-exaggerated smile.

"One moment please."

Jarod turned his back to look out the large window as she did whatever she did. Within moments he heard, "You can go on back, second door on the left."

With a curt nod of his head and scowl fully in place, Jarod followed her instructions, not bothering to knock when he arrived at the close door. He opened the door and let himself in noticing Dylan was not alone.

"Jarod, come on in. I'd like to introduce you to my friend and partner, Seth Finn. Seth, this is Jarod Gates."

Jarod extended his hand to the other man, noting this guy could be his friend Buffy's twin. This guy was as tall as a sequoia redwood, and just as wide. Very few men had a height advantage over Jarod, but Seth Finn did. Not that it mattered; Jarod wasn't here to throw down, just his constant observation quirk.

"So you're Gates. Nice to meet you, man. I appreciate the help you gave us a while back on that lawsuit. Without your assistance, we probably wouldn't have dug ourselves out of that very big hole."

"My pleasure, as I've told Dylan, I'm always willing to help uncover the truth."

"Good to know. I'll get out of your way." Seth said, as he made his way to the door, but before exiting he turned and said, "Oh and D, one more thing, remember Hawthorne wants us to move our meeting next Saturday to Boston. Mae wants to go to visit some friends, and she wants Natalie to come along. The kids are staying home with Lynne."

"Sounds good, I could use some alone time with my wife."

"Welcome to fatherhood." Seth said on a chuckle, as he gave a two-finger salute before leaving and closing the door behind him.

Dylan's attention shifted from the door to the man who took the seat Seth vacated. Jarod lounged in the seat as if he didn't have a care in the world.

"You mentioned a problem?" Dylan asked as he leaned against the front of his desk and crossed his arms over his chest.

Jarod studied the man that had once been a friend, but had the potential to quickly become a foe, especially if he ever learned the truth about Jarod and CeCe's history. "Depends on your definition of a problem. She isn't exactly warming to the idea of me checking things out and shadowing her."

"Good thing I don't give a shit if she wants you around. I want this issue solved, and fast."

"Understood. I just thought you should know, she's being difficult about your plan."

Furrowing his brow Dylan asked, "and is *that* a problem? I'm paying you for security service and to investigate, I don't believe there was anything in there about her liking it, or you."

Jarod stood, ignoring the throb in his leg brought on by such a quick motion. When they were eye to eye, both reflecting similar glares, he extended his hand for a handshake while saying, "Whatever you say; you're the boss." Jarod turned to leave, but just as Seth did before him, he turned back before reaching the door, "When do you plan on telling CeCe how long you've had me on your payroll where she is concerned?"

"When I figure that out, I'll let you know."

CeCe called Derrick earlier and agreed to dinner. Now that it was time to go, she wished she had gone with Plan B, and rented a movie and getting some Ben and Jerry's. The whole rose-stalker thing, and adding Gates on top of it, was really affecting her. So to shake all the negativity in her head, not to mention the newest delivery of roses, she put a little bit more care into her appearance for tonight. She loved this little black dress; it was the epitome of sexiness. From the tight fit, to the versatility, it just made CeCe feel girlie and desirable. Her boobs looked great in the low scoop neck style, and she loved how her legs looked in it. With the hem falling mid-thigh, she loved how shapely her calves looked thanks to the zebra printed rhinestone strappy sandals. She put her hair up in a twist, and finished the look with chunky zebra print hoops at her ears and a matching chunky cuff on her wrist. Applying the last bit of her makeup, when she heard a knock. Derrick was always fifteen minutes early picking her up, and that time was fast approaching, so she thought nothing of opening the door.

However, it was not dark and handsome Derrick on the other side of the door, but Jarod instead. His blue eyes raked over her body several times before meeting her eyes and raising an eyebrow.

"What do you want, and why are you here?"

"I thought you and I could talk. Clear some things up and make this," indicating with his finger between the two of them, "less stiff."

She couldn't help it; his choice of words had her arching her own brow. Knowing Mrs. Snider across the hall was probably at her peephole watching, she stepped back, allowing him to enter. Aware Derrick would be arriving any moment, she thought it best to speed this along. "Can you talk while I finish getting ready?" Not waiting for him to respond she left him standing in the living room as she rounded the corner to the short hall to her bedroom, needing to grab her bag and lip-gloss. When he didn't say anything, she returned to find he had ventured over to the photographs she had framed on the sofa table. He was studying them when she cleared her throat, "Look, unlike you, I don't have all night. Was there something you wanted to say?"

He turned to face her, and again, unabashedly, he slowly took her in from head to toe. When he spoke, his voice was husky, "Where is the rest of your dress?"

Batting her eyelashes, one hand on her hip she responded in kind, "Oh, it is all here, have no worry; when I dress, I know what I'm doing." Just to be a ball buster, she looked down at her cleavage, adjusting her breasts just to ensure they were perky and showing enough.

Unable to hold back the full smile, he shook his head trying to shake the image, but when he looked back at her, the smile was gone, "Got a date?"

"Not that it is any business of yours, but I do. What do you want?"

For the first time, CeCe noticed Jarod looked uncomfortable. He fidgeted before leaning back on his heels and putting his hands in his pockets causing the corded veins running up his forearms to twitch.

"I get that it may have been a shock seeing me, but Dylan just wants to ensure you are safe. He hired me to do a job the cops can't do. So the sooner you let me do it, the sooner you can say goodbye to me. But until I figure out who this guy is, you are stuck with me, Kitten."

"Don't call me that. You lost the privilege long ago. But it seems I am stuck with you. Dylan called me today and told me either I play nice, or my physical address would be changing." CeCe noticed Jarod's expression didn't show any surprise, which irked her even more. "And since that doesn't really work for me, I guess I will play nice. Well, as nice as I can play with you."

"Oh, you want to play? I can play real nice," Jarod smoothly cooed and winked.

CeCe rolled her eyes.

Slowly, Jarod crossed the distance and, if she didn't know better, momentarily winced, but before she could be certain, he recovered. When he was merely foot away from her, he leaned in and whispered, "Do you have any idea how gorgeous you are when you aren't sneering at me, Kitten?" He knew he just severed any sort of cordiality they would have, but truth is truth, and she deserved to hear it.

Surprised, she locked eyes with him, searching for something—anything—to explain what a statement like that meant, but realized she was just borrowing trouble, so she settled for, "Thank you." Knowing she had to keep him at arms-length she added, "Now, was there anything else?"

"Yeah, who's the guy you're going out with looking like that?"

"Come again?"

"Oh Kitten, I could make you come and come, but wouldn't you like to eat first? I know I would." He bobbed his eyebrows a couple of times to emphasize the sexual innuendo.

"Still an asshole! Who I see personally has nothing to do with your presence and is none of your business. Be sure not to confuse the two. I already have one overprotective man in my life. Trust me, that is more than enough."

"But see, it doesn't work like that. You go somewhere; I go

somewhere. But don't worry I won't be so obvious that your date will feel the need to arch his stream."

"I'm serious, Gates. You are off duty tonight. I agreed with Dylan that you could hang around the store and observe, and do your little investigation, but it's not happening when I'm on a date."

Standing this close, he could smell her perfume, and she smelled incredible. He wondered if she still tasted as good as she did then. He knew he was walking a fine line, "You are missing the point here, Kitten."

"Okay, Slick, you want me to spell it out for you? I have a date, and with any luck—which I don't think I actually need—I plan to get quite the cardio workout in afterwards with multiple orgasms. I'd rather not have you around for that. Besides, I'm sure there is some Barbie around who would be happy to give you a whirl."

Unsure whether it was the mention of what she had plans to do, or her offhand remark about his extracurricular activities that sparked his temper, Jarod barely managed to keep his tone in check. "A whirl? Is that your way of hinting around to my sex life? Don't worry about who's warming my sheets. When I'm on the job that is where all my focus is. And I do mean *all* my focus."

Suddenly uncomfortable, and thrown off her game with this pissing match, CeCe opted for the easy way out, "Doesn't matter…"

"I think it does. Where you go, I go, Cees, so perhaps you should rethink your after dinner activities. I hear there is a Julia Roberts marathon on tonight. See, problem solved, you have other plans now."

The audacity and cocksureness of this one man rendered CeCe speechless. She turned away from Jarod and walked to the door, more pissed off at herself for not having a witty comeback. When she opened it, she was greeted by Derrick's gorgeous smile. He quickly stepped in, wrapped his arms around CeCe, and placed a light kiss on her lips before saying, "I didn't think it was possible for you to get any more beautiful, but you just keep amazing me." It was then he noticed Jarod, "Am I interrupting something?" looking from CeCe to Jarod, and back again.

"No, Jarod was just leaving." CeCe said with a wide smile, hoping to hide that her nerves were completely thrown off of their axis.

Finding immense pleasure in her discomfort, Jarod walked up to Derrick, with nothing but contempt on his face and in his voice, "Yeah, I was just leaving. Don't want to interrupt your date." Turning to CeCe he said, "I'll see you around." Then the bastard winked before brushing past Derrick, whistling unapologetically as he strode down the hall.

Derrick watched Jarod's retreating back, then turned back to CeCe, "Everything alright?"

"Peachy! What time is our reservation?"

CeCe looked at Derricks questioning eye, and knew all hope the date was going to take her mind off everything went completely out the window. Damn, she really wanted Ben and Jerry's now.

To CeCe's shock there were no surprise interruptions in the quaint corner of Giovanni's Derrick reserved for their dinner. Jarod didn't pose as their waiter, nor did he appear snapping pictures of the two of them from the other side of the windows overlooking a beautiful spot in the gorge of the Green Mountains National Park. By the time their meals came—Beef Wellington for Derrick and Scallop Risotto for CeCe—she began to relax and enjoy herself. Derrick was telling her all about his recent trip to California for the software company he works at. He mentioned, more than once, how much he would love to take CeCe to see the Golden Gate Bridge and the extensive vineyards in Napa.

"I found this beautiful little bed and breakfast right in the heart of Napa I think you would love. I will probably be heading back out there the end of August, please come with me." Derrick asked as he took her hand and caressing the top with his thumb.

CeCe looked across the table at the picture he made, his rich chocolate hair and his perfectly trimmed beard, his expensive black dress shirt that was opened just enough at the collar, the Rolex at his wrist and his meticulously manicured nails. Derrick Lowell was a sexy man, and he only had eyes for CeCe. She found herself mentally arranging things so she could get away with him.

"It sounds amazing," she answered back, smiling in response.

"Napa is beautiful, but amazing—that word is reserved for you, beautiful." Bringing her hand to his lips, Derrick kissed her knuckles.

The waitress came by then, "May I get you anything else? Our special dessert tonight is our homemade cannolis."

Derrick looked at CeCe and they both scrunched their noses and lightly shook their heads—it amazed her how in sync they were.

"I think we will do the Tiramisu for two; the lovely lady will have a cappuccino and I'll have an espresso, please." When the server left them alone, he added, "I hope you don't mind me ordering for you. I know how much you love their cappuccino."

"No, it's perfect, thank you. I'm just going to go to the ladies room, I'll be right back."

As she stood and began to walk by Derrick, he grabbed her hand, and once again brought it to his lips, "Be quick."

CeCe's smile stretched from ear to ear and she was in the midst of bliss when she reached the stairs that went up to the ladies room. Her foot on the first step, she glanced to the left towards the bar, and was ensnared by a blue gaze. Her smile fell instantly. Quickly looking over her shoulder in Derrick's direction, she walked with purpose to where Jarod sat at the end of the bar.

"Seriously?" she whispered harshly.

"What? I'm not allowed to eat?"

"You know damn well what I mean."

"So, this is what it takes to get your dress up, huh? Fancy meal and money?"

Every time she thought he couldn't say anything worse, he surprised her.

"Fuck you!"

"Sure. I'm up for a cardio workout." He wiped his mouth with the napkin that was on his lap.

"Never happening, Slick!" she had spun on her heels to leave, when he grabbed onto her hand pulling her backwards, landing her in his lap as a result.

Moving his head so it rested on her shoulder, his lips grazed her earlobe, "Really. I rocked your world once, I'm sure I could easily do it again."

With her fury fueling her movements, she turned her head so they were nose to nose, and she replied, "Rocked my world? The only thing you rocked that night was the car. Don't think it was anything more than that. Now let go of me, before I make a scene."

Instantly, he released her, and watched her walk away from him and toward Derrick…again.

Six

If you walked in the front door to Derrick's home, you would find a clear line of where CeCe and he had been. It would be easy to follow the erotic trail to his bedroom. Shoes and clothes littered the way through the lower level, up the stairs and to the master bedroom where they both lay naked on his king size bed.

With her beautifully bare before him, laid out like a feast for consumption, he began at her feet and slowly worshipped her with his mouth and tongue. When Derrick reached her center and began to delve in, her fingers pushed his head away, causing them to lock gazes.

"What's the matter?"

CeCe couldn't believe she stopped him from the much-needed orgasm she could use to blow the cobwebs out of her brain, but as if taken over by an unknown force, she just couldn't go through with the action.

"CeCe? Talk to me."

When no response came, only a caress of his face against her inner thigh, he sat up resting his ass on his heels, and waited for some sort of explanation. Again, nothing came.

"Is this about that guy in your apartment, Jarod?"

"What? No!"

"Well, then is it me? Do you not enjoy this?"

"You know I enjoy your talented tongue immensely. I'm sorry. I just have a lot on my plate. I'm still getting flowers from the anonymous asshole, and it just has me off my game. Derrick, please don't take it personally."

CeCe was not convinced he wasn't doing just that by his ironic laugh and he added, "And how, exactly, do you expect me not to take it personally when the last two times we've tried to have sex, you wound up pulling away from me? And I'm not just talking about my tongue, or dick, either." He moved so his feet hung over the side of the bed, as he ran a hand through his dark hair.

She was taken aback by his words, but she knew she was guilty, and she'd hurt him immensely. Pulling herself up, she kneeled behind him and put her arms around him, resting her chin on his shoulder and remained silent.

He squeezed her arm, turned his head and looked at her. He must have seen what he was looking for because he pulled away from her and reached for the bedside table, pulling a small box from the top drawer and handed it to her.

Instantly recognizing the blue box and white ribbon packaging, CeCe asked in a small voice, "What's this?"

Giving a one-shoulder shrug, he looked at her hazel eyes, searching for something, then answered, "Coming back from San Francisco, I flew into New York to attend a meeting. It was uptown, so on the way back I stopped in at Tiffany's and found something I wanted you to have. I was hoping to give it to you in the glow of orgasmic satisfaction, but that just got blown out of the water."

Extraordinary fear raced through her as she digested his words. Suddenly, the small box was extremely heavy.

He chuckled, "Okay, the look on your face kind of makes up for the bruise to my ego. It isn't *that* kind of box, CeCe. It is just something pretty I thought you would like."

Taking refuge in this assurance, she sat back and gently pulled the ribbon. She took the lid off the top and saw a beautiful circle of intricately set diamonds on a black silk cord. She ran a finger over the gorgeous piece and raised her eyes to his, "Derrick, it is gorgeous."

"I'm glad you like it. It reminded me of you. May I see how it looks on your sexy neck?"

"Please."

He extracted the cord from the box, and effortlessly placed it around her neck, where it rested between her collarbones. "Perfect," he spoke, being sure to rest his gaze on hers before adding, "the necklace is nice, too."

CeCe fingered the expensive piece while she returned the look in his deep brown eyes that clearly showed how much he wanted her.

Those eyes came closer to her, and when his lips were barely touching hers he whispered, "Let me…"

Why should she deny him, or herself?

Jarod could feel the adrenaline as it pulsed through his veins. Here he was, outside in his truck, with no air conditioning, in this ungodly heat and humidity, while he watched Derrick Lowell's home like a fucking peeping tom without the binoculars, knowing what was going on inside. Seeing CeCe with this Lowell guy didn't sit right with him. Yeah, he was a successful software engineer, with a nice six-figure salary, and he owned property here, along with a condo in Aruba. On paper, he looked like a decent guy; hell, even off paper, and through lesser known channels, the kind of places where dirty little secrets tend to be found, where Jarod was quite familiar with, this guy was a straight shooter and clean as a whistle. So what was it about CeCe dating him that stuck in his craw? *Well, that's an easy one, dickstick!* CeCe was dating him. Hell, he knew she dated and screwed men, but seeing the type of guy she was with only reminded Jarod of his stupidity. Fuck, he was far from celibate, but he also knew, one way or another, he compared every woman to CeCe, in and out of his bed.

Tipping his head back to rest on the seat, he squeezed his eyes shut. He needed to get his head back in the game. He needed to stop thinking of Lowell sucking on her tits, and start figuring out who was stalking her. With one last look at the house and low lighting on in the master bedroom, he picked up the papers on the passenger seat. Background checks and financials of the last ten guys CeCe dated. As he read the info, he couldn't help but smile, thinking how pissed she would be if she had any idea the extent of how well he did his job. If only she knew how much income came into *Gates Investigations and Private Securities* at her expense. But that was between her and Cross.

Looking up from boyfriend #6's hidden Cayman account, Jarod took a swig of his Red Bull, and was glad he did. Derrick and CeCe were on the move. Lowell was carefully backing up his Porsche 911 Carrera Cabriolet out of the drive.

"What's the matter, Lowell, couldn't get it up? Or is it more of a two pump hot injection? Fucktard!"

Once the high-end sports car passed him, Jarod pulled out and turned around to tail. Quickly reaching CeCe's apartment complex, he pulled in and parked in the same spot as when he spoke with CeCe this morning. He had a perfect view of the Porsche idling, and the two passengers still inside. Jarod could clearly see, through the back window, as Lowell ran his hands through her hair and pulled her towards him. Suddenly, Jarod began to clench his teeth so tightly his jaw cracked under the strain.

After what seemed to Jarod like an infinite game of tonsil hockey, Lowell got out, rounded the hood and opened the passenger side door. He extended a hand, which she quickly accepted and he walked her into the building.

Taking the opening, Jarod was out of the truck double time; walking to the Porsche, he made quick work of the lock thanks to his handy pocket tool he never left home without. It was Jarod's experience that most men with something to hide, they tend to hide it in their car. Quickly, he rummaged through the glove compartment and the sports jacket, which was in the back, and came up with nothing. He locked the car again, and had just made it back to his pickup when Lowell reappeared.

Without any fanfare, Lowell jumped back in and Jarod watched as the taillights faded into small dots. Redirecting his attention to CeCe's second floor apartment, he noticed she'd just entered her bedroom. *Dammit, Cees, ever hear of a shade or blind?* Not that he minded the show, CeCe was a gorgeous woman and she knew it, but if he could clearly see her disrobing, then others could too, and that didn't sit well with him.

Before his mind could even process his feet's actions, he was out of the truck and jogging up the steps to the security door. *This could pose a problem.* A petite blonde came down the stairs and without even asking, held the door for Jarod. *God must like me tonight.* Taking the stairs two at a time, his thigh protested, but he didn't care. He reached apartment 221 and pounded on the door then placed his hands on each side of the doorframe.

He could hear CeCe cursing on the other side, just as he could hear her grumbles when she looked through the peephole. She opened the door, and his mouth went dry. There she stood, in nothing but an obscenely short lime green silk robe that hardly covered the black lace bra she was wearing.

"Gates, I should have known. What do you want?" She leaned against the door, crossing her arms and exposing even more of her fantastic cleavage. The obvious expression of annoyance at his presence only fueled his own that much more.

"Oh sorry, am I bothering you, Kitten? I'm hired to find out who the creep is sending you flowers, and here you are, putting on a show for the entire town of Appleton!" Even he could hear his own voice echoing down the hall.

She fisted his t-shirt and yanked as hard as she could, causing him to fall into her apartment. She slammed the door and turned on him. He didn't think anyone's face could get that red without actually exploding.

"Who the fuck do you think you are, and what the fuck are you talking about?"

"I'm talking about the fucking strip show you just put on for everyone within eye shot." Emphasizing his remark, he pointed toward her bedroom, when he saw the flowers.

"Where'd those come from?" He asked as he strolled over to the boxed arrangement and searched its contents.

"There isn't a card. There never is."

"How many of these have you gotten here before?" He whirled around to face her, as he felt his fury build.

"Four, this one makes five."

"Dylan told me all the deliveries to your home were left between the doors in the security hall," he crossed his arms over his chest, as he clutched his fists tight and tried to remain calm.

"Well, that's because that's what I told him." She explained further, with her chin lifted defiantly.

"And lying about this shit seemed like a good idea to you, why?" he seethed. *Of all the stupid things for her to do!* How the hell was he supposed to do his job if she wasn't honest? Looking at her standing there, in minimal clothes, with that look of absolute disgust on her face and all Jarod could think was *why was it when she was annoyed she looked so damn sexy?* His hands itched to touch her. He would need to see a dentist soon if he kept up grinding his teeth at this rate.

"I asked you a question, Cees!"

"Because I knew if Dylan had known the truth he would have gone off the deep end. And what do you know; you're here, so I guess I was right." Walking back to the door, she opened it and motioned with her other hand for him to exit.

With ease he reached over her head and closed the door again, "I'm not leaving until you tell me everything!"

She suddenly looked so drained, but yet still so beautiful. She belonged in the finer things, like silk, and with that little bit of sparkle at her neck, she looked like a Hollywood housewife, and that thought infuriated him more. She should be treasured and spoiled, free to enjoy life, not have to constantly look over her shoulder. She shouldn't be dealing with this kind of shit. Any man that did this kind of thing wasn't right in the head. Yeah, it was just flowers now, but too many cases had Jarod seen where this kind of thing quickly escalated to something more, something sinister, something that could harm her. *Over my cold dead body!* Repeatedly he had to stop his hand from reaching out to touch her cheek. Just to have some sort of physical contact with her. So she would know, truly know, he would not allow anything to happen to her. She didn't deserve this; she was being coveted by this asshole. *Well if that isn't just irony. Pot, kettle; kettle, pot!*

In a meek voice, as if all the fight rushed out of her, "What do you want me to say? Derrick walked me to my door; the box was leaning against it."

"And the turd, Lowell, just said, *oh well*...my date's got flowers from some creep, but I got my rocks off, so see ya?"

He watched as her hazel eyes filled red with emotion, "Leave Derrick out of this! This has nothing to do with him." CeCe walked past him into her living room, where she looked out the window into the dark summer night.

Noticing she didn't deny the 'rocks off' part, Jarod buried the unpleasant and internal rage the thought created and tried to move on. Knowing this couldn't be easy for her, Jarod followed and stood behind her, fighting the temptation to reach out and have some sort of physical connection, "A guy that would leave like that, without even checking things out, is that really the kind of guy you want?" He held his breath against the possible answer.

CeCe turned to face him, not realizing he was so close, her breasts grazed his chest and readiness rocketed through his body.

CeCe's vision remained downcast for multiple moments, before she turned her gaze upward, where it once again stalled at his lips. "Not that it is any of your business, but Derrick wanted to stay; hell, he insisted, but I told him I needed some space." She swallowed hard, and finally raised her eyes until they connected with his. In a firmer, stronger voice, selling her own conviction to them both, "I was perfectly safe here. I promised him I would call the police."

"And did you?" he whispered.

Her gaze never wavered, "I never said *when* I would call them."

He let out an ironic chuckle, before rubbing his hands over his face. "I don't know who to be more pissed at, you for playing the stupid, coy, manipulating female, or Fucktard, for not realizing he has a set between his legs." Trying to defuse the moment Jarod added, "Wait, he does have a pair, right?"

"Still an asshole." But this time, she could not keep the small smile from her lips.

"Yeah, Kitten, but I'm your asshole." Jarod's own cocksure smile graced his face, and for once, he could appreciate and relish CeCe's smile that was only for him.

Breaking the visual connection, she took a step back and tried to get some physical space from the intensity and proximity of him. Cece walked around his towering form and headed to the door, "Okay so you know the story, now can you leave?"

As much as he was enjoying the small amount of headway he was making in cracking her hard exterior toward him, he also could see the fatigue all over her face and in the lines of her fine body. Jarod knew he needed to give her a break.

"Yeah, let me just check out the place, make sure there isn't any boogeyman in the closet, and then I'll head down to my truck."

"Don't you mean home?" she asked, fingering the circle at her neck.

Jarod let his eyes take in their fill again, perusing her body before he answered, "No, I mean down to my truck. I'm not going anywhere." *I'm here to stay, but you aren't ready to hear that yet.* "Look, it isn't like it's the first time I've slept in my truck and trust me, compared to some other places I've slept, my truck is like the Hilton." The pain in his thigh screamed out at the mention of less than favorable memories. His hands flexed in reaction, but he refused to show her any weakness. He chose this moment to head to her bedroom and start his safety sweep.

"That is ridiculous. Just go home," she called out to him from where her feet were rooted by the door.

"No can do, sistah!" he yelled back. She listened as he opened her closet doors, checked the spare room she used as a home office, as well as moved her shower curtain in the bath. He joined her a few minutes later, "All clear."

She stared at him while waging a decision making war in her mind. She did not look happy about the victor. "Now why did you have to be all nice and worried about me? You know, Gates, you are really screwing with my self-centered bitch beacon!" She turned away from his confused face. A few moments later, he assumed when she felt she had control over herself, she turned back and said, "You can sleep here," so softly, he thought he misheard her.

Needing to know she was sure, as well as keep up the pretense he was a bastard, "Did CeCe Cervetti just invite me to spend the night? Now that's what I'm talking about!"

Letting out a huff, she pushed past him and disappeared down the hall, just to reappear moments later. She carried a pillow and blanket, "You are couch-bound, Slick!"

Taking the bedding from her, he couldn't help but goad her again, "Admit it, I make you feel all warm and fuzzy."

"Yeah, like an ugly Christmas sweater, but I won't sleep knowing you are down there cramped in that shitbox you call a truck."

"I like my truck." He answered, feigning outrage.

She rolled her eyes, "Anyways…good night," she turned walking back to her bedroom. When she reached the door, she stopped and turned to him, "And…thanks, Jarod."

Being sure his gaze never faltered he answered, "No need to thank me, Kitten, but I meant what I said, you really should draw the shades when you are in your bedroom."

"I like them open, it's freeing."

"It's asking for trouble."

"Dually noted. Well, anyways, thanks"

"I'm just doing my job. Plus, it's a gentleman thing."

"Gentleman? Who sees a gentleman? All I see is you," she retorted.

Enjoying the verbal sparring, Jarod placed his hand over his heart, simulating a direct hit, "You wound me."

All fun and airiness dropped from her face, "You'd have to have a heart to be hurt."

Jarod was afraid to consider what her words meant, and he hoped another jest would bring her back around, "In the last twenty-four hours you have accused me of having no heart and no dick, I can't wait to see what you conclude I'm missing in the next twenty-four."

She answered by stepping into her room and closing the door.

Well shit!

Seven

CeCe woke to a strange sound. She listened in the darkness; just when she thought she imagined it, she heard it again. *What is that? It sounds like a wounded animal.* She got out of bed and walked to her window and looked out trying to see anything that could be making the noise. When nothing registered as out of the ordinary, she heard it again, but this time she was able to tell the cry wasn't coming from outside; it was coming from her living room.

She padded to the door, opened it and listened again. The yelp was now accompanied by mumbles. She moved down the hall, stopping when she reached the corner where the hall met the living room, remaining in the shadows. She could clearly see his large form on her couch. With the minimal amount of light coming through the window, she was able to tell he had taken off his shirt. The ridges of definition along his arms, chest and abs were captivating by themselves, but add in the provocativeness of the moonlight seeping through her blinds, and Jarod looked like the perfect cover model for one of those Mommy Porn Smut books.

As if reacting to her silent thought, he called out in undistinguishable words before his body stretched out in the most grimacing of ways. CeCe had never seen anything like it; it looked like an electric current was stunning him. With his limbs curled inward and his head thrown back, there was no doubt he was experiencing physical pain, but then he woke, pulling himself out of whatever nightmare he was having. He sat up, thanks to his position his back was toward her, he looked around, cursing quietly before settling back down.

CeCe tiptoed back down the hall and when she reached her bed, she decided this was his one free pass. Come morning, she needed to keep him at arm's length. She couldn't allow him to weave his way back into her life, in any form. If she gave him an inch, he would take a mile, and she just couldn't go back to that vulnerable girl again. She hadn't allowed anyone to alter her course, so why should the one man that made her choose it, be the one to implode it?

The sound of the shower mixed with the smell of heavenly coffee roused Jarod. With a quick glance at his phone, he couldn't believe the time. He very rarely sleeps this late, and 8AM is late for him, let alone the fact he very rarely sleeps. When he sleeps, he falls victim to the nightmares. The fact both occurred while he crashed on CeCe's couch had him considering things that shouldn't be considered.

By the time she came out of the shower, hurried across the hall to her bedroom, and quickly closed the door, he had already folded the blankets and poured himself a cup of morning fuel. He walked to the closed door and lightly rapped his knuckles, "Mind if I take a quick shower?"

"Go ahead. Towels are in the hall closet," came back through the closed door.

When Jarod closed the bathroom door behind him, he was surrounded by the smell of CeCe. The warm air, thick with moisture, filled the small space with the comforting aroma. A quick inspection of the room and cabinets confirmed another fact that Jarod had already concluded in the rest of her home—CeCe liked her space. There were no signs of any usual co-inhabitants, no male razors, shaving cream or even a toothbrush.

The fact was not surprising to him, but still gave him a feeling of satisfaction. He stepped beneath the spray and enjoyed the knowledge this fact would not be a roadblock for his real intentions.

Refreshed and alert, he pulled his jeans back on and exited the bathroom. CeCe was standing in the kitchen, rinsing out a coffee cup before she placed it in the dishwasher, then walked to the table and was rummaged in her bag.

"Good morning, Kitten," he said as he walked back to the sofa where his shirt, socks and boots were.

"I've asked you repeatedly not to call me that. I know it is hard for you to be decent, other than what I'm sure are rare moments, but could you at least be courteous enough to abide by that one wish. It creeps me out." She never looked towards him or up from looking for something in her handbag.

That wasn't the response he was expecting. He finished tying his boots, stood and walked to where she stood. He let his eyes take in their fill of her beautiful form. She wore a black and white second skin style dress. The three quarters sleeve showed off her choice of tropical colored bangles, which were echoed at her ears. The keyhole cutout at her breasts had a magnetic effect on his eyeballs. The skirt hit just above the knee, and her feet wore those kinky-fuckery ankle wrap shoes she wore the night Dylan reintroduced them. Her hair was pulled up in a classy ponytail and her makeup was flawless. She was armed with the weaponry that all women had: the ability to make a man lose his mind. When she still didn't look in his direction he knew something was up. The question was what?

"Looking for something?"

The rummaging was now getting harsher as she snapped, "Obviously, Slick."

Guess all advancement from last night was gone.

"Who put sand in your vagina?"

"Excuse me?" she gawked at him.

That got her attention.

"I asked, who put sand in your vagina? Only reason I can come up with for why you're being such a bitch."

She turned to face him, and he confirmed his thought from moments ago. Her arsenal was full, and ready to make mincemeat out of him. "You have some nerve. *You* are the one that accused me of being a whore for a nice meal, and *I'm* the one being a bitch?"

Purposely, he dragged out his raking gaze from head to toe, stopping at her feet where he pointed, "If the fuck-me-shoe fits."

Forgetting her bag, she slowly and methodically took the four steps that separated them. She carefully placed her hand on his chest, and ran her fingertips down over his abs, further down past the buttons of his jeans, over the hidden zipper until she cradled his hidden member, all the while never breaking eye contact from him. When his nostrils flared waiting for her next move, she began to squeeze.

"Take a good, long look at these shoes because as far as a fuck me invitation goes, this is as close as you will ever get to one." She released him, turned on said heels, grabbed her bag and walked out the door.

That sounds like a challenge, and I just so happen to have time for a challenge in my life, Kitten. When I am done, the shoes won't be the only things asking to be fucked.

Today had been a revolving door, so to speak, at CeCe's. Already today, Fucktard-Derrick had been by when she had opened to deliver coffee. His stay was longer than Jarod thought was necessary to deliver coffee, but given the look of disappointment on his face when he left, Jarod was willing to give him a pass on the time thing.

Jarod had just gotten off the phone with a friend of his who was helping him with prints on the florist box, when there was a rap on his truck's door.

"Yo," he answered to the two rent-a-cops trying to be authorities, that couldn't be old enough to wipe their own asses.

"We've received a call that you've been loitering, sir. What is your business here?" the one on the left asked, as he held onto his belt buckle, in more of a holding it up sense than one of intimidation.

Jarod looked from one to the other and answered the only way he could, dryly, "Well, kid, my business is my business. I'm not breaking any laws. I am a sufficient distance away from the storefronts, and I've had no contact with any of the patrons. So thanks for swinging by and saying hi, but it's time you go ride your Security Segways elsewhere."

"Sir, you are going to have to tell us your business, or you will leave us no choice but to escort you to our security office while we call the police."

"Well, as fun as that sounds, I think I'll pass."

"Sir, you are leaving us no choice."

Jarod rubbed his hands over his face—it was too hot for this shit. He leaned over, pulled the glove compartment open pulling out his license. The action was obviously questionable to the guards, since they both grabbed for their radios. When Jarod straightened he said, "Now come on fellas, let's not get itchy with those radios. No need for them."

He handed the license to the one closest to the window. The kid looked it over and then back to Jarod, still confused.

"It's a Private Investigator and Security Service License, kid. Let me dumb it down for you, this says it's okay for me to be here."

When Barney Fife I and II left, Jarod admitted he didn't need to be such an ass to them. But he was just so jacked up from CeCe's version of a blow off that he decided it had been too long since he had gotten a dose of CeCe. And what perfect timing, no customers and her employee, Kelleigh, was heading out for lunch. CeCe was alone.

He walked to the store and was met with a full view of CeCe on a ladder in the window. Even on the opposite side of the glass he could clearly see the much-discussed shoes wobble on the small ladder step. He pulled the door open, stepped in and inquired, "What are you doing?"

"I'm trying to hang a promotional banner, what the hell does it look like I'm doing?"

He stepped over to at least hold the ladder so it wasn't so shaky, "It looks like you are giving anyone who walks by a view of your slit."

"My dress doesn't have a slit."

"I wasn't referring to the dress!"

The audacity of the statement caught her off guard and she lost her balance. She was unable to regain it herself before he offered up a strong forearm to steady her.

"You are so crude! With that kind of vocabulary, the panties must be dropping in all directions for you, Gates"

His mind wandered back, all those years ago, when he taught her how to shoot pool and they would talk about anything and everything, "As I seem to recall you enjoyed our talks."

"Is that how you remember it?" she mumbled, while she stretched to reach the ceiling hook.

Watching her struggle only annoyed him more, "Will you get down before you hurt yourself!"

"I can do it, Gates."

"Cece, get down. I'll hang the fucking banner!"

"What? Just because you have a penis, you think you can hang it better than I can?"

"Well at least you're admitting I have a penis. It's a step up from yesterday. And as far as how it hangs, I'm happy with it."

Finally able to hook the last pin in the ceiling hook, she smoothed down her dress and avoided his offered hand as she stepped down the ladder. Jarod watched as she walked away from him to step back and look at her new sign.

The remark about their talks irked him as well, "You telling me you don't remember our hour long talks about just about everything?"

He honestly didn't think she would respond when she said in a less stern voice, "Yeah, well, as far as those talks, I was young and stupid; I had an excuse." As soon as the last word was spoken, she turned her back on him and headed into her back office.

Jarod folded the ladder closed and carried it back. The back room, or office, wasn't exactly what he expected. In the middle of the room sat a feminine looking white desk. Strewn out on top were papers and sketches. Along the back wall were boxes he assumed were new shipments of merchandise. However, the spot that held his attention was the large table that held a state of the art sewing machine, an open cabinet with baskets filled with fabrics, threads and other paraphernalia. Next to the desk were two freestanding wire dress forms, one bare, while the other had an unfinished dress of white lace.

He could feel her eyes on him as his feet explored the space.

"Are you done, Nosey?"

Without turning to face her inquisition, he off handedly said, "Being nosey is part of my job." When he had taken in everything, he turned and added, "I remember you wanted to design. Good to see you never let go of that dream."

He watched as she swallowed hard as something crossed her face, but she remained mute. He was just about to probe further when the front door chimed, announcing a customer entering the store. Before CeCe could take the three steps to enter the store floor, the sound rang again.

Gates was reading the shipping invoice adhered to the side of one of the boxes when he heard CeCe shriek, "This is getting old, really fast!"

Double time, he exited the office to find CeCe holding an arrangement of white roses. He ran past her and out the door. He looked left then right, but there was no one walking away from the store. No more than fifteen seconds had passed. Jogging around the immediate parking area, there was no movement, or any cars exiting the lot. Returning to the store, again passing CeCe without a word he went into the back where the video feed was. Jarod ran the feed back and found his first piece of evidence. The male seen entering the store was between 5'11"and 6'2" and wore a dark hoodie over his head and had a stockier build. He obviously knew where the cameras were because he kept his face averted. He used the sleeve of his sweatshirt to enter and leave the store as well as to hold the florist papers. He played it multiple times to ensure he didn't miss anything.

When he returned from looking at the feed, the flowers were on the counter next to the register and CeCe was at the front window with her cell phone to her ear. He walked towards her, but when she looked over her shoulder and saw his approach; she quickly ended her call, "…talk to you later."

"Everything alright?"

"Peachy! This flower Casanova of mine seems to know just when to enter and leave. He comes into my business. He comes to my home. Why wouldn't everything be anything but alright?" She gripped her phone as she watched life continue on through the large storefront window.

She was pissed, that was obvious, but there was something else beneath the fury. He needed to reassure her she shouldn't be scared, "It's just a matter of time, before I catch him, Kitten. I'm not going to let him get anywhere near you." Her gaze never wavered from the unknown spot she was looking at outside. "I'm going to head over to the Security Office and check out the outside cameras. I'll get him, CeCe. I promise."

Finally turning her beautiful hazel eyes to him, she said sternly, "Fuck your promise, Gates. I want results."

Jarod's trip to the Security Office took longer than a root canal should, thanks to Barney Fife I and II. Unfortunately, the outside feed showed nothing different than the in-store feed. There were two more shots of the suspect leaving the store, but he went to the location of the parking lot blind spot. Jarod had had enough of the Barneys interference, so he called the Security Manager himself and was on the phone with him when he headed back to *CeCe's*.

"You have a major security breech and a tenant that is being harassed, that isn't enough for you to rearrange your security cameras?"

When the manager explained about building funds and whatnot for the umpteenth time, Jarod's temper exploded, "Listen, I'm telling you I don't care if you have to raid your kid's piggy bank, just figure it out, and have the cameras fixed by tomorrow, or you will be hearing from Ms. Cervetti's attorney about a public safety suit. I'm sure building owners, and the town officials you keep saying are restricting your ability to do so, would not want to hear they were the reason behind such a lawsuit."

When he returned to the store, he found CeCe using her flirtation abilities at full power as she stood close to a man that was returning his own megawatt smile. The man's clothing and how he carried himself was similar to Lowell's, confirming to Jarod that this must be her type. The two were laughing, and she grabbed hold of his forearm when she seemed to have lost her balance, apparently from laughing too hard.

Jarod cleared his throat and then ground his teeth. *I have to remember to call the dentist.*

"Am I interrupting?"

The man's back was to Jarod, and he turned, immediately sizing Jarod up in return.

Jarod walked toward the duo, crossed his arms over his black clad chest, and arched a brow as he waited for an introduction.

He didn't miss the exaggerated eye roll CeCe gave or the masculine sizing-up look Max wielded, "Gates, this is Max, I mean Lieutenant Idarraga. Max, this is…"

"…The private investigator Cross sicced on you." Max finished for her, as he placed his hands on his waist, giving more prominence to the badge he wore on his belt.

"And you're the Podunk cop that can't solve this case, hence why I'm here."

The two men stared at each other; plainly evident they didn't care for one another.

Max was the first to break the staring challenge, he turned his attention back to CeCe and said in what Jarod was sure was an over-emphasized accent, "I'll go check out the security feed for the plaza, but I doubt we will get anything more than your video got. This guy seems to know what he is doing."

"Good thing you are here to tell her everything I already confirmed, *Max*." Jarod snarled.

Max turned his attention back to Jarod and licked his lips before tonguing the inside of his mouth, "Do you have a problem with how I'm running *my* investigation, Gates?"

Jarod walked past the man, turned his back to the counter and hoisted himself onto it, like he was comfortable here, before retorting, "By problem, do you mean doing nothing and just keep giving this guy the ability to do his stalking thing, then no, not at all."

Max was just about to clarify his opinion when CeCe spoke up, "That's enough. Look, I'm stuck with him, Max, so you might as well play nice."

Jarod smiled from ear to ear, listening to her reprimand of Idarraga, but the laughter died when she rounded on him, "And you, stop being such an asshole, as usual. The faster you do *your* job the faster you can leave *me* be. I just want to know who this prick is so I can turn him down and get back to my life."

After a few more moments of Max giving CeCe the standard police blah blah blah, he exited the store. When he reached his car, CeCe turned away from the window and walked with purpose back to where Jarod sat, "What is your problem? You know, not every man is a dick-length challenge? How the hell did you make it through the Marine Corps? Or are all you Jarheads sarcastic twit-twats?"

That got Jarod's back up. Why was she so touchy about his behavior toward Idarraga? Maybe CeCe had already found her next conquest. The idea was enough to make Jarod see red.

"Kitten, every man is a dick-length comparison when in your vicinity. Don't fool yourself into thinking otherwise." He hopped down and stepped close enough to inhale her wonderful scent.

Her hazel eyes searched his, waiting for him to say something else, and he wanted to, but he chose to remain mute, knowing she wouldn't appreciate hearing the truth.

"Oh come on, spit it out...why stop now?" she motioned with her hand for him to continue.

"Fine you want it, here it is..." he stepped right up to her, so she had to look up at him, and he whispered in her ear, "Idarraga wants you bad, Kitten."

"You are certifiable!" She bit back, trying to walk away; he reached out and grabbed her arm, firmer than he should have.

"Oh...I get it, it's one of those, been there done that situations."

"Let. Go. Of. Me!"

He did, but the glare continued. As if her easy brush off of her sex appeal and the constant chemistry between them, whether she was willing to admit it or not, wasn't bad enough, the fact that he was finally within arms-length of her after all these years he needed for her to feel some of the pain he felt.

"Tell me, is there a cock in this town, or the surrounding three states, you haven't taken a ride on?" he shouted to her retreating back.

She turned around instantly, silent and shocked, fingering the circle at her neck. Then the take no shit pride crossed her face. She marched right back up to him, poking him in the chest causing Jarod to back step several times.

"That is none of your Goddamn business! Besides, what, are you jealous?"

Her pupils darted back and forth as she searched his blue eyes. She must have seen what she wanted because she walked backwards with a triumphant smile on her face, "Your silence speaks volumes. Careful, Gates, you might actually be showing an emotion of some kind. Jealousy does not look good on you."

Eight

CeCe finished out the rest of the day on her own. Kelleigh had called right after the flowers had been delivered stating she wasn't feeling well. Kimmie had come in later in the afternoon and worked until close. When CeCe walked Kimmie out so she could lock the door behind her, she noticed Jarod's truck in the parking lot. His large form was hard to miss behind the wheel. She could see he had his aviator glasses on, and they were staring directly at her. With a final wave to Kimmie, CeCe locked up, and headed back to her office.

She changed into the yoga pants and oversized shirt she kept at the store. She sat down at her desk, knowing she needed to draw out some of these crazy emotions that were circulating through her. Between the latest flower deliveries; the fact she had been a mere twenty feet away from the guy; the knowledge this was becoming more than some random flowers; and the ramped up interchange with Jarod, she needed to just zone out with her designs.

She replayed his words over and over again in her head. Did he really think she was such a tramp? Was she a tramp? Just as the thought crossed her mind, her phone buzzed. It was the tenth text from Derrick. Like all the others, she ignored it. She knew she was being unfair to him, especially after receiving the necklace last night and when they tried again for intimacy, she stopped him, again, and asked to be taken home. Always the considerate gentleman, Derrick obliged. Now he was texting her, but it was confining to her, almost suffocating. Knowing he would continue, she responded quickly with a working late excuse then turned off her phone.

CeCe picked up her pencil and just let her creative juices flow. Apparently, time got away from her because when she next looked at the clock almost ninety minutes had passed. Rolling the muscles of her neck, she jumped when there was a bang at her back door. The sound startled her. There was no window and no peephole for her to look through. She grabbed her phone and sat, not even breathing, hoping she imagined it.

There was another bang, this one longer and harder.

Standing, with her phone firmly in her hand, she walked to the door still unsure what she should do.

"It's Jarod. You know, the asshat. I have come with food and beer. Open the dang door!"

Removing the securities, she opened the door and found him standing there with a takeout bag from her favorite Chinese restaurant.

"You scared the shit out of me. Ever heard of calling?"

Jarod walked in and placed the take out on her desk, careful not to put it on any papers, then turned back towards her and replied sarcastically, "Ever heard of turning on your phone?"

CeCe looked down at her phone and realized he was right; she had turned it off. Chagrinned, she threw the phone onto her desk before walking around and sitting in her chair with her legs tucked underneath her.

She watched as he emptied the bag's contents, including plates and plastic utensils. The aroma wafting toward her nose was heavenly.

"What's this for?"

Jarod opened the containers as he answered, "Consider it an apology. I was out of line earlier."

Taking the closest container to her, she began to load her plate up,

"I'll just chalk it up to the fact you're an asshole. We're square on that front, now." Jarod walked over to her workstation, he rolled the computer chair back, straddling it backwards as he made his own plate.

She was enjoying the silence when he broke it.

"What is going to make us square on all fronts?" He pulled the cap off the bottle of beer and took a long swig, waiting for her response.

"I don't know." She chewed her food before reaching over and taking his already open beer and swallowing a long pull. "I suppose an apology for your accusations on my sex life would be a start." Taking another swig of the frothy coolness, she added, "Then there is the whole breathing thing."

"Breathing thing?"

"Yeah, you're breathing, that's enough to piss me off."

Jarod let out a deep belly laugh at that. He twirled some noodles on his fork, messily stuffed them in his mouth before grabbing back his beer and tipping it in her direction, "I'll see what I can do about that, Kitten."

They ate in silence until most of the containers were empty, as well as several beer bottles.

Pencil in hand, CeCe was deep in thought, sketching her current design and Jarod was over by her workstation looking at the designs she had tacked to the wall.

"These are really good, Cees."

She looked up and found it extremely funny that Jarod's big form was moving his head back and forth in different angles as he tried to interpret the designs.

"I particularly like this one." He pointed.

Unable to see what he was pointing to, she set the pencil and pad down and walked over to stand next to him. He was looking at a design for a bra and panty set she had drawn.

"Typical," she lightly laughed as she stood with him looking at all the designs that she was starting to feel would remain just paper thoughts.

"Can I ask you something?" Jarod asked, now with his full attention on her. Standing this close to him, in her bare feet, their height difference was so evident, almost a foot.

"What do you see in Lowell?"

She looked at his direct blue gaze and suddenly, the room felt small.

"Just tell me, is that what you want? I'm sorry. I'm just curious." He stepped away from her, running his hands over his face, he'd taken a deep breath before turning back to face her. "From the outside looking in, I don't like him with you. He isn't right for you."

She should have known he would turn this cordial meal into anything but. Raising her head and praying for strength, even though she knew she would never wait for it. "How the fuck do you know who is, or isn't right for me?" her breasts heaved from the seething shout. Breaking the distance, she poked his chest again with her index finger emphasizing every word, "You've reappeared in my life, what three days ago? And all of a sudden you're an expert on who and what is best for me?"

Grabbing her finger with a gentle hand, he tried to stay calm, but whenever he is around her the fury just exploded out of him, "I don't like him with you!"

She laughed a malicious laugh, but didn't move, "And why the fuck not?"

"Because he isn't me! Alright?" he shouted.

"What?"

"You damn well heard me," he said softer, but closer to her. "You are just as much affected by me as I am by you. Admit it."

"You are fucking insane, that is what you are." She pulled away, taking refuge over by her workstation.

"Are you denying it?"

"You are damn right I am!"

"I'll prove it to you." Then he converged on her. Pushing her against the wall with a thud, he covered her curvaceous body with his larger one. Their bodies touched on every line. His demanding mouth descended on her lips, with his tongue he forced her mouth open, but once it opened, there was no force on his part at all. She was in this just as much as he was. Her tongue mingled with his in a classic fight for dominance. His taste was incredible—better than she remembered—mixed with beer and Chinese food. Moving his hands from her face, they roamed down her sides, swiping across her gorgeous tits, forcing a moan from her lips. Finally, they came to rest on her hips, where they rotated around to her ass and pulled her up, closer to his throbbing cock. The yoga pants offered her very little shielding from his firm member.

He was everywhere; she couldn't get close enough to him. Reading her mind, he lifted her so she could wrap her legs around his waist as he continued to knead her ass. His mouth moved along her jaw, down her neck where it currently sucked and bit the spot where her shoulder and neck met. Using the wall to help support her, he raised his large hands to her tits where they squeezed and plumped before they pulled on the tight points. Her core ignited with sensation as it naturally prepped itself for what this was leading to.

"Stop, stop…I can't!"

"Why?" he asked between licks and nips leading back up to her mouth, where he inserted his tongue and began his version of the tongue tango.

She participated, hell she was the one who held his head to hers, but she was experiencing an interior battle. She had to stop this; she had to stop him. This would only lead to disaster. This would only lead her to where she swore she would never go again. This was weakness on her part, that's all it could be.

"Gates! Stop!" She pushed hard with her hands on his shoulders and unhooked her legs from around his waist.

He wasn't as accepting of the halt of action, but he respected it. He leaned his chest into the wall, and now that her feet were on the ground, she ducked out from under him and to the safety of the other side of the room, one hand at her lips where she could still feel him, and the other clutching the silk cord at her neck.

He turned to face her; his hands on his lean hips and breathless, he said firmly, "I won't apologize for that."

"I didn't think you would."

"Kitten..." but she held her hand up, stopping his words.

"I need some space Gates. Thanks for dinner and thanks for...for that, but it was a mistake."

He dropped his head, shook it side to side slightly before he walked over to her. Tipping her chin up with his forefinger, he searched her eyes and said, "Call it what you want, but that was as far from a mistake as one can get."

He followed her out front, when she opened the door; he stepped close again, and just looked his fill. Her eyes returned the gaze, but where his spoke clearly hers spoke coldly.

"I meant what I said."

"So did I, Kitten. I may have climbed my way out of hell, but for you, I'm willing to go back at a moment's notice."

"Well, you are going to have to find another one way ticket because I can't, and I won't."

"One person's hell is another person's heaven." He breathed as he rubbed his nose along her cheek, before stepping out and turning to lock eyes with her as she locked the door and fled from his prying gaze, returning to the safety of her office.

Nine

Ten days had passed since Jarod came back into her life. The weather was hot and oppressive, mirroring CeCe's disposition. Two more arrangements of white roses arrived: one anonymously delivered to her store when CeCe wasn't there and Kelleigh had left the floor for a moment, and the other delivered to her home, laid on her doorstep. It was beyond frustrating, and in a way she wished this guy would grow a pair and just say, "Hey, I'm the one." But no such luck.

After the night Cece asked Jarod to give her space, and labeled their hot make out session a mistake, he had kept his distance except to perform his job. Every morning he was parked in the same spot on the street, waiting for her to leave her apartment and head to the store. He would remain in the parking lot, sitting in his truck or walking the perimeter. Then every night, he would follow her home and metaphorically stand guard, never exiting his truck. And let's not forget everything in between, whether it was grocery shopping or going to the bank, all CeCe had to do was look over her shoulder and she would see those aviator glasses, never very far away. She had to admit he had an uncanny ability to know when she was looking for him because he dissolved into the shadows whenever she wasn't looking.

Derrick was still in the background, either blowing up her phone, or arriving at her store unannounced. He said he was okay with space, but CeCe could tell he really wasn't. She just couldn't deal with him on top of everything else right now. Honestly, she couldn't understand why he was still sticking around, with the amount of blow-offs and excuses she had come up with; if the shoe were on the other foot, she would have said, "see ya" a while ago. However, in true Derrick fashion, he graciously accepted her terms, always with a smile on his face and a compliment and promise on his tongue.

The latest visit was today, while CeCe was on the floor and Kelleigh was in the back, he arrived just prior to close with bruschetta and chicken marsala from Giovanni's and a bottle of Pinot Grigio. He looked incredible and the aromas wafting from the bag and him were mouthwatering.

"Hey, beautiful, I assume you are working late again tonight, but I just wanted to make sure you ate dinner."

Putting down the unfolded shirts, she greeted him with a kiss on his warm lips, "Derrick! Will you stop being so sweet?" *Especially since I'm being a bitch to you.* "Want to stay?"

"I'd love to, but I also don't want to pressure you, either. I get it; you need time and space to deal with all this craziness, but I'd be lying if I said I want to leave. Are you in the mood for company?"

CeCe wanted to say yes, but honestly, she really wanted to work on some designs. She scrunched her nose as she pondered a time line to spend time with Derrick and get all she wanted to accomplish with her sketches.

He laughed, "I can tell by your lack of jumping at the offer you really don't."

"No! It isn't that…" she grabbed his arm.

He removed her hand from his arm and brought it to his lips, kissing her knuckles before saying, "I get it, beautiful, no worries. Nevertheless, let me just tell you, I'm here for you whenever you need me, and I really wish you'd let me help you. I could stay at your place…just for company," the way he smiled let her know he wanted to be more than that. "Or you can stay at my place, just let me in, CeCe."

Looking at his dark, caring eyes and amazing smile, something just clicked for her. She needed to give him something, something to show she did care for him, and appreciated how wonderful he was being, especially with her arms-length behavior.

"Rain check on the company, but book the trip to Napa," she whispered as she touched the circle at her neck.

His faced searched hers, and then broke into an undeniable *I just won the lottery* smile, "Really?"

"Definitely! *It* and *you* are just what I need to look forward to. If you can just bear with me until then."

Pulling her into his arms he answered against her lips, "I think I can make it work, as long as you don't mind occasional visits."

The smile spread across her face, giving him a gentle peck before finishing, "Absolutely not. In fact, why don't we have dinner this weekend? Saturday night?"

"It's a date." He kissed her, expressing his happiness.

"Cees, the negligee shipment seems to be wrong…oh, I'm sorry I didn't mean to interrupt."

"No, you are fine, Kelleigh, I was just delivering you ladies dinner." Derrick moved his attention from Kelleigh back to CeCe, whose attention was on her employee trying to signal her not to say anything.

"Thanks. I'm just going to get back to the shipment, we can talk about it later, CeCe."

"Sure, no problem." *Phew!* Sending a silent prayer toward Kelleigh for not saying anything, CeCe said goodbye to Derrick with a promise to call him tomorrow to iron out details for their Saturday night date.

With Derrick gone, and just a few minutes left before locking the door and closing up shop, CeCe entered the back room with an explanation on her tongue. "Thanks, Kelleigh, given all that has been going on, and me staying and working on my designs, I just thought it was easier to tell

Derrick, you and I were working than telling him I've been holed up here like a recluse."

Kelleigh laughed as she clutched a skimpy purple silk nightgown in her hand, "Oh, is that what you were doing? I get it, I guess, but I can't figure out, for the life of me, if someone like Derrick wants to spend time with you, why you aren't jumping at the chance?"

"Yeah, well…me either." CeCe laughed at her idiocy for not doing just what Kelleigh pointed out.

"It's none of my business, but this wouldn't have anything to do with a certain PI would it?"

"No," telling herself it was truth, just like she was telling Kelleigh.

"Uh huh, sure, Cees. I bet Jarod could make a nun go weak in the knees," Kelleigh said, letting out a laugh as she went back to sorting the shipment.

CeCe needed to change the subject from Jarod's arousal ability, "So tell me about the new boyfriend."

Kelleigh's face warmed with a smile of new attraction and happiness, "He is a really cool guy. We are still at the getting to know you stage, he is quite a bit older than me and seems to have his shit together, which makes me want to get my shit together. I know it sounds stupid and silly, but he came into my life exactly when I was sure I would be alone forever. Spoke all the right words and everything. He not only reenergized my faith in the human population, but in my own personal fairy tale, too."

"Sounds like true love. And any man would be lucky to have you." CeCe added, as she smiled at her friend and began to unpack the delicious smelling food.

"I don't know about that, but I'm hoping it is something with long-term potential."

Just then the front door chimed, indicating a customer, "Never fails, guess food will just have to wait," CeCe turned and headed out onto the floor, where a man held at least four dozen, long-stem white roses.

"CeCe?" he asked, honestly unsure. He was about 6'2" and young—CeCe guessed his age to be early 20's—pretty-boy handsome with inky black hair and icy blue eyes. He took in CeCe's appearance and a slow cocky smile grew on his face.

Keeping her distance, she responded, "You've got to be kidding me!"

Suddenly, the door sounded again, and Jarod walked in, weapon in hand. He stalked slowly toward the younger man, arcing around to the left so he would end up in front of him. His gaze wavered for a moment from Casanova Joe to CeCe and back.

"Yo! Dude! What are you doing?" the younger man dropped the blooms, raised his hands in the air, and turned white as a ghost.

"I have to ask, dicklick, after all the anonymity, why pick now to show your face?" Jarod was now only feet away with his Glock still up and aimed at the boy.

"Dude, I don't know what you're talking about! Some guy paid me two hundred bucks to deliver these flowers to a woman named CeCe. I swear!" he cried with a quivering voice.

"What guy? What was his name?" Jarod and CeCe asked in unison.

"I don't know, I answered an ad! He told me where to pick up the flowers and there was an envelope with the cash with them when I arrived. I swear!" The young man looked from Jarod and the gun still pointed at him, to CeCe and unwisely added, "I mean she's hot, I'd tap that, but I swear this guy paid me to bring her roses."

Jarod lowered the gun, holstering it in the back of his waistband, rolled his eyes as he walked the few steps to Casanova and smacked him on the back of the head, "Be respectful, fucktard!"

"Am I free to go?" Casanova looked from Jarod to CeCe, then back again.

"Not quite, we'll need to verify your story first, starting with proof of the ad. Second, where did you pick up the roses?"

The young man looked physically ill, CeCe kind of felt bad for him at being under Jarod's scrutiny.

Kelleigh picked now to come out onto the floor. "Is everything alright?" she asked, but then noticed the roses and she pulled on CeCe's arm, offering herself as protection.

CeCe placed her hand over Kelleigh's, "Everything is okay; this is just a delivery man. I'm going to close up shop Kel. I've had enough fun for one night. Why don't you head on out."

"Are you sure?" Kelleigh asked

"Completely."

Kelleigh reluctantly agreed and CeCe walked her out, watched her get into her car before she locked the door then returned to where the two men stood. Jarod had his phone to his ear while he swiped through the young guy's phone.

"…Yeah, he isn't going anywhere. Just don't take your friggin' sweet-ass time." Jarod disconnected the call and continued search the other phone.

Since Jarod didn't even look up, CeCe looked toward the other guy and asked, "You sure you don't know who posted the ad?"

"No idea. I knew it sounded too good to be true," he looked to Jarod's dominating form that outweighed him by at least seventy pounds and then back to CeCe, "No wonder this guy didn't want to bring you flowers himself."

Jarod spoke up then, "Okay your story checks out. The owner of the florist shop confirmed it was a phone order. He wasn't very forthcoming with the news that he overcharged the caller two hundred dollars to make up the cash in the envelope. Apparently, he has some other kind of plant business going on there as well."

CeCe didn't even want to know how he obtained that kind of information while on the phone. "So if it was an electronic transaction, they can trace the card, right?" she asked hopeful.

"No such luck there, Kitten, a buddy of mine just ran the card. It was a prepaid gift card and the call came in from a burner phone."

"Can't he trace where the gift card was bought from?"

"Look at you...you thinking of changing career paths to private investigating, or is it more likely you watch too many crime shows?"

"Very funny," CeCe made a mocking face.

"You are right, though, he can and did trace it. The card was purchased in Burlington over two years ago. It was a cash transaction. And before you ask, yes we know the store, but there is no way they have video feed for that long ago, so it is a dead end."

Well damn!

He rested his hands on his hips, and searched her face. For some reason, she was unable to break his stare. The way Jarod looked at her was intimate and filled with a million questions; questions she didn't want to hear or contemplate answers for.

A fist pounding on the front door broke the moment; it was Max, along with two uniforms. CeCe hurried to the door, unlocking it and allowing them to enter.

"Max, how did you know?"

"Gates called me." Apparently shock displayed on her face because he added, "I know, surprised the heck out of me, too."

CeCe looked back to Jarod, who was now in his usual stance—feet spread with those massive arms crossed over his strong chest. It hit her then, he looked like a force to be reckoned with, and she was sure many men crumbled under that glare. When his eyes drilled into her, it wasn't fear she felt, but something else, but she'd be damned before she would give it a name.

"About time, Idarraga! I pretty much learned everything about this kid here, including his birth weight, in the amount of time it took you to arrive."

"Have to give you a head start, Gates, or otherwise it is an unfair fight."

"Yeah, that's it."

CeCe listened while the young guy told Max everything, duplicating what he told Jarod and herself. Max asked the exact same questions Jarod did, and it gave her ego a boost because he asked the same questions she did, too. Before too long, Max and the uniforms were escorting the kid out, followed by Jarod, who stopped to speak, civilly, to Max before he returned to the back room where CeCe had retreated.

She packed her things, suddenly feeling the need to take a long hot bath and forego the sketching for a night. Her tension level was at its peak, and she just wanted to be alone, but for the first time, not here.

She could feel his eyes on her, watching her. Finally, unable to stand the silent inquisition, she turned and huffed, "What?"

She could tell he wanted to say something, but to her surprise, he remained silent and left her office to answer his phone. She repackaged the takeout food, placing it in the small refrigerator in the office. She grabbed her bag and shut the light off and joined Jarod.

"Not going to burn the midnight oil tonight?"

"No, suddenly, I don't want to be here."

"Let's get out of here, then." Taking the keys from her hand, they exited and he locked the door to the store, before returning them back to her. Instead of walking her to her Mustang, he directed her to his pickup.

"My car is over there."

"I know, let's leave it here tonight," he said as he draped an arm lightly around her shoulder.

"Uh, let's not," she answered as she freed herself from his embrace.

Half way to his truck, he stopped and turned to her and asked, "Afraid to be alone with me in my truck?"

His blue gaze was vivid, even in the twilight; his breath smelled minty and his cologne swirled around her at his close proximity. When she didn't answer he just raised an eyebrow, waiting.

"I'm not afraid of you."

"Good, then leaving your car here and riding with me won't bother you in the least." Lightning fast he squatted down, threw her over his shoulder in a firemen's carry as he jogged to the passenger side of the truck cab. She, honest to God, giggled at his audacity. "If I put you down, are you going to comply and get in the truck?" The giggles continued. "Well?"

Still laughing, she tried to sound stern, "Fine, I'll get in this poor excuse for a truck. Will you just put me down?"

He did, and as he opened the door for her, he whispered, "Spoilsport."

He pulled out of the parking lot without a word. Ten minutes later, CeCe watched as he passed the turnoff to her to her place, "Where are you taking me?"

"My place."

"I don't want to go to your place."

"Then it's a good thing I didn't ask."

When he didn't respond to the first two miles of her insisting he take her home, she gave up. To her surprise, he pulled into a parking spot on Main Street in Hamden, in front of the old Mom and Pop hardware store owned by Mr. Burns.

"Come on, or am I going to have to carry you?"

CeCe exited the car and followed him in her heels, up the side wooden steps to what appeared to be an apartment over the store. As she took one step at a time, she couldn't seem to drag her eyes away from his incredible ass and how it filled out his jeans, but then she noticed the bulge above the waistband—his gun.

They reached the landing, where he easily unlocked the door and switched the light on inside. She had no idea what to expect when she stepped inside, but what she saw certainly surprised her. The small studio apartment was pristine. The large bed dominated the space, and was made with quarter-bouncing accuracy. A small kitchenette was on the far wall next to a life-worn recliner and a small TV, opposite that was a small room she guessed was the bathroom. Nothing was out of place, no week-old takeout cartons or clothes thrown about. The room was cool, confirming the air conditioning worked quite well. Jarod closed the door behind her, halting her inspection.

"Meet your approval?" he asked.

She whipped around, not realizing he was that close, her breasts grazed his chest and her body's reaction to the touch set off warning bells in her brain. She stepped back, putting distance between them, giving her mind the chance to form a sentence.

"Approval? You don't need my approval for anything."

"You're right, I don't *need* it; doesn't mean I don't *want* it."

"I don't understand you." She turned and walked further into the space, putting more distance between them and the Pandora's box of meaning in his comment. She thought he would pursue her, but to her surprise, he ventured into the room she pegged for the bathroom.

She heard him rummaging in a cabinet before the sound of water running. He reemerged and said, "Why don't you strip down and get into the bath I'm running. It'll help you relax."

"Excuse me?" asked both for his nerve, and for the fact his train of thought was exactly her plan for when she went home to her apartment.

Crossing the small distance, he leaned down and looked into her eyes before he spoke, "That was intense back at the store. I just want you to relax, and try not to worry. I'll be a gentleman, I promise." Leaving her eyes, his eyes focused on her lips before he added huskily, "Unless, you don't want me to be."

Not waiting for an answer, Jarod reached over to the small dresser, pulled out a t-shirt and handed it to her. CeCe took it without a word before she locked herself in the bathroom and submerged herself in the water.

Ten

CeCe soaked herself until she was pruned everywhere in the antique claw foot tub. She admitted she was worried about sinking into the water, concerned Jarod would come barging in, but he never did.

Just when I think I have him figured out.

Climbing out of the tub, CeCe wrapped the surprisingly soft terry cloth towel around herself, tucking it in between her breasts. She examined her reflection in the small vanity mirror, which showed exhaustion. Her eyelids were heavy, not to mention the dark circles underneath, now that she was devoid of makeup. She thought over the events of the last couple of hours; now she could admit when she saw the latest delivery of roses, before the anger, she was scared. Scared knowing who was behind it wouldn't bring her the comfort it should. Fearful, that without the case, Jarod would disappear, out of her life, again.

That's what you want right?

Even as she thought the words she wondered if she believed them. Strange, since his arrival, she has wanted him banished, but when the moment presented itself, his departure was the first thing she thought of.

When he came in, his gun aimed, he looked intense and completely focused on his target, but then he looked at her, and that single ounce of concern she saw in his eyes confirmed she was in trouble. It wasn't the first time she saw the look, opening her mind to the part of her she turned off, all those years ago.

"So what is an innocent pretty little thing like you, hanging around a no-good guy like me?"

"Innocent? I'm not so innocent."

"Kitten, you are the 'no' in innocent," he smiled his sexy smile.

CeCe looked around the quiet and darkened parking lot of Chase's, where she stood against the side of his Camaro, and he sat on the hood, his legs dangling over the wheel well. They were alone, but she was constantly concerned someone would come along and interrupt their private moment.

After Dylan introduced her to Jarod, she found herself spending a large amount of time at Chase's, all in hopes of seeing him. She quickly learned Jarod's intentions and admirers were plentiful. His reputation preceded him, but there was something about him that called to her. It was obvious he was gorgeous, any female with a pulse could confirm that, but there was something deeper about him, at least to her. She would watch from across the billiard hall as he effortlessly spun an erotic spell over every female. They all vied for his attention; clinging to any morsel he would throw them. However, one day she was pulled into the beam of his pure blue gaze, connecting for what seemed like hours and ending with a smile that was meant only for her. From that moment on, he always seemed to seek her out, but continued with his flirtatious character, unless they were alone. Those times seemed to increase, whether it was later than she should be out, or in the parking lot where she just couldn't seem to get into her car and drive off. In those moments he would flirt with her, but there was more to it. He talked to her, listened when she talked, and made her feel like she was the only girl in the world. Troy and his ultimate betrayal still so fresh in her mind, but bad-boy Jarod comforted her when he should have scared her and had her running for the hills.

"Your opinion of me is flattering," CeCe answered, trying to hide the hurt she felt from his words.

There was no humor on his face when he slid off the hood, and turned to her placing his finger under her chin, making her unable to look anywhere but directly into his eyes, "It should be; temptation at its finest."

"I don't know what you mean." she said, unable to help the huskiness of her voice, or the quiver that moved throughout her body at his touch.

"Patterns are hard to break, and even if it seems you're happy, you rarely are. I wonder if the grass is really greener on the other side of the fence." He lowered his mouth and claimed hers, sweet and slow. It was the first of many kisses, and private moments, leading to the backseat of his Camaro; then he vanished from her.

The sound of muted voices and the apartment door opening brought CeCe back to the present and the seclusion of the bathroom. She pulled the t-shirt over her head, suddenly engulfed in his scent. She found herself squeezing her eyes shut, letting her sense of smell take over. The light tap on the door once again brought her around.

"You alive in there?"

"Yes, I'm coming," she called out only to have a low sexy chuckle respond with something she couldn't quite make out. CeCe opened the door to find Jarod putting together an impromptu picnic on the bed.

"I thought I was going to have to send in a search party," he joked as he opened the final item's wax paper wrapping before turning his attention to her. His eyes raked over her, from her naked feet all the way up to her damp hair; she felt his gaze everywhere. "I ordered sandwiches, come have a seat."

"I think it's best if I just go home."

Jarod walked the short distance separating them, and pulled her along by the arm to the bed where he gently pushed her down. "Eat first, then I'll take you home." Jarod walked to the small fridge, taking out two bottles of beer, popped the tops and tossed them into the sink. When he reached the bed again, he handed her a bottle before taking a long pull from his.

CeCe gentled sipped the frothy drink, and got up to stretch her legs in the confining space. "Look, I don't know what this is supposed to be, but whatever it is, I don't think it is such a great idea."

Jarod sat down on the edge of the bed, leaning his elbows on his knees and dangling the bottle between his legs before answering, "Why do you think this is something, it's simply old friends sharing a meal."

She couldn't contain the sarcasm, "Old friends? Friends like you, who needs enemies?"

She watched as he shook his head lightly in exasperation before he took a long drink of the beer, draining most of the bottle. He stood, but stopped, momentarily grimacing, then quickly recovered.

"I get it, you think I'm an asshole, but for the next thirty minutes, can you put that thought aside and just eat, drink, and talk with me. We can talk about anything you want; hell, I'll even let you do all the asking, I just reserve the right to ask one question. Please." As if he thought the change in position would help his cause, Jarod actually folded his hands, tilted his head and stuck out his bottom lip in a pout.

Rolling her eyes and smiling in spite of herself, CeCe walked back to the bed and answered him, "I guess there are worst ways to spend an evening."

"That a girl."

After she nibbled on half of her roast beef sandwich, and he devoured his pastrami with mustard, she decided she couldn't handle the quiet anymore and asked the first of her questions.

"I didn't know you had a gun."

"I'm licensed to carry a concealed weapon."

"Why private investigation?"

"When my last tour ended, I bummed around for a bit, but found myself bored. I knew any formal law enforcement would have too many rules for me, so I decided to go out on my own. It started as more of a security specialist. I traveled a bit, got my name out there, thanks to some fellow Marines. I found myself working details for some pretty big celebs. But after the nightclubs every night, paparazzi stupidity and arrogance, I decided that kind of security really wasn't meant for someone like me." He drank the rest of his beer before continuing, "I started taking some more investigation jobs, and wouldn't you know, it's something I'm good at. It's steady work, allows me to pick and choose the work I want, not to mention keeps my pockets filled."

It was nice to hear him explain his start up; she knew about the celebrity thing, especially after she Googled him and saw some of the photos with some of the biggest names out there. From other info she was able to gather, he downplayed the success of his business.

"So where is your business home?" she took a pull of her beer

He smiled that cocky one-sided smile, "My office is where ever I am." He winked. Their thighs touched, and she felt the connection radiate through every pore of her leg.

CeCe looked away, trying to focus on the old wood paneling covering the far wall, thinking of her third grade teacher who looked like a toad— anything to distract her from Jarod being this close to her. *Stay strong, girl! You can do this!*

"But my main base is my place in Burlington."

Burlington? How long has he been that close to her, logistically? The way her attention returned to his face, eyes wide, must have pleaded enough for more info.

"I bought the place about six years ago, and have slowly made it everything I need."

"Six years…wow," was all she could say.

"Before showing your hand, you need to ensure you have the best hand in the game. The pot isn't worth nearly as much if it isn't raised and called until the very end."

What the hell did that mean?

"Anything else you'd like to know?" Jarod asked as he tucked a flyaway piece of hair behind her ear. The action caused goose bumps to form all over her body.

At the moment, she couldn't think with her body's reaction to him, so she just shook her head, ending her round of controlling the conversation.

"Good. Can I ask mine now?"

"One was the agreement." She could handle one; hopefully, it would be an easy one as far as what she had been doing the last thirteen years.

His eyes burned into hers, and just when she thought he wouldn't ask, he looked at her lips and inquired, "May I kiss you, Kitten?"

That is his one question? She was stern, "No."

"Do you want me to kiss you?"

"That is two questions."

He smiled his devastating smile, continuing to study her lips before raising his blue gaze back to hers and whispering, "Fair enough…and you're lying."

No shit!

"Come on, I'll get you home."

Just get through the ride home, Cees. When you are behind the security of your door, you can forget these moments of weakness, and resolve to keep Jarod in your past, where he belongs, and where he should remain.

"You are making a habit of this," Dylan said as Jarod arrived in his S&E office. Neither man bothered to sit, just took identical power stances, with their arms crossed and most sinister expressions.

"I'm going to cut through the bullshit and get right to the point, with everything going on, I think it would be good for CeCe to get away for a few days."

"I agree. What do you have in mind?"

"The other day, when I was in your office, I heard Seth remind you about a meeting in Boston? You wanted to bring Natalie along; I assume the girls are going as well? Why don't you imply, or straight out ask, CeCe to accompany you to give you and your wife some alone time."

Dylan pondered the idea before examining Jarod and asking, "And what are you going to do in the mean time?"

"I have some feelers out, but I don't need to be here for them. I'll tag along to ensure the problem remains here.

Dylan looked at the other man, trying to gauge his intentions, but Jarod was right, CeCe needed out, even if it was just for a few days. "Okay, I'll talk to Cees. But is there anything else I need to know about?" Dylan asked as he stepped into Jarod's personal space, blatantly trying to intimidate him.

Jarod was well aware what Dylan meant, and implied, but damn if he would discuss what was going on between him and CeCe with Cross. Especially considering he was still trying to convince CeCe to just *want* to be in the same room with him. "When, and if, you need to know something, you will know."

"And that is supposed to mean, what, Gates?"

"It means just what you think it means, Cross."

After another moment mutual glaring, Dylan gave a curt nod before walking off.

Eleven

In the Old Colony Harbor Hotel's bar CeCe, Mae and Natalie sat with an unobstructed view of the gorgeous hotel's vast open lobby. From the beautiful wall of windows that looked out over the harbor, to the lavish and classic leather furnishings, everything just screamed luxury. Boston was one of CeCe's favorite destinations.

Dylan's demand of her attendance on their trip put her off, but then he played the softy card that he was hoping to get some private time with Natalie. Since the twins have arrived, that kind of time is rare for them. Needless to say, CeCe agreed to come along, even knowing she had to back out of something she shouldn't want to.

Even though she was having a fabulous time with her friends, drinking and girl talking, she felt extremely guilty for canceling her date with Derrick for tomorrow night. At first he was upset, but he recovered quickly and said he understood. *What a guy!* In a way, she didn't know what her problem was as far as Derrick was concerned. Maybe it was time to reconsider her unattached life. Derrick made her happy, and she had a blast whenever they were together, maybe it is time to really consider it.

"I still don't know how you do it," Natalie complained as she placed her martini glass down on the mahogany bar.

"Do what?" Cece inquired, rubbing lint off her navy blue capris.

"Sit there and look stunning, basking in the attention of every set of male eyes in a six mile radius." Mae offered up, as she emptied her wine glass, motioning for another to the bartender.

"Exactly!" Natalie said, pointing to Mae.

CeCe looked from one friend to the other and then shrugged her shoulders and said offhandedly, "What can I say…it's a gift."

All three women laughed at that.

Taking a sip from her drink, Natalie explained further, "When Dylan and I first got together, and we met up at Cal's, I was so envious of your flirting capabilities, including getting phone numbers and scoring free drinks."

"I think it has a lot to do with her fantabulous body and those great ta-tas she was blessed with." Mae added.

CeCe looked down at her cleavage and said, "They are pretty fabulous aren't they?"

"I would agree," came a deep voice from behind the friendly female giggles. A voice she was way too familiar with.

All three women turned toward the man joining them. CeCe's mouth went dry. He looked different from the way he has looked since invading her world these past couple of weeks. He was clean-shaven and wore a blue button-down shirt over khaki cargo pants and polished loafers. He looked nice, really nice. Sexy. It annoyed her.

Standing so his hand rested casually over the back of CeCe's bar stool, his fingers grazed her silk covered back, sending a tingle through her body at the contact. Once his blue eyes met hers, she couldn't look anywhere else. Apparently, he found it humorous because he raised his eyebrow in question.

"Sorry, thought the statement was open for commentary." When she responded with a quirk of her own eyebrow, he gave an exaggerated smile, before adding, "It would be nice if you introduced me."

It didn't go unnoticed by CeCe that both Natalie and Mae were staring at Jarod with goofy smiles on their faces.

"Mae, Natalie, this is Jarod Gates. He's the Private Investigator."

"Oh, yes. It is nice to meet you, Jarod." Natalie was the first to extend her hand, followed by Mae

"Likewise, Mrs. Cross, Mrs. Finn."

"Oh none of that Mrs. crap! Come, join us, we were just basking in the glory CeCe brings to all womankind." Mae said, as she moved down a seat giving Jarod the stool next to CeCe.

Flagging the bartender, he motioned for a draft beer then nonchalantly said, "Oh, I agree, she definitely demands attention, but she isn't the only one. All three of you ladies are very easy on the eyes. Trust me, I'm male…I know these things."

And so it began; Mae and Natalie were eating out of the palm of his hand. They hung on his every word. CeCe admitted he sold a good game. Complimenting in excess, God, he was almost endearing. CeCe watched sourly as he easily flirted with her friends. Even though she knew it meant nothing, it was just how Jarod operated, it still irked her, and the fact that it irked her, irked her even more.

"Well, I should be getting back upstairs to help Dylan get the girls to bed." Natalie said, as she reached for her handbag.

"I got it," Jarod said, quickly pulling his credit card out, and telling the bartender, "for the entire tab."

"Well thanks, Jarod. Thanks for the drinks. It was nice meeting you," Natalie said as she hopped down from the stool.

"You know what, Nat, I think I'm going to ride the elevator up with you. Thanks Jarod, you are a sweetie." Mae said, placing a kiss on Jarod's cheek before adding, "Cees, we'll meet for shopping in the AM, okay?" Not waiting for an answer, Mae added, "Have a great night; come on, Natalie."

Well isn't that just great!

Suddenly, CeCe was mesmerized by her martini glass, along with everything to the left side of her seat, the opposite direction of him. The unmoving and uninteresting painting her eyes were currently transfixed on was causing her eyes to strain.

Jarod snickered, "WOW! I take it, you are not happy to see me."

Back to the imperfect martini glass her hazels went, "Happy is definitely not the word I would use."

"And why is that?"

He wants to hear it then, by God, she will give it to him straight.

"Because what good can come of you being here? Hell, I don't even know why you are here."

He searched her eyes, and feeling bold, he lifted his hand and touched her face, caressing her cheek, like it was the most precious of treasures.

God, he smelled good. He smelled of excitement and danger, of memories and of desire. His touch was electrifying, igniting every nerve ending in her face, and throughout her body. Her body was responding to him, ultimately betraying her. She didn't want to have this reaction to him. She didn't want him to have this power—any power—over her. She clutched the cord around her neck.

"Is it so difficult to believe that I care about you? That I want to be here?"

"Yes it is."

His body flinched as if her words cut him.

"What is it going to take to get you to see I'm not the person you think I am? The person you need me to be so badly, so you can ignore the obvious connection we have."

"What connection?" She asked firmly, knowing the lie was transparent.

His thumb rubbed once more across her cheek, before he removed it. She expected him to place it back on the bar, but he surprised her by placing it on the seat of her chair, pulling it so she sat between his straddled thighs. She could feel his breath on her neck, his smell surrounded her; the musky cologne was intoxicating and clouded her brain. It muddled her desire and ability to keep denying what she knew would ultimately break her. But even as her nipples hardened and her core quickened its already heightened preparations, she clung to the small amount of resolve she still had.

"Notice you didn't pull away from me. Oh, I'm not denying you want to throw that drink in my face, but your conscience is winning out with the help of your body. You want me here, almost as much as I want something."

"And what is it you want?"

"Doesn't take a rocket scientist to figure out what I want, but let's discuss what it is you want."

Now his hand was resting at her waist, almost like he knew the proprietary touch was igniting a fire she was helpless to fight.

"What. Do. I. Want?" She emphasized every word, trying to focus on her thoughts because honestly, she was imagining scenarios that she shouldn't.

"Me." That one simple word was so cocky, so full of assurance, yet so true.

She did want him, more and more with every passing second, and she hated herself for it.

I can't!

"You think so?" she drained the remainder of her martini.

"Oh, I know so. I'm ready. I've been ready. Room 504, your play, Kitten." He leaned in and grazed his teeth on her earlobe, and lightly flicked it with his tongue before standing and leaving the bar.

CeCe watched his powerful retreating back and that Grade-A ass walk into the lobby and press the button for the elevator. While he waited, he locked gazes with her, and never wavered. When the elevator arrived, he quirked that eyebrow of his in the sexiest of ways, raised his hand and saluted her before stepping in and disappearing from sight.

Fuck me! CeCe squeezed her eyes shut, trying to mute the voice in her head screaming for her to get her ass of the stool, and up the elevator to Room 504.

Taking a deep breath, she stood and grabbed her bag as she said goodnight to the bartender. She walked to the elevator, rolling her eyes as it miraculously opened just as she reached it. *Figures.* She stepped in and pressed the button to floor five, which coincidentally, happened to be the same floor her room was on.

As she rode the elevator up, even the instrumental music felt sexual in nature. She stepped off the elevator and her body prepped for what was to come. As she walked closer to his room, she could feel the moisture pooling below. Her nipples ached as they strained against the lace of her bra. Her body blushed as warmth covered her skin and sweat began to bead at her temples, her neck, and between her breasts. She stopped just outside his room and looked at the door. She raised her hand to knock then she lowered her hand, turned and ran to the safety of her own room. She could feel the tears building in her eyes, and it just pissed her off even more. Placing the keycard in the lock, she opened the door and stepped into the dark room.

"Six minutes, I'm impressed," came from the darkness before she was pushed against the closed door.

His mouth hammered down on hers, his hands everywhere. With the door at her back, she felt every line of him. His hardness consumed and thrilled her. He lifted her thigh in his large hand, pressing his throbbing cock to her center. His lips left hers, traveling along her jaw, down her neck, kissing every ounce of exposed skin.

Breathlessly, she confessed, "I don't even want to know how you got in here."

Chuckling while his lips still moved erotically around her neck, he said against her skin, "Probably not."

She pushed his shoulders, causing him to lift his head. As her eyes adjusted to the darkness, she found his. Needing him to know this was only physical, she proclaimed, "This is sex, Gates. That's it."

"Whatever you say, Kitten," his eyes focused on her mouth as his hands covered her breasts plumping as they went. His tongue invaded and sought no prisoners. He was ruthless in his ability to drown out any thoughts not involving what he was doing to her body. His teeth bit lightly where her neck and shoulder met, followed by his tongue as he ran it along her collarbone, using his nose to move the silk cord and mimicked his movements on the other side. His hand touched her waist, sliding slowly up and touching her bare stomach, ever so lightly with the back of his fingers. But that one moment of gentleness was gone in an instant as he grabbed the hem and pulled up, moving his head just in time, and had it over her head and off in a nanosecond. He dipped his head low, so he could lick the top of her breasts where they spilled out over her demi cup. Nibbling on the soft skin his hand pulled down, freeing them from their lace prison. His mouth seemed to cover her entire breast, but then he tongued her nipple, circling it in expert fashion. CeCe couldn't help the moan that escaped her lips, or the plea for him to continue. Never had she peaked just from her breast, but like her virginity, this moment may be another first, and all because of Jarod Gates. The contact was incredible, even through her clothes. Her moisture flowed freely, confirming he knew exactly what he was doing. She held his head as it moved from breast to neck to breast. If he continued like this, her drought would end in a matter of seconds.

Jarod's hand ran the width of her thigh, squeezing and moving around to her backside, where it was joined by the other, "God, how I want you," he breathed. He used his hands to spread her thighs wide lifting her off her feet completely.

"Take me."

Jarod held her firmly to him, as he walked from the door to the king size bed. He laid her down in the middle, and quickly went to work on the closure of her capris. With a flick of his thumb and finger, he had them undone and pulled down, leaving her in a bra that no longer held her, barely there panties, and stilettos.

He stood in the middle of the room, unmoving just watching her on the bed. CeCe wished she could see his face, to tell what he was thinking, but it was just too dark from this distance.

"I need to do this," he said quietly in the dark.

CeCe was confused by the way he sounded, were those words for her, or him? Just as she thought he would remain rooted to the floor, he slowly followed her down onto the bed, covering her body with his. This kiss was different, it was sweet and drawn out, as if it could go on forever. His tongue swept in and brushed against hers, communicating without words. He did not touch her except for where he held her face between his palms.

Lifting his head just enough to allow her to look into his eyes, he spoke softly, "This is for you; all for you, with no expectation of reciprocation. Let me do this for you; let me make you feel good." He leveled himself off her with his strong forearms and kissed his way down her body, giving thorough attention to all that came across his path.

Jarod knelt on the floor; he spread her thighs with ease, maintaining eye contact with her as he pulled her panties down until she was completely bare to him. He positioned his hands under her ass, lifting her to him then he leaned in to her, all the while keeping his blue eyes locked on her hazel eyes.

"Why?" was all she asked, but no other words were needed.

"Because it's unselfish of me," he answered, blowing warm air against her stimulated skin. She responded only by biting her lower lip and he added, "I need you to know I'm not the selfish man you think I am."

He shifted attention from her face, and an instant later she felt his tongue glide in and taste her. With rhythmic sweeps, he licked and devoured her, consuming her essence. Soon, she was pulling on her own nipples to relieve some of the building tension.

"Oh God!" she moaned as she arched her back in pure decadent satisfaction.

His tongue honed in on her clit as two of his fingers entered her, flexing and curling right where she needed them. Tipping her head back, she called out. As if he'd been holding back, everything increased tenfold. The speed of his tongue, the depth of his fingers, and the reaction of her body, she saw the peak just as she crested it, but he had no mercy. He continued his oral assault with a vengeance. Using his strong forearm, he held her hips down as his mouth ravaged her over the first wave, quickly building her to another.

CeCe gripped his hair, hoping to guide him to a halt, but he didn't take the hint. Her entire body was vibrating with sensation. Everything he did to her center radiated throughout her body, especially her nipples. Her mind was so muddled with immense pleasure she could not be sure of anything. Was the bed still attached to the wall, or like her, was it floating somewhere in the stratosphere, between the clouds.

Her body reached its limit once more, launching her over the edge into complete triumph.

She called out again and again, fully aware there wasn't a person on the hotel floor that couldn't hear her screams of ecstasy.

His fingers were no longer moving, only his tongue, twittering back and forth over her clit; just enough to prolong her climax from incredible into my-body-can't-take-anymore. Finally, he relented, leaving her wasted, no longer with any sense of feeling throughout her nervous system.

CeCe lay spent, motionless except for her heaving chest, covered in sweat from the exertion, and unable to form a coherent thought. She watched as he stood and used his hand to wipe his mouth before taking each one of his fingers in and licking them like they were a dripping popsicle melting in the summer heat.

He walked to the head of the bed, and leaned down. She anticipated the kiss, but it never came. Instead, he studied her face, taking in every pore. This close, she could smell herself on him, and it turned her on.

Fine! He wants me to make the move, I will!

She moved her head the scant few inches that separated them, but he moved away.

What the fuck?

He let out a loud exhale of breath before he kissed the tip of her nose then turned and walked out of the hotel room.

Twelve

It took CeCe many hours to fall asleep, even after the incredible multiple orgasms, not because she wasn't tired, but because her brain was running a mile a minute—all because of Jarod. *Talk about wham bam, thank you ma'am, I'm outta here.* But CeCe wondered why he only pleasured her. He said he wanted her, but yet when she was ready to deliver, he just casually kissed her nose and walked away? She lost count of how many times she picked up her phone looking for a text that never came. Every time she heard motion outside, she would run to the peephole, but there was no tall, dangerously handsome man on the other side. When she finally did find sleep, it was restless laced with vivid memories of the past she tried so hard to keep dormant interlaced with repeats of what happened hours ago. Talk about fucked up!

She had just gotten out of the shower and was towel drying her hair, when her phone finally buzzed with an incoming text. She rolled her eyes in annoyance.

Oh, now you want a booty call!

Ready to hit Newbury Street in 20? ~ Mae

As she responded back, her disappointment rose! The fact he could disappoint her once again just pissed her off. But as she dressed, applied makeup, and slipped into her flip-flops, CeCe began to contemplate if she was really disappointed at him, or because of him. She wanted him, bad. Even considering her body's triumphant climaxes minutes apart, she was ready to spend hours acquainting herself with the sensation over and over again, but this time she wouldn't be alone.

Damn him!

She grabbed her bag, made sure her keycard was in it and headed down to the lobby to meet her friends. Some retail therapy was just what the doctor ordered.

Yeah, you just keep telling yourself that, Cees! She wanted hard and sweaty physical exertion, and not the kind from lugging around boutique purchases.

"So why didn't you bring something to wear?" CeCe asked a perplexed Natalie.

"Well, I didn't expect to have any alone time, let alone a *putting on the ritz* kind of date night." Natalie answered as she swished metal hangers along the bar, perusing the sixth boutique's selection. "Besides, even if I did, why would I purchase something here when the greatest place is in Appleton? I would have had no problem finding the right dress there."

No matter how many times she heard her friends' compliments, it still tickled her that they genuinely felt her store was the best. Natalie, Mae, and their other friend Lola, have become quite the regular clientele at *CeCe's*. And to be honest, CeCe adored it. It was like playing dress up, only for adults. Each of her dear friends had amazing, but different bodies that were just so much fun to dress, while remaining true to their styles and personalities, CeCe nailed it, every time, if she did say so herself.

Mae was the epitome of a curvaceous full figure. Some women with her figure would want to hide under layers or frumpy styles, but not Mae; she rocked and embellished every beautiful curve. Natalie was the petite and understated, all over perfect female body. She could carry the classics pieces just as easily as she could the trendy ones; a class act all around and beautiful, no matter what. Their newest friend, Lola, was what CeCe considered a moving muse. She had curves, but the best thing about Lola was she was hard core edgy. She loved to mix things up, like pairing dingy denim with sequins and silk, balancing the opposites perfectly. Or, her go-to attire of vintage concert t-shirts with a flowing lightweight skirt. Lola was toughest for CeCe to wear down as far as just standing still and letting CeCe do her thing, but after months of whining and a roll of duct tape, CeCe finally got Lola to come around.

"Any luck?" Mae asked as she checked the price on a sundress.

Letting out a moan of desperation, Natalie turned away from the rack she'd looked through four times and headed over to a display of camisole and boy short pajamas before saying, "No, I'll just have to tell him to cancel dinner at the Prudential building, and just take me to one of the bars in Quincy Market. Better yet, room service, so we can hang out with the girls."

"Oh, no you don't! Your inner pajama goddess is just going to have to wait a little bit longer," CeCe walked over, grabbed Natalie's arm, and dragged her to a rack by the window overlooking a beautiful sunny summer day on Newbury Street. "Here, try this," CeCe handed her one piece from the closest rack and another from a table display.

"You want me to try on a shirt and a scarf?" Natalie asked, confused.

"No, I want you to try on a dress and a shawl."

Mae laughed as Natalie's eyes bugged out, lifting the garments up to examine them closer.

"Now! No lip, Nat, go! The dressing room is that way." CeCe shooed her friend, secretly knowing this ensemble was going to look fabulous as long as they found the right shoes and jewelry.

CeCe focused on the small selection of shoes, hats and jewelry the store offered. She had a couple of jewelry pieces, and three pairs of stilettos in her hand when she noticed the cream colored leather fedora on a stand in the center of the display. With a trick of her hand, CeCe put it atop her head and was adjusting the fit and admiring the look in the display mirror, when her quiet moment was interrupted.

"Need a hand?"

Never turning to face him, she met Jarod's intense blue eyes in the reflection of the mirror. She watched as his jaw worked, and admired how his shoulders and chest looked large and firm in the white t-shirt he wore. His aviator glasses hung in the collar of his v-neck shirt. The short sleeve showed just the hint of his tattoo on his left bicep as his hands rested casually on his hips. Funny, she had forgotten about his tattoo.

"I asked if you needed a hand. You seem to be juggling an awful lot there," he asked again, firmer this time as he moved closer to her, still holding her gaze in the mirror.

"I'm good," she answered huskily, touching the corded circle between her collarbones, not knowing where her voice had gone.

A gorgeous, panty-dropping smile crossed his face as he leaned down, remained in the view of the mirror, and whispered into her ear, "Good? Oh, Kitten, you are better than good, your taste was incredible. Something I will binge myself on again, very soon." His tongue shot out and traced the lower lobe of her ear before they were interrupted by Mae's shriek of delight.

"Damn, Natalie!" Mae giggled as she admired her friend, unaware of the private erotic challenge that was just issued yards away.

Natalie turned this way and that way in front of the mirror outside the dressing area. The black mini dress covered her efficiently yet indecently, paired with the hot pink shawl, which hung loosely over her arms.

CeCe joined them, balancing everything effortlessly. She handed

Natalie a pair of hot pink lace stilettos as well as a matching chunky pink beaded long necklace.

CeCe used her professional eye, changing out the necklace for another before proclaiming, "Perfect!"

As if CeCe's seal of approval wasn't the deciding factor, Jarod chose this moment to let out a wolf whistle causing Mae to whip her head around, and Natalie to blush from head to toe.

"Excuse me," CeCe said as she put everything down including the fedora and grabbed hold of Jarod's beefy arm and walked outside. When the boutiques door closed and the sun beat down on her face she unleashed her annoyance on him, "What do you want, Gates?"

Placing his aviators back on, Jarod rubbed his lower lip with his thumb erotically before answering, "I thought I made that clear, Cees."

She looked up the street, trying to gather herself so she could battle him. Once again touching the black cord around her neck she expelled a deep breath, she turned back to him and said, "What are you doing here?"

"My job."

"Look. I get you need to keep an eye on me at home, but don't you think this is excessive? I don't even know why you are in Boston."

"Nope, and because you are."

Why did the combination of those words have her thinking of stripping him down, right here on the street?

"The only thing excessive right now is the amount of clothes you are wearing. We will have to rectify that sooner rather than later."

He is just too cocky! The fact everything coming out of his mouth is making her wet is beside the point.

"And what if I've changed my mind. I got what I needed last night, why the hell are you so cock sure there will be a next time?"

He ducked down close, but before his lips could touch hers he spoke, "Because I was there, Kitten, I felt everything you felt. The question isn't *if* sex will happen between us. The question is *when*. As I said last night, your play, Kitten. All you have to do is tell me you're ready."

Good luck waiting for that to happen, Slick. Her will tried to remain strong, but even as she thought the words, her mind betrayed her, vividly remembering all he did to her last night, and how much she enjoyed it.

As if he could read her mind, "You were ready last night, but I want to make sure you come to my bed one hundred percent willingly because once I have you there, neither of us is going anywhere for a while."

CeCe swallowed hard as his words and their meaning settled over her.

Placing his hands on her hip he shifted his head so his mouth now lay against her earlobe," I'm going to fuck you so hard and thoroughly, there is a damn good chance one of us won't walk away unscathed." He turned and strolled down the street with a swagger that spoke volumes.

And by God, she was panting at the notion of such a promise.

Something happened in that moment. Her will cracked, and her libido won out, her decision was made. He wants her to be ready. She has the perfect way to tell him she is ready. The sooner she gets him out of her system, the sooner she can forget about him. Again.

Thirteen

CeCe cinched the belt on her coat, double-checked her lip-gloss and sexy tousled locks in her compact before she knocked on the door of Room 504. She knew her choice of outfits would be all the answer he needed. She had to admit it was fun. The short trench coat covered only enough to make her decent and the matching fedora and large round sunglasses added to the role perfectly. He answered the door casually enough, as if the fact he was glistening wet from his shower and wearing only a towel didn't matter in the least.

"I like the fedora and trench coat," he breathed huskily, as his eyes roamed over her multiple times.

"Isn't this what you PIs wear?" she retorted, ducking under his arm and walking the length of the room, stopping in front of the picturesque window before turning to face him.

Jarod closed the door, and held the towel at his hip as he lightly chuckled and walked towards her, "Yeah, when Columbo made it glamorous, but the look kind of died with him. But damn, he never made it look anything like that." He continued to stalk towards her with a Cheshire cat grin, "You, on the other hand, make it look sexy as sin. What do you have on underneath that coat, Cees?" He lifted his hand to move the short hem that rested high on her stocking covered thigh.

She swatted his hand away, "I don't think so, Slick, I'll be the one doing the investigating."

His smile confirmed he was enjoying this verbal sparring, "Oh yeah? What do you want to investigate?"

For fun and emphasis, she looked out the window as if someone was watching before whispering, "I'm looking for something...hard. Rigid. I heard it is hard to conceal. I haven't seen it in years, but I've recently been teased with it, and I've decided it's time to reacquaint myself."

Jarod let a hand rest on each hip as he dipped his head trying to mask his smile and amusement, "and what do you plan on doing with this thing, if and when you find it?"

"Hmmm...well, if it is found, and it will be, thanks to my private dick expertise, I plan to see how much stamina it truly has...all...day...long." CeCe took off the glasses, tossed them on the bed before she undid the belt of her coat, letting it fall off her shoulders and pool at her feet.

The smile and playfulness present moments ago had been cleaned off his face. His eyes raked her body, beginning at her sky-high stiletto covered feet, tracing up over her lace lined thigh highs, the clasps of her miniscule lace garter, over the barely there thong all the way up to its matching cream-colored lace pushup bra.

CeCe began to feel her body hum to life just by his visual assessment. Mission accomplished. However, she was not prepared for the severity of his expression to remain. It scared her, heightening her arousal even more.

He let the towel drop and proved all humor had fled the moment. His cock was rigid, and as erect as she had ever seen. The engorged head and deep purple veins running up his long shaft were impressive, but paled in comparison to the marred and deformed skin, showing a major injury and muscle loss on his left thigh and hip, the ugliness continued up his side all the way around his shoulder. Her breath caught and her mind clouded wondering why she didn't notice it when she first walked it, but then it came to her. Taking inventory of it all, she raised her gaze to his and was met with a challenge in his quirked eyebrow.

She answered in kind, raising her own brow, stating plainly it didn't matter.

He must of accepted their nonverbal exchange because he added, "Private Dick Expertise, huh? Well, Kitten, I don't think it will be too hard to find; in fact, I happen to know it has no plans to elude you."

She closed the few feet of distance, signaling this is what she wanted. She wrapped her arms around his neck before answering, "Good, I wasn't looking forward to wasting my energy on the hunt." She rose up on tiptoes to kiss him when he pulled away ever so slightly.

"You sure? I won't stop," he searched her gaze looking for any doubt.

"It's fucking, Gates. Nothing more."

"You just keep telling yourself that, Kitten."

And then it began. His mouth closed over hers as he picked her up and pushed her back into the wall, none too gently. He nuzzled her neck kissing her everywhere as she gripped his head, giving him access to everything. His large hands held and kneaded her ass, as he pushed his throbbing cock into the cradle of her womanhood. With only the lace as the barrier, he made quick work of the scant piece of material, ripping it effortlessly as he said, "I'll add these to the others," before he dropped them to the ground. With his cock at her opening, he lifted his head catching her gaze, "Do I need a rubber?"

Breathlessly she answered, "Not this time. I'm protected. I trust you. In me, now!"

"Yes ma'am," he rammed into her, burying himself to the hilt.

They swore in unison as he began to move inside her. He hammered into her, knocking her against the wall with every thrust. His mouth closed over a nipple through the fabric, biting and sucking, stimulating her close to the edge. He maneuvered her legs farther apart, needing to be deeper insider her with each stroke. He quickened the already fast pace, throwing her over the peak and had her begging for mercy.

"Oh, God!"

Mercy he did not grant. He continued to thrust into her as his mouth moved from her breast to her neck, up her jaw to bite on her lower lip.

All the feeling left her limbs; he remained unrelenting in his promise to fuck her hard and thoroughly. Just as CeCe was sure she would split in two, his momentum slowed, almost teasing, but just as torturous, his movements building her to her second orgasm. The moment his warm seed spilled into her, she claimed ecstasy again.

They remained against the wall, leaning into each other for strength to remain upright as they panted and tried to regain their breath.

"You can put me down, now," CeCe stated, hoping her legs would not turn to wet spaghetti.

A low chuckled replied, as his face remained buried in her neck, "I like you like this."

She snorted, unladylike, "Up against a wall not touching the ground?"

"You can't run away from me like this."

His words hung heavy in the air. *What did that mean? Why did he think she would run away? He couldn't be referring to years ago, could he? If so, his memory is distorted, she wasn't the one that fled.*

She tapped him on the shoulder, trying to bring the lightness of the moment back, "Come on, Slick, time to move."

He picked his head up and looked her in the eyes. The blue of his irises were so vivid, the color would make Crayola jealous. He wore his half-cocky grin, but remained in place. He really was a gorgeously sexy man. She knew it, and he knew it. This might not have been the brightest idea, but to hell with the consequences. She would deal with them tomorrow; today was about taking all the physical release she needed, and when they got back home it would be strictly business.

Raising her eyebrow at still being pinned to the wall, she ran her finger over his lip and his cheek, rubbing off the smeared lip gloss.

Jarod spun them around and stepped twice to the bed and lay down with her still entwined around him. "Warmed up yet?" he asked with a wicked grin before kissing his way down her neck, tonguing the circle that lay there before venturing lower until he had one still covered semi erect nipple in his mouth.

CeCe thought her eyes were going to roll back into her head. He couldn't possibly be ready to go again, nor could she…could she? Suddenly, her limp limbs began to hum to life as her blood began to pump and arousal took over. Her core pulsated and she found her fingers moving of their own accord, pushing him over onto his back. She followed, straddling his hips where his limp member lay.

"Kind of false advertising, isn't it, to ask if I'm ready if you are currently unable to perform?" she inquired playfully as she ran her fingertips down both his arms and over his washboard abs, ignoring the cratered and pitted skin on one side.

The smile that grazed his face was like none other she had seen on him, this one was both playful and completely sincere as his own hands rested on her hips, "Unable to perform, huh? Does what's pressing against your fine ass feel limp?"

At his words, the sensation of the firm warm flesh now making contact with her, registered. She wiggled her bottom just enough to confirm he was, in fact, hard again. Reaching behind her, she undid her bra exposing herself to him, for the first time in the light of day. Usually, she would sit proudly, but for some reason, she felt shy.

He sensed her sudden nervousness and covered the gorgeous mounds with his hands and reverently breathed, "Beautiful. Better than I remember." Sitting up, he replaced a hand with his mouth and began admiring the hard nub with his tongue.

She held his head to her, completely wrapped up in the sensation. He moved his free hand, skimming it along her side and belly until his thumb found her clit. She bit her lip at the contact. With his rigid cock firmly pressing against her backside, his thumb massaged her hidden bud while his tongue suckled deliciously on her nipple. It wasn't long before she thrust against his hand, reaching the crest of another orgasm.

"Oh yeah, right there."

"Come for me, Kitten." Jarod commanded.

He increased his speed, inserting two fingers into her and curling upward, touching her magic spot. Her moan of her pleasure went on and on as she plummeted over the edge. She curled into his shoulder, allowing her body to vibrate and convulse against him in pure bliss. The fedora fell off and lay next to his hip on the bed.

He held her to him, running his hands up and down her back soothing her as she regained her equilibrium. When she was sure she had control over her skeletal system, she sat back and cupped his face in her hands then leaned in and kissed him, in control for the first time. It wasn't sweet, but neither was it harsh; it was the perfect balance of gratitude and lust. When she thought to end the kiss she found herself thinking of more reasons to continue. Finally, she mustered the will to pull back.

"What did you mean earlier, when you said you'd add my ripped panties to the others? If you tell me you have a shoebox full of ripped panties, I may just vomit."

Her words amused him and a megawatt smile crossed his face, so huge it creased the edges of his beautiful eyes in a mix of age and sexiness only men can get away with.

"I only had one talisman I carried around the war zones; these will be added to those since they came from the same woman."

CeCe's eyes widened at his words, the air suddenly thick and intense. Choosing to ignore the bigger meaning of his comment, she brought the conversation back around to what this was all about: sex.

"You certainly are a man of your words, aren't you?"

"I am. But what word are you referring to?"

Picking up the fedora, she placed it back on her head, pulling it down low and adjusting the rim she answered, "The promise of my brains being thoroughly screwed."

"A Marine's honor is his word."

"Well, Marine, I thank you for your service."

"But since we are discussing promises, let's discuss yours."

She looked at him quizzically. "Mine?"

Lightning fast, he flipped her over so she lay on her back, the fedora falling to the floor. He slowly crawled up her body, until his cock aligned perfectly with her opening. "Yeah, something about becoming reacquainted with what you've been looking for."

"Ooohh, that. I guess I should focus on the job then, huh?" she answered playfully as her hand explored south.

"Never stop until a job is done."

"Then let's quit with the clit chat and let me do just that."

He covered her body, and reintroduced her to every inch of him. He took all that she offered and all he desired.

Jarod lay on his side watching CeCe sleep, the smell of sex heavy in the air. She'd drifted off about thirty minutes ago, after two more rounds of reacquainting their bodies. His leg throbbed from the workout and his back and shoulders bared multiple scratches and nail indentations, but he wouldn't trade it for the world. Finally, CeCe was in his bed, where she belonged. His heart had just about stopped when he'd opened the door and saw her standing there in that getup. He knew she'd struggled to accept their off-the-chart sexual attraction; hence, the reason she made it a role-playing game, but if this were his offered opening he would take it. He would never look this kind of gift horse in the mouth.

His eyes drifted over her, and the obvious fact was she was beautiful, awake and asleep. She slept peacefully, obviously finding comfort in her dreams, something he was envious of. Like so many other aspects of his life, being a Marine taught him to live and function on minimal sleep, which helped keep his demons at bay. Demons that seemed more alive and gripping, now that he'd opened the Pandora's box of being with CeCe. But, dammit, he would willingly accept the licks of Hell's fiery fury for one moment of her sweet taste.

Leaving her last night was the second hardest thing he had ever done. How he wanted to take her right then, and physically show her everything she refused to see with her eyes and heart. But he wanted—no, needed—her to see he wasn't the man she thought he was, and if that meant he had to deny himself, then so be it.

Nevertheless, his fear surfaced and slid off his tongue so easily when she came to him today. He'd faced the enemy head on, was willing to die for someone else's war and he survived, wounded and scared, but alive. But that was nothing compared to the power this beautiful creature held over him. Soon it would be time for her to understand just what that power was, and how he meant every fear-filled word.

Unable to resist being this close and not touching her, he leaned over and kissed her soft, swollen lips. As he tongued the soft line, her eyes fluttered open, focusing instantly.

"Hey."

"Hey, yourself, I must have really worn you out," Jared stated, brushing away the soft lock of hair that had fallen across her face.

"Seven orgasms will do that to a person," she leaned up and over him to look at the bedside clock. Jarod took the exposed breast that dangled in front of his face as an invitation, as he glided his lips over the soft point. "None of that." She said as she pulled away from him before adding, "I have to go." She slid out the opposite side of the bed, quickly retrieving her discarded lingerie.

"Got a date?"

"As a matter of fact, I do," she answered not even looking in his direction.

"Excuse me?" he barked, suddenly furious.

She cinched the tie on her coat before turning to him and laughing at his expense, "I've told you before, jealousy does not look good on you, Gates"

Shit! We're back to Gates again. Dammit! What does she mean she has a date?

"Mind explaining why you are rushing off?" he tried to sound unaffected, but he knew it sounded just as he meant it.

"Well, I came, I conquered, I came again," enhanced with a wink, "now I'm leaving."

"You think so, do you?" He shot out of bed reaching her easily, but what he hoped would be a romantic wrestle back onto the bed, became him losing his balance as slicing pain shot through his thigh, causing him to collapse back onto the bed as the cry of agony ripped from his mouth.

"Oh my God, Gates, are you okay?" she asked, as she kneeled in front of him trying to look at and touch his thigh.

"It's fine!" he bellowed, embarrassed for her to see him at a weak moment.

At the tone of his voice, her eyes met his, and the fury in them couldn't mask the fear of her pitying him.

"Obviously, it isn't fine. Were you going to tell me about this?" she asked pointing to his thigh, her unwavering gaze demanding an answer.

He continued to rub at the excruciating pain out of habit, even though it never helped. Dammit, he didn't want to tell her about the ugliness of his body, nor did he ever intend for her to see him broken by it. He wasn't an idiot, he knew when he dropped the towel she saw it, but that was all the attention he'd planned on her having of it. *Didn't that just get fucking blown to smithereens?*

"I'm waiting!" she snapped, standing with her arms crossed over her chest and her hip jutted out.

Squeezing his eyes shut against the pain, he knew he had two options;

tell her, or don't tell her. When Jarod raised his head and met her annoyed gaze head on, he made the decision…to go right down the middle.

"Not now." And with that cowardly, backdoor answer, the pain increased and began to burn.

CeCe threw her hands up and rolled her eyes, irritated, as she marched to the door. Every heeled step emphasized her annoyance.

"Fine! Whatever…like I said, I have somewhere to be. See you around, Gates." She said over her shoulder, never looking toward him as the door closed behind her.

Well isn't that fucking perfect! Three steps forward, twenty steps back. Gates, you are an asshole!

CeCe had quickly showered, changed and was just on her way out of her room, heading up to Dylan's suite, when she noticed Jarod casually leaning against the wall across from her door. Their eyes connected—his full of inquisition, hers of annoyance.

"You going to tell me where you are going?" he asked, not moving.

She crossed her arms over her chest, raised her eyebrow and countered, "you going to tell me about your leg and hip?"

"One has nothing to do with the other. One is my job."

"Job Schmob!"

A smile spread across his face at that, melting a bit of the ice inside her chest.

CeCe honestly didn't know why him keeping something from her bothered her so much, but it did. It felt like a betrayal of some sort. She realized how foolish such a concept was, but there was no other word to describe the feeling.

He pushed himself off the wall with his foot, stepped slowly towards her and let out a loud breath, "You aren't going to drop it, are you?" CeCe batted her eyelashes in response. "God, Kitten, you certainly are infuriating.

Let's just leave it at a story for another time. I'm just not ready to share that with you."

"But you will?" she pushed.

"I will."

"Alright then." One small victory for her, but it felt important.

"Now your turn…where are you going?"

"We are going upstairs."

"We?"

"Yup! You and me, Slick. How good are you with diapers?"

CeCe laughed aloud at the priceless look on his face in response.

Fourteen

Two hours later, Jarod was on a hotel bed with rumpled sheets and a happy female...three actually. The evening was the furthest concept possible of how Jarod thought his night with CeCe would go. But he was enjoying himself. Currently, he was the foundation of the Cross twins' nighttime entertainment.

"Come on Gates, let's see how many pushups you can do with forty pounds of wiggly, giggly little girls on your back."

"Pfft...easy," Jarod pushed off his forearms as Cat and Ria sat on his back, laughing from their bellies as they went up and down, falling off then climbing back up as quickly as they could. By the time he counted out one hundred reps, only Ria remained in place and was happily pretending he was a horse, kicking his ribs to get him to "Gibby um orsy, gibby um orsy!"

"You heard her!" CeCe said through her own deep laughter, as Cat sat between her legs on the bed watching the huge flat screen television.

Making sure Ria was secure, Jarod climbed off the bed, adjusted to the pain in his leg, and galloped around the room, making what he thought was a convincing horse sound, but CeCe told him it was pitiful. With the ranch activities occurring in the room, soon Cat's attention was diverted from the television and she wanted her turn on "orsy man".

After many more rides, switching off between giggling little girls, when it came time for bed, he was happy CeCe told him to head out to the living room of the suite so she could put the girls down. His leg and hip were screaming, and he went without argument, but not before Cat and Ria insisted on hugs and kisses. By the time Jarod left the bedroom, his smile was a reflection of the two smaller ones about to go to sleep.

He was sitting on the uncomfortable couch when CeCe emerged twenty minutes later. She looked fantastic, mouth-watering. Regardless that he had her not even four hours ago, he wanted her again and again. Her taste was the most addictive kind of drugs, and he was ready for another hit. Her long hair was pulled up in a high messy bun; her shapely legs showcased in short cut offs she wore. Her bra could easily be seen through her white scoop neck tee and her feet were bare displaying her French manicured toe polish. She sat next to him tucking one leg under her and pulling her other knee to her chest. CeCe wiggled her toes, unknowingly tempting him.

"They asleep?"

"Goodness, no," CeCe removed her hair from its high knot, letting if fall as she combed her fingers through the tangled locks, "but hopefully they will be shortly."

God, could she get any sexier? The more she ran her hands through her hair, the more her sweet smelling scent wafted to his nose, increasing his already revved libido. With his eyes openly roaming her leg, Jarod slowly moved his hand over, watching and waiting for her denial, which never came. Jarod gripped her foot, pulled it towards his lap, where her foot rested high on his thigh. He began to rub her foot, pressing deep into her arch. Her head fell backwards to the cushion she leaned against.

"That feels incredible," she moaned.

He continued to rub and enjoy the pleasure she was receiving at his strong hands. He stopped only long enough to pull her other foot from under her ass so he could alternate from one foot to the other. After several minutes of finger work, he brought her left foot to his mouth, running the tip of his tongue along the top of her foot, from her big toe nail up to her ankle, continuing up to her knee and back down. All the while never breaking eye contact with her, fueled by the aroused fog clouding her beautiful hazel eyes. When he returned to the starting point of her toe, he began to rub its arch again with one hand while the other gently massaged behind her knee. Somewhere along this journey, her nipples hardened against the tight strain of her top, calling to him for attention. The diversion of his attention from her face to her chest apparently was abrupt and lengthy, causing CeCe to laugh. That sound was one of the best sounds to him, only topped by her moans and screams of pleasure.

He didn't complain when CeCe shifted her position and straddled his lap. Her smile matched his own. Her hair hung around both of them, making a curtain in which only the two of them existed. He was consumed by her mouthwatering scent, her kissable plump lips. Not to mention those pebbled hard nipples now pressing into his chest, and her barely covered warm heat pressed into his cock, straining against his zipper.

"I want to bury myself in you for just a short while," he whispered as his hands roamed around to her ass, pulling her even closer.

She snickered before rubbing herself against him some more, "Only a short while? Jeez, Gates, didn't we talk about this stamina thing."

He smiled between light bites of her lip alternating with each word, "Oh, but by a short while, I meant we will start with infinity, and work our way up." The instant he finished his statement he noticed the change in her.

She straightened her back, sitting upright and breaking their intimate position. She ran her hand through her hair, the way she does when she is annoyed, before placing her arms across her chest under her breasts.

"What?" Jarod huffed, pissed she pulled away from him. When she didn't answer, but instead just sat there, stone still, he asked again, louder this time, "What the hell happened, Cees? What I do this time?"

"Lower your voice!" she snapped before climbing off his lap and walking to the closed bedroom door to check on the twins; they hadn't stirred.

Jarod watched as she paced the room, simultaneously giving him a wide birth. This only fueled his pissed off mood. He was off the couch in a nanosecond, refusing to give into the scream of pain that sliced though him. He reached her in another moment, catching her off guard at his speed, as he grabbed her upper arm.

"Don't shut me out. Tell me what just happened, Dammit!"

"Let go of me, Gates!"

He did not comply, his anger continuing to fuel him, "There we go with calling me Gates, again! My name is Jarod! You know that is my name; hell, you called me it all the time back then, why is it you refuse to call me it now?"

What he saw in her beautiful face at that moment was worse than the pity he was so afraid of, this was unadulterated hatred. He recognized the bone deep anger; it was the same mask and mentality of so many fellow Marines, as well as his own haunting demons.

"You have two seconds to get your hand off of me before you no longer have your fingers, *Gates!*" she seethed.

He released her, crossed his arms over his wide chest, and waited for an answer to his questions.

After several seconds—that felt like minutes—of the stare off, she decided to tell him the truth and get it off her chest, "I call you Gates as my defense mechanism."

"Defense mechanism?" he was confused at the unexpected response. "Why the hell do you need a defense mechanism for me, and what did I say to make you pull away?"

"I told you this was sex! That's it!"

"I don't believe you," he countered.

She ignored his response, searching his face for something he couldn't even fathom. Not finding it, she looked down at her feet before continuing,

"Yeah, a defense mechanism to make myself remember how you gutted me," she said, with less steel in her voice, raising her gaze to him, allowing him to see the scars he left on her soul.

Shit! She no longer was the pissed off combatant she had been, but rather gave glimpses of what he had done to her all those years ago. Maybe his dream and hope would never come true. Maybe his biggest fear—that he could never make up for his cruelty—was about to come to fruition. The justification for his actions back then no longer held the same importance today. Instead of the hot, amazing sex bringing them closer, maybe it was her best weapon; her weapon of mass destruction. At a loss, he ran his hands over his head before shoving them in his pockets. He was just about to speak when she walked to the door and opened it. She waited, never looking toward him.

He knew, in this moment, how he responded would either sink him, or allow him to sail another day. Perhaps if he gave her time, she wouldn't shut him out just yet. Silently, he walked to the door, stopping in front of her, still refusing to look at him. And he admitted it hurt. Slowly, he leaned down and kissed her forehead and whispered against her soft skin, "I'm sorry. You have no idea how sorry I am."

He saw her squeeze her eyes shut, and he decided to walk out and come up with another way to break down her wall.

As he stepped into hall, she spoke, the steel returning to her voice, "That time in my life was both one of the worst, and one of the best; the latter because of Dylan and because of you. I never thought I would be able to trust a guy again after Troy, but Dylan showed me I could. With you, it was different; I felt things for you I never felt for Troy, even after all the time we had dated. I always knew I was just another notch in your belt, but you sold a good game, and I actually believed I was different. How stupid of me. Granted, you didn't hit me like he did, but you left me. Disposed of me, like I was nothing. Like my virginity was nothing to you. From that moment, I swore I would never allow myself to be the victim again. *That* is why I need a defense mechanism against you." She finally looked at him, her beautiful hazel eyes met his, and the ache it caused in his soul was worse than the shrapnel ripping through his skin and muscles like butter. "I need to remember that Gates," then she closed the door leaving him stunned.

He remained there, looking at the closed door, for several minutes, before finally turning and walking down the hall. *Her defense mechanism might just be his self-destruct button.*

Fifteen

Why is it, after saying what she had wanted to say for years, she felt so terrible? Perhaps it was the quiet of the room, or guilt for being mean, or for missing out on the sure-thing orgasm she was heading for with that little foot rub; regardless, she felt like shit now.

Ducking out on Dylan and Natalie, after their multiple invites to stay, CeCe only had one thing on her mind; numbing herself with liquor. Even the silence in the elevator grated on her nerves, the God awful instrumental music apparently taking a break. True to the saying, the silence was deafening.

When she reached the bar, it was fairly busy. She found an open stool at the bar and sat, quickly ordering a shot of Patron and a Dirty Martini. While she waited, she looked around and felt a tad underdressed. Maybe she should have changed out of her t-shirt and shorts before coming down, but she'd just wanted liquor. *Oh well.*

"Here you go, Miss," the bartender said with a kind smile as he placed the two glasses in front of CeCe.

"Thanks. May I start a tab, please?" she asked, before tossing back the shot.

"Rough night?" The fiery liquid still licking her throat, she just rolled her eyes at the voice to her left.

"Kind of," CeCe answered, looking in the other direction, hoping he could take a hint.

"What could possibly be wrong with a fine looking thing such as yourself?"

Yeah, no such luck on the taking a hint. Fabulous!

CeCe turned back to speak with the gentleman addressing her. Usually, she could probably find something appealing about his runway model looks and extremely fit body, but right now, all she saw was a penis on his shoulders. The last thing she needed in her life was another one of those.

"Look, Prettyboy, rule number one in how to pick up a chick: Only go for the ones looking to be picked up. That is not me, so move along."

She didn't even find humor in his appalled expression, or the derogatory name he called her under his breath. She quickly drained her martini glass, asking for a refill of both. When the bartender placed both glasses in front of her again, she downed the shot, finally feeling the numbing sensation she was going for.

She had just plucked the second liquor-infused olive off its pick, when the bartender placed a huge Caesar salad in front of her.

"I didn't order this."

"I know. The man over there did, saying if you were going to consume so much liquor, you needed to have something in your stomach. Please, don't shoot the messenger."

CeCe didn't need to turn around to know who it was. The fact he was right—she had hardly anything in her stomach—pissed her off that much more. When she did turn around, those dangerous blue eyes were trained on her. Suddenly, every pore in her body swelled with goose bumps, her mouth went dry, and her panties became wet. Jarod Gates was a gorgeous man, the kind that only got better looking with age. His short light hair looked even lighter with his darkened tan. A tan that proved he spent a lot of time outside, or on a beach. His eyes were the color of an ocean, brighter and more vivid as if the color were taken from the waters of the Caribbean. His muscles bulged beneath his black t-shirt; visually indicating he could handle anything that came his way. She had firsthand knowledge on both their strength and their gentleness. His veins corded down his forearms and pulsated in his hands with every flex of his muscles. His muscled thighs looked strong through his jeans, but she wondered if he was in pain.

She didn't move from her bar stool, nor did he from his wingback leather chair, where he sat with one ankle resting on the opposites knee. It was a position indicating relaxation, but she knew he was anything but. He was always on his toes, he was always aware of everything and everyone around him. It was...sexy. Just like he was. Her body remembered what it was like to be filled by him and began to crave and demand a repeat performance, regardless of her mind and heart's continuing opposing vote. He rested a glass filled with amber liquid on his raised foot, rotating the glass so the liquid swirled in constant motion.

Not caring if it was the alcohol, or her mind's way of gaining ground, or just the pure sexuality of it guiding her, she brought the plastic pick with the last remaining olive to her lips, and slowly surrounded it with her teeth, gradually drawing the salty fruit down the pick and into her mouth, never moving her eyes from his. CeCe watched as he swallowed hard and his jaw twitched, feeling empowered and vindicated.

Jarod rose from his seat and slowly stalked toward her, in no rush as he closed in on his obvious destination. When he reached her, he didn't even stop to ask permission, or wait to gauge her reaction. He simply placed both hands on the bar, caging her in, and took possession of her mouth. He tasted of strong whiskey and heated intent. His lips and tongue were anything but gentle; they were demanding and unequivocally speaking a language of their own; a language she was fluent in. His tongue stroked the inside of her mouth, claiming it all. His hands never moved from their grip on the bar, and no other part of him touched her; just his mouth, but it was so erotic. It was apologetic, promise filled, proprietary, and all consuming, all at the same time.

So many emotions ran through her; she knew this was wrong, she knew this would leave her emotionally bleeding, but she just couldn't deny what her body wanted, what it needed. Somewhere in the back of her head, she imagined the show they were putting on, but she just couldn't ask him to stop. To stop would mean to break contact and take in air, and that just wasn't possible at the moment.

When he finally did stop, never paying heed to the snickers and mumbled-under-breath comments, he didn't speak, only handed her the martini glass, and lifted his own. He clinked his glass to hers, and they both drained them. He took the empty glass from her, set both next to the untouched salad on the bar, threw multiple bills down, and pulled her off the stool and along in his wake. CeCe had to walk fast to keep up with his long, hurried stride. Her heart raced at the eroticism of his dominating actions, making the decisions. And she was letting him. She didn't want to think; she didn't want to be aware of the complications, or the open wound she would ultimately give herself, all she wanted was him inside her. He walked past the elevator, past the stairs, she wanted to ask where they were going, but knew he wouldn't answer if she asked.

When they reached the lobby, she thought he was heading outside, but instead he veered toward the ballrooms. Events were taking place—weddings most likely, given the attire guests wore. Just as they reached the area, Jarod pulled her down a small hallway. They walked to the end and he opened a closed door. He ushered her in to the dark room, closing the door behind them. She couldn't see anything except for the few windows that showed the darkened sky over the calm harbor.

Her attention was focused on the quiet night outside the windows of the darkened conference room when she felt Jarod in front of her. Her eyes finally adjusting to the darkness, she was able to see his face. He placed a warm, strong finger under her chin, lifting her gaze to his eyes as her bottom touched the large oval table and she felt the cool leather of one of the chairs against her bare thigh.

"You deserve better than me. You deserve all the happiness in the world, and if I had even a shred of decency in me, I would walk away from you, but I can't. I would rather saw off my own limbs than walk away. I know what I did to you then; by God, I thought I was doing the right thing, but all I did was make us both miserable, and both of us miss out on time. That was the worst mistake of my life, and I swear to God, a day—hell, a fucking minute—has not gone by that I haven't regretted saying that to you, from the moment the words left my mouth."

Could this be true? Did it change anything? She honestly didn't know; all she knew was the demand her body, and its sexual needs, put on her. Here, in this room, there was no history, there were no bad decisions, or regrets; There was just a man and a woman who wanted each other in the most primal of ways.

"I'm every bit the asshole you accuse me of being, but please, just let me experience peace again," he whispered as his fingertip ran from her chin, down her neck, swirling around the circle there and lower, until he was gently following the seam of her t-shirt where it touched her breasts.

Between the warmth and liquor smell of his breath, and the feeling his touch caused, she was amazed she could form a thought. Surprised by his choice of words she was compelled to ask, "Sex is peace to you?"

He cocked his head to the side, focusing his attention on the track of his finger before returning his gaze to hers and replying, "No. Sex isn't my peace; you are, CeCe."

He lifted her up, setting her on the edge of the table, placed a hand on each side of her face and kissed her. If his kiss in the bar was demanding, this was its opposite. There was no rush; there was nothing to prove, just flesh ready to touch flesh. Her nerve endings pleading and waiting to feel every ounce of stimulation they could.

CeCe wrapped her arms around Jarod's neck, pulling his head closer, as she wrapped her legs around his waist, reveling in the hardness that pressed into her. Her mind took her back all those years, reminding her she'd experienced this gentleness, this tenderness, before; many times, in fact. Every time he touched her, all those years ago, he was always gentle with her, never demanded anything, and if it got too intense, he always withdrew, sometimes leaving her to wonder why. Every time, but the last time—that night, he took. He showed her the side of him everyone else saw, the reputation which preceded him, the side that she had since concluded was the true him.

Until now. Now, she took too. Every time they were intimate, she took her pleasure; maybe she needed to show that she could be unselfish. Perhaps she needed to prove something to him; that she was capable of acting on desires, regardless of the ramifications of emotions. She owed him that much, she owed herself that much. She had been given a redo, so to speak, a second chance to take what she wanted from her first lover, but also a chance to give pleasure, for both of them to carry on when they part ways, again. She pulled away from his embrace, taking his roaming and magnificent hands into hers, keeping them still.

Jarod let out a long held breath, and rested his forehead against hers. She knew the thoughts he had, and the vixen in her let him think them. "I don't blame you," he breathed, "I made my bed, now I need to lie in it."

"I don't plan on letting you be alone in your bed, just yet."

"What?" his blue eyes searched her face, trying to decipher what she could possible mean. She was truly a horrible person because she relished in his confusion.

She leaned over, pushing the closest chair out and with a light shove to his hard chest Jarod fell backwards into the waiting chair. CeCe slid off the table and with her arm draped across the back, she swiveled the chair around so he faced the windows.

CeCe enjoyed Jarod watching her as she stood in front of him, her back to the harbor, and deftly pulled her t-shirt up and over her head. His eyes took her body in, the smile on his face growing, but quickly vanished when she dropped to her knees before him.

"CeCe, you don't have to…" she cut him off with a gentle hand to his mouth.

When she was sure he would remain mute, she went to work on his belt. Quickly and expertly, she freed his hardness of its prison. He smelled incredible, like musk, sex and anticipation. With a final seductive stare, CeCe let her gaze drop to her new focus. She bent her head over his hard rigid cock, letting her hair fall to his abdomen and thighs. CeCe licked the head like it was a dripping ice cream cone.

A moan of pleasure ripped from his throat, and at the sound, she adjusted her head to the side, so she could watch him, watch her orally satisfy him. She took him into her mouth, shallowly at first, lightly sucking on the head, then taking in more and more of him until he tickled the back of her throat. Slowly, she worked him, over and over, driving them both insane. She could taste the salty secretion that began to bead on him and its taste only fueled her to continue.

Jarod gripped the back of the chair, the muscles in his forearms tightening, manifesting her effect on him, physically and sexually. *Talk about empowering.* She increased her pace, adding more suction, rolling her tongue around the head and along the shaft, thrilling in his moans of pleasure and his pleas for her to continue.

She caressed his balls with her hand before moving to his shaft, mimicking the movements of her mouth causing him to buck in pleasure. Breathlessly, he begged her to stop, "Kitten, I'm going to come. Stop your talented mouth right now unless you plan on taking all of it." She responded by sucking him harder; exploding a moment later, he let out a guttural moan at the release.

The first blast of hot salty cream hit the back of her throat and just kept coming. His entire body constricted, and his teeth ground together, making the veins his neck throb. When he was finally spent, he collapsed back against the chair, heaving for breath and covered in a film of sweat.

CeCe sat back in triumph; using her thumb, she wiped the corners of her mouth and waited for him to regain his bearings. God, he was sexy when he was sated. Seeing Jarod like this made her feel sexy, ultimately female.

"Kitten…" he began, still breathless.

Coyly, she stood and placed her hands in her back pockets of her shorts, knowing full well this position caused her breasts to thrust forward. *He always was a tit man.* Her breasts threatened to spill out over the plunging cotton cups, and her hard pointed nipples could be seen easily even in this low light.

"That was as much for me, as it was for you," she explained, feeling her own sexual excitement reach a fevered pitch. CeCe always enjoyed giving oral sex, but this experience was beyond her usual enjoyment of giving a blowjob. The intensity of her arousal was threatening to make her self-combust.

As if he could read her mind, he stood, ignoring the cry of pain from his thigh. He grabbed her around the waist and whispered, "I want to take you, now; this wasn't supposed to be about me."

"Then take me," she answered firmly, issuing the challenge. She stood up on tiptoes and kissed his lips before blazing a path to and from erogenous zones.

He could only take her torture for so long before he stepped behind her, directing her to the large table. With her back to him he served up his own torture, kissing and nipping along her neck. He pressed his chest against her back, gradually increasing the pressure, bending her forward until her chest rested on the table. He slowly ran the tips of his fingers down her spine, until they reached the waistband of her shorts. His hands slid around to her front, easily unsnapping them. He eased her shorts and thong over her hips, letting them fall to pool at her feet. Jarod reversed the motion of his fingers along her spine, and CeCe felt the goose bumps again. The cool table felt amazing against her overheating skin. He flicked open the clasp of her bra then replaced his fingers with his mouth, continuing the exploration of her succulent skin. Wet open kisses ran from her hairline down to the curve of her lower back, occasionally venturing from side to side, to kiss her outer rib cage.

"I want you like this," he mumbled against her back.

She could only answer with a "Mm hmm."

Her entire system was in overdrive. The unyielding table heightened the sensations racing across and through her body, showing no mercy to her aching breasts and nipples. Jarod's once again rigid and stiff cock pressed against her ass cheeks, as her own equally ready and waiting scent filled the room. She heard the sound of foil being torn as he quickly sheathed himself then she felt his head probe her entrance, sliding in slowly, only allowing the tip enter her, toying with her. Then, with exquisite control, he filled her, inch by glorious inch. He reveled in the sensation of filling her this way for the briefest moment before he flexed his lower body, brushing his hips against her ass, shattering his control. Soon an aggressive pace was set. The sound of skin slapping skin filled the room as the scent of sex increased in intensity. CeCe pushed her palms down on the tabletop, levering up to counter his demanding thrusts. His hands clamped onto her hips as he repeatedly drove himself into her, hard. She was so full and he was so deep, the only word fit to describe this kind of connection was ecstasy. He was as unapologetic in his demands as she was. Harder. Faster. Deeper. Both repeating those words to each other multiple times.

"FUCK!" he groaned.

CeCe felt her body build to its peak, but every time she thought she would shatter, her body played a cruel joke on her and just kept enduring and building again.

Jarod's pace slowed as he laid his chest against her back, sliding in and out of her torturously, yet erotically, slow. He slid his right hand around to her front and applied pressure right where she needed it. He strummed her engorged tissue, and soon she was screaming out in climax. He followed right behind, and together they rode the wave of their passion on and on, Jarod gently covering her mouth with his hand to stifle her screams before someone investigated.

Both remained bent over the table, heaving breaths and unable to talk or move, just reveling in complete orgasmic pleasure. Jarod regained his composure first as he kissed her back, shoulders and neck, anywhere his mouth could reach.

"That feels nice," she mumbled, her cheek pressed against the solid table.

"I want you to feel a whole lot better than nice, but what I have in mind should probably be handled in one of the hotel rooms, rather than in here." With one final kiss to the base of her neck, he slapped her ass before fastening his pants. He bent down, pulling her thong and shorts up her smooth legs. When her ass was covered, he stepped away to retrieve her shirt from where it landed, a few feet away. When both were dressed, he kissed her forehead, and once gain grabbed her hand, pulling her along in his wake, out of the room and back toward the elevators.

When they reached the waiting elevator and stepped inside, he pulled her into his embrace, holding onto her waist possessively. Without even asking he brought her to his room, opened the door and ushered her inside. When the door swung closed, he clicked the deadbolt, ignored the light switch and bent down picking her up, cradling her in his arms, as he carried her across the room. Jarod laid her down on the bed, quickly removing their clothes. Once they were both naked, he covered her body with his, and set out to rid her mind of all the mistakes he made in the past, hoping he was replacing them with promises of a future.

Sixteen

The bedside clock read 2:43AM beneath the soft glow of the lamp next to it on the side table. CeCe gently turned her body so she faced Jarod, who was lying on his back with his left arm tucked under his head. His eyes were closed and his breathing even. She was able to see just the edge of the tattoo on his bicep. With great care, CeCe pulled back the sheet that covered his waist so she could examine his skin. High on his left side, around where his ribcage began, the skin was pitted and discolored. The pattern continued down to his waist and farther beyond to his hip and thigh. His thigh was the worst. CeCe had never seen badly burned skin, but she guessed it looked something like this. The rigid and jagged scars along the marred skin looked painful. She wanted to touch it, not to bring attention to it, but so she could hopefully take away some of the agonizing pain he felt. Such scars must never truly heal.

CeCe replaced the sheet and let her eyes roam north, taking in his strong, carved abdomen, his sculptured chest, and his gorgeous face that now had two concerned blue eyes watching her. She felt her cheeks redden for being caught.

"Find anything interesting?" he asked, sounding upset.

She steeled herself not to get riled over his tone, she was sure if the roles were reversed her feathers would be ruffled, too. "Yes, a gorgeous man," she answered honestly.

Bringing the attention back to the top half of his body, she touched his bicep. "Tell me about your tattoo."

Jarod moved his arm enough so she could see the unusual design. It had deep, thick lines running from his low bicep up to his shoulder, but it made no image or sense to her.

Sensing her confusion he explained, "It's an ambigram."

CeCe studied the tattoo that much harder, "So it is supposed to look the same to me as it does to you from a different angle."

"Right, but given the hard look on your face you can't tell what it says."

"Sorry," she whispered as she continued to try to figure out his ink. "Okay, I give up!"

"It's a reminder of what I have to live with, day in and day out." His intense eyes stayed focused on her upturned face. Suddenly, the lose sheet that covered them both felt like air and all of her was exposed to him. His eyes turned back to his own bicep and remained focused there before he said, "One regret."

The moment he said the words, CeCe's eyes could clearly see them in the bold script. She itched to know what his regret was, but considering he caught her examining his scarred body, she only could guess.

"We all have regrets," she said hoping to leave her assumption on a good note.

However, his eyes seemed to say something else. Time to press.

"You know, it is 'another time.' I'm awake, you're awake, so we might as well talk," she let her fingers lightly walk up his chest where they found his chin and pushed gently.

Jarod rubbed his hands over his face multiple times. It didn't take a brain surgeon for her to deduce he did not want to have this conversation. However, to her surprise, he let out a long heavy breath, pulled her so she lay with her face resting on his chest. CeCe waited as his hand ran the length of her arm back and forth. The action of comfort and calming, she wasn't sure if it was meant for her, or him. Just when she decided he wouldn't tell her, he began to speak.

"I thought I knew my direction in life. I grew up in a military family; so going into the service was drilled into me for as long as I could remember. Honor, courage, service, that was our creed and it was a path I fully intended to follow. It was also a path that required very few emotions from my father. Mom was the emotion that held our family together. She was his opposite in every way. He was a Marine to the letter, and she was full of life and laughter. Don't get me wrong, he loved me and was proud of me, but she was the one that handled all the messy emotions."

This wasn't what CeCe was expecting, but she was hanging on every word.

"Then, the fat lady sang; a drunk driver hit my Mom's car on Christmas Eve of my junior year as she was driving home from working at a Soup Kitchen. Christmas was her favorite time of year. She always said the greatest thing one could do for another is just help with a smile." Jarod got quite for a moment, before he cleared his throat and pushed on, "She held on until the following night, but her injuries were too severe, and she died. I sat in a cold sterile hospital room on Christmas and watched my Gunnery Sergeant Father, whom never showed any sort of feelings, cry like a baby over his wife's lifeless body." The emotion in his voice he tried so hard to mask still slipped through. CeCe placed a soft kiss on his chest offering sympathy for the devastation he went through.

"After her funeral, my Father returned to his emotionless Marine self. It happened. Time to move on, end of story. Being upset would not bring her back. He replaced his home time with base time. I knew he just couldn't look at the walls where her spirit was so strong, but in grieving in ignorance, he shut me out, too."

CeCe's heart ached for the young man left alone, and for the man beside her now that carried this with him.

"I started lashing out, cutting school, getting into fights. I was just so damn angry; I hated everything and everyone. By some miracle, I passed my junior and senior years, but I honestly think it was more that the school just wanted me gone than a stellar academic performance. Anyways, when I did graduate, my old man never said anything to me except to ask me when I was meeting with the Recruiter. I told him he was out of his tree if he thought I would enlist. Our relationship became nonexistent; he gave me an ultimatum, the Corps or my ass on the street. I took the street. I didn't need him, or the service to tell me how to live my life. For the two years before, he couldn't give two shits less about what I was doing."

Jarod stopped speaking for a bit and returned to rubbing her arm. CeCe had so many questions she wanted to ask, but she somehow found the strength to remain mute. She'd pushed him to spill; the least she could do was let him tell her how he wanted to.

He turned his head and kissed her forehead before telling her the rest, "Three years later, I was making decent money and supporting myself, but I wasn't happy."

That hurt. Her fears were just confirmed, she hadn't made him happy. She'd known what they had wasn't a whirlwind romance, but she did think it was something tangible, but he was just sowing his oats. Tears pooled in her eyes.

"Then one day, it just clicked. I needed to man up, be a better man than I was, than I was heading for if I didn't change."

The silence that hung between them was thick with things unsaid.

CeCe ran her finger over the lines of his abdomen before asking, "And the scars?"

"Convoy patrol when an Insurgent bomb went off. They disabled six of us with that bomb, but the fuckers didn't live to see three minutes after the fact. I took shrapnel to thirty percent of my body. Overall, I'm lucky; I walked away, so to speak, some in my platoon lost limbs right then and there. My hip and leg sustained the most damage. Along with major muscle and nerve damage, my femoral artery was punctured. The medical team worked miracles, and I was able to keep my leg, so vanity over the scar never came up. After my medical discharge and years of therapy, the pain is manageable as long as you can ignore excruciating pain."

She knew he said that last to be funny, but she found no such humor in it. It was amazing he could walk two feet, let alone what he did daily. She needed to process all of this. Without a word, she rolled over to turn off the light, but then returned to Jarod's embrace. In the darkened silence, they offered comfort to each other with their bodies. When they were through he spooned against her and CeCe replayed everything he told her in her head. Fitting the pieces together in the timeline she knew. There was something he wasn't telling her, that she was sure of, but as minutes turned into hours as she lay in his arms, she made a decision. She'd known the consequences of crossing the line with Jarod, but she'd done it anyway. They were attracted to each other physically, but she had to think of her life. The life she worked so hard to build. The life she swore she would accept nothing short of completely on her terms. She knew her actions would display her as an uncaring bitch, but she needed to convince him it was for the best. Convince herself it was for the best, too. Tomorrow she would go back to Hamden and focus on that life, considering this merely an interruption. She just needed to steel herself that this was the only option she had, a decision that she would never get to make again.

Jarod woke feeling refreshed; more refreshed than he had felt in a long time, and he knew it was because CeCe slept next to him. Honestly, he couldn't remember ever sleeping this deeply, or this long. It was as if his body was heavy with deprived sleep, deciding to catch up all at once. With his eyes still closed, he reached to embrace her and revel in the moment, but his hand encountered nothing. He opened his eyes and noticed she was nowhere in the room.

"Cees?" No one answered back.

He climbed out of bed, checking the bathroom to find it dark and empty. Fury began to build inside of him, but it was laced with something else, something worse; fear. Jarod grabbed his phone and dialed her cell, it went directly to voicemail, he disconnected the call and grabbed for his discarded clothes, quickly dressing before he ran from his room. He reached her room and pounded on the door. His gut told him that she was gone, but he just continued to pound on the door, physically dealing with the panic that was overtaking him.

Ignoring the pain from his leg, he ran like he was back in boot camp. Ignoring the elevator because it was too slow, he raced down five flights of stairs. By the time he reached the desk in the lobby, he was grasping at straws, "Room 526, did she check out?"

"Sir, I can't…" the desk attendant began.

"Just answer the question, dammit!" he bellowed.

"Is there a problem here?" an older man in a suit came from the back, confronting Jarod.

Before Jarod could respond to that question, he felt a small, warm hand on his shoulder.

"Jarod? Is everything okay?" Natalie asked with obvious concern in her voice.

Jarod turned to face Dylan's wife as fury replaced the panic. *She left him! She snuck out and left him!* He felt the sweat bead at his temples and his heart constricted. After all they did and talked about last night; hell, less than twelve hours ago, she left.

"Where's CeCe?" he yelled, aware he was taking his anger out on her, but not caring.

Natalie jumped at his tone and volume, but she still remained polite,

"She caught a ride home with Seth and Mae, and headed out a couple of hours ago."

What the fuck? Of course she did! With an ironic shake of his head, Jarod turned and headed back up to his room, saying nothing else to Natalie.

As Jarod stepped into the elevator, ignoring the stares and comments, he knew her disappearing was not a rash decision All the ground he thought he gained, letting her see him vulnerable, that he was wrong all those years ago; that now he only had good intentions—all that work for nothing. Hurt and panic was quickly replaced with anger and betrayal. He would not allow her to make this decision regarding their future without understanding the ramifications. Some would call it desperation, but he chose to call it changing his strategy: Operation CeCe and I Belong Together.

The elevator doors opened to the fifth floor, stepping out, Jarod headed straight for his room. He quickly packed his bag and schemed how their next confrontation would go down. Whether she liked it or not, he would not allow her final response to be her sneaking out. If she wanted him gone, she damn well would have to say it to his face. As he grabbed the door handle to leave and return to Vermont, he paused. Closing his eyes, he asked for strength, what he had in mind would require her to be stripped bare emotionally, only then would he accept her choice. Of course for her to be so vulnerable, he would have to be, too.

Seventeen

When CeCe arrived back in town and picked up her car at Dylan's, she knew she should have gone to her apartment, but she found herself driving to her store. She had shut her cell phone off a while ago and was still nervous to turn it back on, imagining the number of texts and voicemails that were waiting for her.

When she pulled into the parking lot in mid-afternoon, she was pleasantly surprised to find the plaza, and her store somewhat busy. She pulled into to a parking spot and killed the engine. She picked up her phone where it lay on the passenger seat, flinching as she powered it up. After the tone sounded she had to wait a moment longer for all messages to register. With no way of knowing how many calls she missed, she was surprised to receive only a text from Natalie and one voice message. She steeled herself, as she dialed up her inbox and listened.

You are going to have to do better than that, Kitten. You and I are not through…yet.

She rolled her eyes. *Of course he would make this difficult.* But she had to admit, she expected more than a cryptic message.

No! CeCe don't go there. You've made this decision, and you need to stick to it.

The further you keep him from your thoughts the better, and safer, you will be.

CeCe left her car and walked through the front door of *CeCe's*. There were a fair number of customers and she was happy to see both Kelleigh and Kimmie being attentive and professional. Giving a quick hello to both her employees and the regular clients in her store, she ducked into the back office.

Throwing herself right into work, she looked through the computer, reviewing the sales for the last few days. She was thrilled with the numbers. Kelleigh came in shortly afterwards.

"How was your weekend?" Kelleigh asked.

"Good. I was going to ask how everything was here, but looking at these numbers, I don't need to. Looks like you gals had some rocking sales." CeCe said astounded, she checked the figures three times.

"Yes, yesterday, a shotgun destination bride came in with her honor attendant and mother, and bought her entire trousseau, as well as their dresses."

CeCe watched as pride crossed Kelleigh's face.

"That is fantastic! I'm sorry I missed it, but looking at these figures you handled it amazingly. Just for that, why don't you get out of here? Go spend some time with the new man. I'll close up shop; getting right into the thick of it here is just what I need after being away for a couple of days."

Suddenly, Kelleigh's face changed, "Oh no, I couldn't do that, but if you want to let Kimmie go, that would be fine." She said, looking down at her feet. CeCe watched as her friend's glee left her face, replaced by worry.

"Everything okay, Kell?" CeCe asked as she got up from her desk and approached her friend.

"Uh, yeah, just would rather stay here, if that's okay."

CeCe didn't like the sound of that, but she didn't pry any further. CeCe went out onto the now quiet floor and found Kimmie and told her she could head out. Her boisterous employee was more than happy to leave early.

The next several hours went by easily as customers continued to filter in. Kelleigh kept all talk work related and CeCe was happy for the subject. She was concerned for her friend, but keeping everything about the store helped her to focus as well. By the time closing came around CeCe had almost put aside the feelings she couldn't ignore, and began to feel she was making the right decision.

With the lights turned down in the front, CeCe and Kelleigh each sat in the office, happily tired and comfortable in the silence.

CeCe looked at her friend and knew it was time to find out what was eating at her.

CeCe pulled her weary bones out of her chair, walked over to the small refrigerator and pulled out the bottle of Pinot that she was happy she kept there. She filled two hefty plastic cups, and handed one to Kelleigh. When she returned to her own seat, she took a long drink.

"You okay, Kelleigh? Did something happen with the new man?"

Kelleigh sipped her own cup and looked to her boss and friend, "I feel foolish, honestly, but I thought things were going great. We were seeing each other pretty regularly, but these past few days I haven't heard one word from him. No calls, no texts; heck, not even a Dear Joan email." She took another sip of her wine, got out of her chair and paced the small space before continuing. "I'm so embarrassed to say I think I've, once again, been too clingy and spooked a really awesome guy. I just want to get my shit together, and get on the path I'm supposed to be on. Is that too much to ask?"

CeCe listened as her younger friend voiced the fears of so many women: the fear of being alone, and taking all the responsibility of something going wrong in a relationship. CeCe had made it her mission to keep herself away from this particular abyss, but her brain was flooded with everything she had done this weekend that sucked her right back into the center of this group.

"Anywho, I'm just getting tired of the dating game. It's a game you need talent to play, and I apparently have no such talent for it."

CeCe watched as Kelleigh drained her glass, her heart breaking for the younger woman. She was just about to pull some *I'm no one to be giving out advice* out of her ass when the space filled with a current Top 40 song.

"Oh, I'm sorry, that's my cell phone," Kelleigh said as she threw the now empty cup into the trash and went over to the cubby she used for her stuff while she worked.

CeCe finished her own cup and contemplated refilling it, when she noticed Kelleigh's face go from self-loathing to instantly happy.

"Oh my God…it's him."

And then the Earth is righted back onto its axis and the abyss closes until the next moment it's needed. CeCe was happy, Kelleigh deserved to be happy.

"Go! Get out of here, but make him work for it. Fancy dinner, and fulfilling all your wants," she answered with a wink, watching the younger woman respond to the text and pull her bag out and head out the door.

When Kelleigh was on her way, and the front door once again locked, CeCe decided to indulge in the second glass of wine. She would pay some bills, play one of those annoying social media games—anything to keep her mind off of the images and memories of the weekend that were trying so hard to infiltrate her thoughts.

She had just finished the second cup of wine and was really considering just drinking straight from the bottle when there was a pounding from the back security door.

Gates!

Reprieve over.

Another pounding, this one firmer and angrier. CeCe rolled her eyes and was happy for the wine in her system to help her deal with him. She undid the security locks and pulled the door open, confusion suddenly overcoming her.

Jarod wasn't there. No one was. Only warm summer humidity and the fading sun.

Then she noticed the three white roses on the ground. These ones were shorter, but the same bloom. They sat on the ground in some sort of vase. Not knowing where the bravery came from, CeCe squatted down and panic gripped her throat, knocking her on her ass. She crawled backwards like a clumsy crab, knowing she should slam the door shut, locking it, but she remained frozen to the spot.

The slogan on the vase had her blood running cold. Old Colony Harbor Hotel, Boston, Massachusetts. Her vision filled with images of herself, admiring the same little vases in the quaint hotel gift shop just yesterday.

In the next several minutes, when no boogeyman appeared, CeCe's fear began to lessen. She climbed to her feet, slowly making her way to the door. Looking around the back lot of the plaza, making sure she wasn't being watched, she quickly bent down, picked up the vase, then closed and latched the door. She carried the vase to her desk to examine the roses closer. They really were beautiful, in a completely fucked up and freaky way. Whoever this jackass was, he didn't mind spending the dough.

Annoyed with herself for getting scared, but also completely pissed off this guy was still playing this completely aggravating game. *Grow a pair! Seriously!*

The longer she stood there looking at the blooms, the more irritated she became. She was so over this. It was because of this dickless asshole Jarod was thrown back into her life. She would not give this asshat another ounce of her fear.

In a moment of complete wrath, she picked up the vase and threw it against the wall. She watched as the glass smashed into a hundred pieces, as the once manicured flowers lay broken on the floor.

Bringing her hand to her head, as her heart beat rapidly under her breast, she tried to calm herself.

Great! Now I have broken glass to clean up.

She walked over, and began picking up the larger shards of glass. She had a handful when she was, once again, startled by a loud banging, this time coming from the front door.

Jumping at the sound, she dropped the handful of glass, a shard slicing her palm in the process.

Really!?!

She knew who it was before she even left the office, and thankfully, she had the fucked up flower fucker to thank for the proper attitude to deal with Jarod, once and for all. She walked with purpose to the door and opened it, allowing his intimidating body to enter.

She was neither intimidated, nor put out by the scowl on his face; if anything, it only fueled her fury.

He wasted no time invading her personal space, sneering at her, his blue eyes the smallest of slits. "You mind explaining what the fuck that was?"

You want full-on bitch mode? You got it! "You'll have to specify what you are referring to."

"Not funny, Cees!"

"I didn't intend to be," she pushed on his chest.

He took the hint, backing off, but just barely. He stepped away from her, walking in a circle before turning back toward her with his hands on his hip and a softer tone to his voice, "I thought we would make a go of this?"

"This?"

"You know damn well what I mean. You and me, together."

"I agreed to no such thing, I made myself clear, it was sex."

"Amazing sex," Jarod clarified.

"Yes, amazing sex, but it doesn't mean it was anything else."

He didn't respond for several second before saying ever so quietly, "You just keep telling yourself that."

"You are impossible, you know that? I knew this was a mistake!" She began to make her way back to the back room, but didn't get very far. He used his longer strides to cut her off.

He was in her face in a heartbeat, "Don't you ever call anything you and I do a mistake. The fact you refuse to see it is the exact opposite of a mistake makes me pity you."

You Mother Fucker! "Pity? I don't need your fucking pity?" Her astonishment at his stupidity froze her where she stood.

"You know, I should of known." He said as he shook his head with a smile on his face that was nothing close to happiness.

"Known what, *Gates?*"

"I'm not going to lie, it hurt; fuck, it gutted me to see you with all those guys, never one for long. Mostly rich pretty boys that liked you on their arm, I thought it was just fun to you."

What is he spouting about now? "What guys?"

"All the guys you've been with for the last three years. And let me tell you, you can pick some doozies, money launderers, dead beat dads, oh wait, the adulterer was my favorite."

"I don't know what the hell you are talking about," but her gut began to cringe.

"You can't be stupid enough to believe everything everyone tells you. Think of what's his name, the one that only brought you to a hotel for your nights together. The reason he didn't want to bring you home was because he didn't want his wife and nineteen month old baby to know about you."

This wasn't about confronting her, and being upset about her decision, this was about hurting her. About giving to her a taste of the pain he was feeling. She knew in a way she deserved it, but this was just cruel. She honestly didn't know how much more she could take, the crazy emotions, her brain and heart constantly at war, wanting two different things—things she knew would destroy her. Add in the flowers from minutes ago and the knowledge her sick fucker stalker not only followed her, but wanted her to know. CeCe had nothing, no more to fight with, nothing to wield as a weapon to defend herself. "How could you?"

"I was just doing what I was paid to do."

"What?" she must of heard him wrong.

"You are as smart as you are beautiful, I'm sure you can figure it out."

Oh my God! Dylan! "Dylan paid you to spy on me?" she wrapped her arms around herself, her last attempt at self-protection.

He leaned down close again, pressing his nose to hers and whispered viciously, "You're damn right he did. And after learning what I did, he was right to do so, you apparently can't tell a liar from an honest man."

Her hazel eyes widened and she was shoved into silence. Her tongue couldn't form a single word.

"Now don't get your panties in a twist, it isn't like I took pictures looking in windows. I just run background checks every few months on your employees and your boyfriends. Some financial checks and immigration status, when necessary."

Her mouth bone dry, when she could finally speak the words were raspy, "Oh, is that all? How could you?"

Jarod's face changed, no longer the cruel assailant of last few minutes; instead revealed a man exposed, "How could I make sure you were safe? Because it was the only way I could be near you." He squeezed his eyes shut, grimacing in pain before opening them again, the bluest blue eyes piercing her. "Did you think I was kidding when I said you have been my beacon for thirteen years? You've gotten me through the worst and darkest days of my life."

She couldn't believe her ears. How dare Dylan? How could he? Suddenly the pain from her bleeding palm served as a point of reference for everything that had occurred.

But he wasn't done, "So excuse me if I don't just step aside, and say thanks for the screw, and let you out of my life again."

She looked down to her palm and saw all the blood pooling and now dripping onto the store's carpet, "Well, you are not going to have a choice."

He missed her attention diversion, "When are you going to get it? I'd crawl over hot coals for you!!" He finally looked down to where she was looking. "CeCe, what the fuck?"

"GET OUT!"

Blue eyes met hazel, glare for glare, as he said, in his most vicious of voices, "Not until you tell me why you are fucking bleeding!" he pulled her palm to him and examined the cut.

"I cut my hand on some broken glass."

"Broken glass? What happened?"

"I threw the most recent delivery of roses against my office wall." She said calmly.

Now it was his chance to be shocked into silence. "When, exactly, were you going to tell me about the roses?"

"Well, you didn't exactly give me an opening, now did you?"

She relented, giving in, and lead him to the office. He insisted on taking care of her cut first. As he cleaned the cut and bandaged it, she explained to him about the pounding on the back door, leaving out the part about thinking it was him. He calmly examined the flowers, only to morph into a caged animal when she told him the vase came from the hotel in Boston. He was on the phone within a minute, relaying everything to Idarraga. When he was done there was no sign off just Jarod disconnecting the call.

"He'll be here shortly."

He watched her like a hawk, and it annoyed her. How they could go through the gamut of emotions in the span of fifteen minutes? It was wrong and exhausting. "Since Max is on his way, and you've said what you apparently wanted to say, it is time for you to leave."

"Not happening."

"Well, as you've pointed out already, I don't give a fuck and I'm an idiot, so get out."

"I never said…"

"Oh, you said more than enough, now leave."

"Look, I'm sorry I laid into you. If I had known about the flowers, I would never have done that."

She did not respond to his appeal, just asked again for him to leave.

"You don't know what you are saying."

"I know damn well what I'm saying!" Suddenly the tears began to fall, the dam unable to hold them back any longer. "Jarod, if I've ever meant anything to you, please, just leave."

"That is not fair!" he said, wounded.

"Neither is what you are doing to me."

The expression on his face signaled her final plea as a bull's-eye.

Without another word, he turned around and left the office. A few moments later, CeCe heard the front door chime, signaling his departure. She slid to the floor and cried out everything she had been holding in for so long.

Eighteen

"So are you going to tell me why you're so grumpy?"

"I'm not grumpy." CeCe responded, never looking up from her block tower creation. Whether it was her intense concentration, or the floor vibrations created by bouncing toddlers, the pink building blocks tumbled to the ground.

"Oh, I must have my dwarves mixed up. I could have sworn the one with the scowl and constant furrowed brow was Grumpy. Oh well, guess I'll have to freshen up on my fairytale characters." Natalie said, matter of fact, without looking up from folding laundry.

"Again! Again!" Cat demanded as she picked up three blocks and shoved them at CeCe's face.

CeCe had come here to give her mind a break from everything that has been suffocating her, getting back to the basics, a task made infinitely easier when in the company of toddlers.

Cat and Ria always could make CeCe feel better with their free spirits and love for fashion, as demonstrated by the fluorescent tutus each wore with the multiple strings of beads, funky colored sunglasses and CeCe's personal favorite, the bling-filled tiaras.

"Okay, okay, little Miss Bossy," CeCe jeered as she began the tower again.

With a white terrycloth towel mid fold Natalie asked, "How are things with Derrick going?"

"Pfft," CeCe said under her breath. When the tower fell again and the demanding toddler didn't look away from the television she was glued to, CeCe pivoted to face her friend. "I don't know why he is even hanging around still."

"Because he knows a catch when he finds one."

"You are biased, my dear. Honestly, he should have given up long ago. I cancelled our last date, a date *I* made with him because I had been giving him the brush-off with the flower stalker thing and the…"

"And the what?" Natalie pressed, but by the smirk on her face, CeCe knew it was rhetorical.

CeCe squinted her eyes in defiance as she grabbed a towel and folded it.

"I'm not going to say it. No matter how much you want me to say it." CeCe said as she grabbed another towel.

She watched as Natalie pinched her lips tightly closed, and in shear frustration and because it was about to explode out of her anyway, she threw the folded towel at her friend and admitted, "Since Gates got thrown back into my life! Happy?"

The smile on Natalie's sweet face proved she was.

"You two obviously have some deep connection. Just sitting next to you at the bar that night, I could feel you vibrating out of the seat."

"That was just annoyance, Nat."

Natalie rolled her eyes and placed the last folded towel into the laundry basket, "Yeah, okay. You do know whom I am married to, right? I'm quite familiar with those kinds of sparks. What is so wrong with you and Jarod seeing each other? I like him."

"You don't know him."

"I know him well enough, and I know you. I also know what I witnessed with my own eyes. I wanted to blush just being next to the two of you. Even the static electricity in the air cranks up when you two are close together.

"I have a good thing with Derrick." CeCe issued defensively.

"That you do, and I like Derrick, but I…you know what, never mind." Natalie stopped and stood up from her perch on the couch, and picked the laundry basket up but CeCe, on her feet now, blocked her and refused to move.

"No! Say it!" CeCe demanded as she crossed her arms over her chest.

Natalie looked to where the twins were happily watching television, oblivious to the intense conversation between their mother and aunt. With one hand she balanced the basket to her right hip and grabbed onto CeCe's crossed forearm, "I've meddled enough already, you do what you want." She stepped around CeCe and started her away across the sunken living room toward the stairs.

"Oh, don't go all Mother Theresa on me. Spill it, Natalie!" CeCe quickly stepped to grab the basket, halting her friend. She looked toward the twins then raised an eyebrow, waiting, when the twins didn't move a muscle.

Natalie let out a huff and swallowed before she spoke from the heart. "From the moment I met you, you've never tried to be anyone other than who you were. You are beautiful, smart, successful, confident and badass, and you know it."

That had the scowl leaving CeCe's face and a large smile appearing in its place. "Badass?"

Natalie had a smile of her own, "Well, compared to me, you are badass, and you have the shit kickers to prove it" indicating the heels CeCe wore. "With all that being said, I just don't know why you would pick now to lie to yourself."

The smile slid from CeCe's face at the accusation, "I'm not lying to myself. If anything I'm being more honest with myself than I've ever been. One hundred percent, in fact."

In her best teacher voice, Natalie said, "You know, the problem with lies is you have a hard time keeping them straight. But with the truth, it just naturally flows out of you. When you lie, you have to constantly remember the lie, and continue to be on the defensive to protect the lie. Seems like a lot of work to me, especially when the truth would be so easy to live." With those parting words, Natalie carried the laundry basket toward the stairs and began to climb.

Needing to prove her friend was misinformed about CeCe's actions, she offered, "I'm going to call Derrick. It's about time we had our date and get back on track. Besides, you never know, maybe it's time I stop with the whole only fun thing, and consider changing my status."

Natalie stopped half way up the open staircase, turned back to her friend and asked, "And you can't do that with anyone other than Derrick?"

"He's the best choice," fell out of CeCe's mouth.

"Best, or safest, choice? Either way, Cees, Dylan and I will support you completely."

CeCe watched as Natalie climbed the remaining stairs, leaving those last statements to hang in the air and bounce around between CeCe's ears.

CeCe drove to her apartment having left Natalie as she attempted to wrangle the twins for bed. She contemplated going to the store to sketch, but decided a bubble bath, a glass—or bottle—of wine and her newest music downloads sounded like a better idea. She had to call Derrick, but first she wanted to be as relaxed as possible. *You can't relax if you're lying, can you?*

When her cell phone rang, she answered, surprised to hear Max's voice on the other end.

"Hello Ms. Cervetti, hope I'm not disturbing you at this time of night."

"No, not at all, Lieutenant, I'm just driving home."

"I wanted to let you know we may have a lead. We were able to retrieve a fingerprint from the glass shards. It is being processed and I'm hoping to have an answer by tomorrow."

Thank goodness for small favors. The quicker she could get stalker guy out of her hair, the sooner Jarod could get out of town, too.

"I look forward to hearing from you then." She disconnected the call and was suddenly eager to make that phone call to Derrick.

Completely pruned and relaxed from her bath, CeCe wrapped herself in one of her lush towels, ready to make that phone call to Derrick. She had just deposited the empty wine glass in the kitchen sink when there was a light knock at the door. She stepped to the door and looked through the peephole, not surprised to Jarod looking back at her.

Glancing down at her barely concealed chest and her still glistening skin, she considered letting him stay there.

He responded simultaneously, "I know you are on the other side of the door, Kitten."

Of course he does.

With the security chain still in place, CeCe hid behind the door and craned her neck enough so she could speak out the small opening.

"Not really in the mood for a social visit, Gates."

His clear blue eyes, locked on her bare shoulder before they returned their gaze to her hazel one, "We need to talk about your case."

CeCe swallowed, weighing his words, he seemed all business, and apparently that was enough to sway her decision. She closed the door, unlatched the chain and let him to in.

"Sorry to disturb your bath. If you want to put something else on, I'll wait."

Um, okay…he is being decent and considerate.

"Uh, yeah, just give me a moment." She turned and made her way to her bedroom, quickly throwing on an oversized cotton shirt and yoga pants. She even went for the security of putting a bra on. No sense in poking the bear any more than she needed to. She left her hair pinned up on top of her head, checking her appearance in the full-length mirror before she left her room.

When she made her way back out to the living room, she discovered Jarod hadn't moved away from the door. He looked weary, tired, and as she rounded the corner, she'd noticed he was rubbing his thigh, guilty struck her for not insisting he sit down. Her thoughts found their way out of her mouth, "Is your leg alright? The pain bad?"

"No, I'm good." He said, immediately stuffing his hands in his front pockets as he continued to look at her.

Breaking the silence she pressed, "So…what did you need to tell me?"

"How well do you know Kelleigh?"

Completely caught off guard, CeCe balked at him.

"Kelleigh?"

"Yes, how well do you know her, or more specifically, her life outside working at your store."

"You think Kelleigh has anything to do with the flowers?"

"It's possible. I've done some digging, as well as observing, and something seems off with her. I'd bet she isn't living the life you think she does. What do you know about her?"

"Uh, well, she has worked for me for three years, she lives with her sister, she has always been trustworthy and a straight shooter. You can't be serious that she would have anything to do with this? It doesn't make any sense."

"Just convenient, every time there was a delivery she was never there, or didn't return. I'm not saying she is specifically sending the flowers, but something just isn't adding up. It'd be good to keep that in mind until we have more information."

Kelleigh? But he had a point. Suddenly CeCe felt cold. She vigorously rubbed her hands over her arms, but it didn't seem to help.

"Do you need some help warming up?" Jarod asked, his eyes explaining the true intent of his words. They grazed over her, from head to toe, before resting on her lips.

Suddenly, the bra wasn't enough of a shield; she felt she needed full body armor.

"Visit's over," she croaked, as he slowly walked toward her, stopping when he was right in front of her, looking at her upturned face. She bit her lip, not knowing why.

"I'll go when you ask me to," he whispered, pulling the pin from her hair, letting it tumble downward. "But you need to say the words aloud."

"You will?"

"I will," he leaned down and kissed the spot right below her ear.

Leave. Get out. Don't let the door hit you in the ass on the way out. All these terms where stuck between her brain and her mouth, but never came out. Instead, she found herself tilting her head, giving him better access.

His mouth began to move lower, and using his nose, he moved the silk cord out of his way, dipping his tongue into the circle that rested between her collarbones, before traveling up to kiss her other ear.

Somehow, her hands lifted of their own accord, resting on his broad strong shoulders. Letting his lips leave her skin, he nuzzled her jaw, inhaling her scent, enticing the most erotic feelings to swell inside her.

Jarod leaned down, placing his strong hands behind each of her thighs, lifting her so her legs wrapped around his waist. He carried her to the couch, turning to sit with her straddling his lap. Her shirt and bra were gone a moment later. His face buried in her breasts, CeCe threw back her head, reveling in the amazing feeling of his touch her as he worshipped her.

His fingers gently rubbed her erect nipples, weighing the heaviness of her tits, as he brought one to his mouth and lavished the nipple with as much attention as a newborn baby would, while his thumb and forefinger rubbed over her other one bringing it to full erection.

Unable to remain still, CeCe found herself rotating her hips into the bulge pressed between her thighs. Anxious to have his tongue inside her mouth, she cupped his face and raised his mouth to hers. Their lips and tongues swirled around, taking all and leaving nothing.

His hands roamed down to her waist, around to her heart shaped ass where he kneaded and gripped as if it was a lifeline. With each squeeze of his palm, CeCe's arousal grew. With ungraceful moves and less than seductive stretches, she was quickly rid of her pants. Fully bared to him and ready to cross the line again, she shut off her brain.

They broke apart long enough to pull his shirt up and over his head and wiggled himself out of his jeans. She found it convenient he was going commando, one less item of clothing to remove. When they were both finally nude, he stopped her kiss.

"Something wrong?"

"Never."

"Then why did you stop?"

"I'm just taking in the moment that reminds me why I open my eyes every morning."

Before she could process his words, or understand their heaviness, he brought her mouth back to his. His tongue swept in and took everything he wanted and all that she wanted to give him.

With his hands behind her thighs, he opened her as wide as she could go, slowly entering her until he was buried to the hilt and she was stretched to the max, and he touched her womb and they both felt it; the moment of absolute penetration, of a complete union. Then with gazes locked she began to move. Rotating her hips slowly at first, then increasing speed and tempo. Using the strength of her thighs she rose up in synch with her rotations, as he continued to thrust. With amazing strength and complete trust, CeCe began to lean back ever so slightly, changing the angle of penetration just enough to reach the sweet spot. He held her with his own powerful thighs, lengthening his strokes and increasing the speed. Soon the frenzy of their thrusts had them both at the brink of oblivion, and Jarod chose that moment to drop his hand to her clit and with just one caress of the engorged tissue, she tilted over the edge, crying out in ecstasy. Her orgasm went on and on and was like nothing she ever felt before. He followed right behind her, emptying himself into her vibrating body. His teeth clenched it agonizing pain as the amazing climax overtook them both.

Both covered in sweat and fluids, Jarod pulled CeCe up, tucking her into his chest as they both heaved from the exertion. He recovered first. With gentle strokes, he brushed her sticking hair away from her temples and asked the one question she didn't want to be asked.

"Why didn't you ask me to leave?"

She searched his face, as if the answer to his question would appear there. Finally, without a reason or word, she pushed herself to her feet, and he willing let her pull away from him. Offering no explanation, she went to her bedroom, closing the door on their tryst, as well as his question.

Nineteen

The flow was off at the store was over the next few days. Whether it was coincidental, or because Jarod had placed the seed of doubt in CeCe's head, she was edgy about Kelleigh calling out three days straight. Being down an employee meant long days for CeCe, it also gave her an excuse to put off an official date night with Derrick.

When she did call him, the morning after her inability to keep Jarod at arm's length, he was thrilled to hear from her as if no time had gone by, and things hadn't been strained between them. Derrick was elated she wanted to reschedule their date, and was beyond excited when she hinted at potentially taking their relationship to another level. She would generally steer clear of bringing up such a topic over the phone, but suddenly the matter seemed very important.

Jarod remained around, but with the long hours at *CeCe's*, chitchat was at a minimum and she decided she would no longer be answering any unexpected or late night knocks on her apartment door. However, whenever she was in the front of the store, all she needed to do was look out to the parking lot and there was his pick up and those aviator glasses looking at her.

The fingerprint seemed to be a dead end as well. Max said it was a good print, but as of yet they hadn't had any luck getting a hit on it. To everyone's surprise, Max actually reached out to Jarod for assistance on it. With Jarod's connections, he was having a friend run the print through federal channels, but nothing came back yet, or so Max told her, since she refused to speak with Jarod.

"Ugh, is it time to go yet?" Kimmie whined. She was grating on CeCe's last nerve, to the point CeCe was tempted to run the store by herself rather than endure another complaint. "It's too hot to work, I should be at the beach rather than here."

That's it! Limit reached. There hadn't been a customer in a couple of hours, and it would be closing time in another hour.

"Kimmie, time to go! In fact, it will be light the next couple of days, and I'm sure Kelleigh will be back tomorrow, so why don't you come back the beginning of next week." CeCe's face hurt from the phony smile, but whatever, she just needed her gone.

"Like, oh my, God CeCe, you are the best boss ever!" Within two minutes Kimmie was out the door and in her Volkswagen convertible. *Good riddance.* Time to rethink her employee choices.

CeCe walked to the back room and grabbed a bottled water to bring out on the floor with her; when she returned, she wasn't alone.

"Malcolm! How are you?" She was so thrilled to see him. She had been berating herself for not going over to say hello, but with everything going on she just hadn't gotten over to the smoke shop.

"Oh you know me, getting along. How are things with my favorite business neighbor?"

"If we could have some more customers, I'd be a lot better, but other than that, all is good."

"Still having problems with how a man is supposed to deliver flowers?"

"They just don't make them smooth like you anymore. Sylvia is a lucky lady." CeCe watched as the older gentleman smiled at reference of his wife, who he's be married to for fifty-seven years.

"Still such a sweet talker, you are, Cecille. You let me know if you need anything, okay?" Malcolm said.

"I sure will. Thanks, Malcolm, for checking on me."

"Anytime," the elder man made his way to the door and when he opened it, a flower deliver man greeted him. Malcolm held the door open for the man, but came back in with him.

CeCe watched as the man came towards her carrying the long white box with a red ribbon wrapped around it.

Within a moment, Jarod was in the store and had the young deliveryman cornered.

"Who sent you?" he barked, as Malcolm walked to CeCe's side and they watched Jarod intimidate the trespasser.

"Uh…my boss." The terrified delivery guy answered.

Jarod took the box, untied the ribbon, and removed the lid and found two dozen long-stemmed white roses lying pristinely in the box. However, there was a note attached to this one.

CeCe watched him open it and read it before grabbing his cell phone and placing a call.

Malcolm kept his hand on her waist, holding her still.

While Jarod spoke into the phone, he handed the computer written note to CeCe. With Malcolm's hand around her shoulder she read the words

It's almost time, CeCe.

Fear shot down her spine at the sinister sentence. Her eyes connected with Jarod's, and she suddenly wanted to launch herself at him.

Jarod questioned the delivery guy for a few more minutes, making multiple phone calls. Soon Max and a couple uniforms were there taking the card, flowers, and box in for evidence."

Malcolm remained with her, even though she insisted multiple times for him to go.

"Really, Malcolm, I'm okay."

"I'll leave when I know you are alright, and not a minute before." Malcolm answered without even looking at CeCe.

Jarod and Max chose that moment to fill CeCe in.

"The delivery guy is clean, we've confirmed he works for Flower Depot out of Burlington. They received an online express order a few hours ago. Apparently, the Flower Depot will an accept order and deliver it the same day, up until eight PM. My guys are chasing the IP address and credit card used for the order in hopes of finding this guy." Max explained.

Jarod didn't say anything, he just watched her like a hawk. CeCe pulled her eyes away from Jarod, turning her attention to Max, "And the note? What does that mean? Almost time for what?"

Max didn't say anything at first but his dark eyes spoke volumes, "We don't know, but we have to assume it isn't anything good. He has gone out of his way to be anonymous. This note indicates he's preparing to reveal his identity."

"Great! So I just get to keep on waiting? The suspense is killing me," the last part was spoken sarcastically, but it was beginning to be too much.

Malcolm and Max jumped to placate her with words of encouragement and reassurances, but when she went to look to the blue eyes she knew would be straight with her, he wasn't there. She turned her head slightly and saw he had left the store and was walking towards his truck.

You probably deserve that, Cees!

His abandonment hurt. CeCe closed her eyes and shook her head, walking away from Malcolm and Max. She paced to the office and back multiple times. Suddenly she heard Jarod call out to Max.

"You might want to have your guys run this, too."

CeCe turned to look toward the door and was snared in a blue gaze.

When their eyes connected calmness came over her.

He didn't leave.

She watched as he returned his attention to Max.

"This was tucked under my windshield." Jarod handed the note to Max.

Keep your eyes on the prize, not the girl.

Max read the words aloud. CeCe's breath caught and all three sets of eyes raced to hers.

Malcolm insisted he would stay with CeCe, as Max and Jarod went to look at the video feed of the parking lot. When they returned, she wasn't surprised they didn't have much to go on. All they were able to tell was a young kid leaving the note when Jarod was distracted. Max had his uniforms patrolling, looking for the kid to question, but neither of them expected much to come of it. They both assumed he was paid anonymously to leave the note.

By the time Max and Malcolm had left, CeCe had no desire to be at the store, or go to her apartment.

Jarod was on a ladder checking the locks and security feed within the store when she emerged from the back room in ripped jeans, and a metallic silver, drape-front tank with a plunging back. He didn't even look in her direction when she came out.

"Look, Gates, I know you see me."

"I do." He continued to focus on the ceiling tile, trying to get to the security camera that was mounted inside of it.

"I'm going to get drunk, do you want to come?"

"That's an open ended question," he responded, now using the side of his fist to get the camera mount to disconnect, still without looking at her.

"I'll buy. I just need to forget about all of this. And I really don't want to go sit at a bar by myself. Can you just be my friend tonight?"

Finally he looked down at her, and she watched as he swallowed hard. He climbed down the ladder, and when he was on the ground, he let out a sarcastic huff and just shook his head while his hands rested on his denim covered hips.

"You really do know how to push a guy to the limit don't you, Kitten?"

She didn't want to admit what she was feeling to him, but she was afraid it was the only thing that would get him to accompany her.

"Please, I just need a friend tonight."

"Fine. I'll be your friend," he answered. As they made their way to the door he asked, "Are we talking friends, or friends with benefits?"

CeCe honestly laughed aloud, "We are talking 'you can borrow my lip gloss if you see a cute guy' kind of friends."

"Oh, great! But I think the color will clash with my shirt."

Twenty

When CeCe and Jarod arrived at Cal's, she was surprised how busy it was, considering it was a weeknight. Seats were at a premium, but they were able to find two together in the original building.

"Wow this place has changed," Jarod said as he looked around.

"It's been a couple of years since Cal added on the new portion, but I'm biased to the original place. This was the first place I ordered a beer. First place I threw a drink in a guy's face, and the first place I come when I want to feel like the old CeCe."

"The old CeCe?" Jarod asked, not understanding.

"Yeah, the girl that appreciated simplicity."

"What the hell does that mean?" he pushed for a further explanation to her cryptic answer.

"It means everything seems so complicated lately."

"And complications are bad?"

"To the simplicity of life, yes, they are." She answered quietly, and more to herself than to him.

The bartender joined them then, and after some small catch up niceties, CeCe ordered a double shot of tequila and a draft beer. Jarod ordered a soda.

"A soda? I told you I wanted to get drunk."

Looking into her eyes he said, "You can get drunk, I can't."

She crossed her legs on the bar stool, turning herself so she faced him and pressed, "Why can't you drink, Gates."

He knew what she was doing, and by God, he couldn't allow it to work. She told him she needed a friend, and as much as he wanted to be anything but friends, he would give tonight to her. She needed it, and deep down he needed it, too.

"Because for me to remain your friend, it is best if I have all my faculties. Not to mention safer."

The bartender returned with their orders, CeCe picked up her shot and brought it to her lips, but before downing it she asked, "Safer?"

Jarod turned his head and focused on the mirror and glass shelves that housed all the different bottles of booze. He could see himself in the reflection, not to mention the beauty next to him, and tried to convince himself his answer was the honest truth, rather than the noble one, he responded, "Kitten, where I'm concerned, you are far from safe. But I know where the line in the sand is, I'll die before you are anything but." He sipped his soda, and only then did he look back to her, and watched her swallow back the shot before taking a hefty swig of her beer.

After that intense moment, they drank in silence for a bit before the atmosphere between them lightened up immensely. CeCe inquired about his time in the Marines, as well as the friends he talked so candidly about.

By this time, she'd had four shots and was working on the same number of beers. Jarod was still nursing the same soda. He looked at her and noticed the redness in her face and the giddiness in her voice and knew she was toast.

"How about we get you home?"

With overzealous emotion and constant touches to his bicep and shoulder, she insisted, "No way, it's still really early. I'm having fun, aren't you?"

He couldn't help but smile, he was with CeCe, so of course he was having fun, but it didn't take a piece of paper and a lot of letters after your name to know she was going to be hurting come morning.

He watched, as she danced in her seat to the jukebox, and conversed with regulars and non-regulars, basically anyone that would talk to her, and the smile just tattooed itself to his face.

When she began to shake her chest in time with the music, he knew it was now or never, or his nobility and promise would go straight out the window.

"Time to go, Kitten."

She stopped and pouted, but something must have told her not to fight him because she succumbed to his direction without an argument. When she attempted to stand, she swayed and wound up right back on the seat.

"Whoa! Head rush," she held her head for a moment as Jarod placed a gentle hand under her elbow, lifting her to her feet. He kept his hand there to steady her, but truth be told, he just needed some sort of physical contact with her.

You can do this, Gates. She needs you to be on your best behavior. I'm sure there will be a throne in Heaven, or a dunce chair in Hell for you for your actions tonight.

Slow and steady, he walked her out of the bar and down the porch steps of the Hamden watering hole. With hysterical laughs from her and many near stumbles, he finally got her to her car. He opened the passenger door, and indicated for her to get in, but she had another idea.

CeCe stood in the open car door with Jarod in front of her, and she touched his chest while the sexiest of smiles crossed her face.

Yup, definitely the dunce chair in Hell.

"You know, it's been a while since we rocked the backseat of a car," she lifted up on tiptoes and brought her lips to his.

All eternity in Hell, would it really be that bad?

"I don't think your backseat should be rocking anywhere tonight," he answered moving his head away from those all too tempting lips of hers.

"Come on, Jarod, don't you want to relive that moment? We could drive back up to that secluded spot you brought me to all those years ago and fucked the brains out of my virginity."

CeCe plastered herself to his front; the low-cut drape of her top exposed her, causing her to giggle and look up at him coyly and say, "See, even my tits think the idea is great. You know your cock wants me."

Nuns. MREs. Ms. Taylor's sixth-grade science class. Colonel, the collie Jarod had when he was six. He flooded his memory of all things that could freeze his impulse to take her up on everything she was offering, damn the consequences.

With quick hands, he fixed her top so she was safely tucked back in, and lightly held on to her upper arms, pushing her backwards, creating space between their bodies, "You don't know what you are asking. It's the booze talking."

With a little bit of fight, he was finally able to get her in the passenger seat and closed the door. He slid behind the steering wheel and put its 400hp into gear. When he finally pulled out of the parking lot and was heading in the direction of her apartment, he let out a relieved breath that he was able to refrain from the ultimate temptation.

As if she read his mind, CeCe removed her seatbelt and shifted her body so she faced him. With a wicked and seductive grin she laid her hand on his lap.

"Hmmm, something seems to want to come out and play,"

With more force than he should have handled her, he threw off her hand and righted her in the passenger seat. "Enough, CeCe!"

With a huff, she suddenly became defensive, "What? Suddenly you don't want in my pants? Once an asshole, always an asshole!"

Jarod locked his jaw together; grinding his teeth to what he was sure would be dust. He gripped the steering wheel with white-knuckle force. The fifteen-minute ride seemed like fifteen hours in the silent car. When he pulled into the parking spot at her apartment building, he exited quickly and took a moment in the night air, where her smell didn't surround him, and his brain wasn't focusing on what they could be doing in the backseat of this muscle car right now. When he finally thought he had enough control, he walked around the car and opened the passenger door. He offered his hand, but she scoffed at it.

He got her into the building and up the stairs to her apartment. When they entered, she turned to him, placing a hand on his chest, "I don't want you here."

"Let me just get you into bed and I'll leave." He said, as her face began to turn green.

CeCe pivoted quickly, heading directly to her kitchen sink, knowing she would never make the bathroom. Unfortunately, she didn't make the sink either. However, Jarod was able to catch her around the waist with one hand, and wrap her hair up in the other before she emptied the contents of her stomach onto the floor and his shoes. She wretched, and wretched. When it finally seemed to stop, saying nothing, he grabbed a towel, poured cold water onto it and washed her face before handing her a glass of water.

She didn't argue, or utter a word. Once she drank the water, Jarod guided her down the hall to her bedroom. Faced with the decision to strip her down, or put her to bed in puked splattered clothes, he knew no man had ever been so tempted before. He lifted the top up and over her head before sitting her down on the edge of the bed. She was swaying so badly, she actually collapsed backwards. With surprising quickness, he efficiently removed her heels and pants, leaving her in just her barely-there bra and silk scrap of panties.

Jarod was rock hard as he looked at her, laid out on the bed in the most delicious of sexual ways, but he held his desire in check as he scooped her up, just high enough to adjust her position, and pulled the covers over her. She was asleep faster before he could click on the bedside lamp.

He went into the bathroom, looked in her medicine cabinet and found the bottle of aspirin. He returned to her bedroom and left two caplets and a glass of water next to the bed. And the wastebasket, just in case.

Jarod watched as CeCe slept. What he wouldn't do for this woman. He leaned down and kissed her forehead with a lingering kiss before righting himself and leaving the room. He cleaned the mess in the kitchen, ensured the apartment was tidy and secure before he let himself out.

As he walked into the warm summer night, he could honestly say he was proud of himself for not giving in. It would have been amazing instant gratification, but in the bigger picture of getting CeCe in his life permanently, she needed to know, and see, that he could do the right thing. That he would always try to do the right thing, even though it was the furthest thing from what he wanted.

That dunce chair might just have to wait a little bit longer, after all.

Jarod was sitting in his truck, reading through some emails from his friends running the prints, when her mustang pulled into the plaza parking lot. Rather than park where he usually did, off in the back corner of the lot, this morning he chose to park in the front row where she parked.

He noticed her high ponytail and dark sunglasses. Her face didn't exactly grimace as she got out of the car, but it wasn't anywhere near a smile, either. She was definitely hurting. His window already down, he poked the bear, saying, louder than he should, "How you feeling there, Rock star?"

"Like I've been hit in the head with a 2x4." She whispered. She started to walk away, but then stopped and turned back to him, "Thank you for getting me home last night. I hope I wasn't too much trouble."

Jarod looked at her and confirmed she looked completely unsure of her actions the night before. But even in the state of complete hangover remorse, she still looked amazing. Her long hair hung from its clasp in a curtain of silk. The black and white paisley dress she wore clung to her curves beautifully and she still opted for four-inch heels. She was a complete pro, through and through. Should he remind her she threw herself at him, or not? He opted for the route that would get him closer to the seat in Heaven, "No trouble at all. After we hung out at the bar, you fell asleep in the car, and I drove you home. You walked up of your own accord, and I left once I knew you were safely inside." *And if you believe that, I have a bridge to sell you.*

"So weird, I don't remember anything after the second round of drinks. When did I turn into such a lightweight?"

"It happens, yesterday was a rough day, and you are entitled." He said hoping this would close the subject.

She must have sensed his closure, opting for, "Well, thank you again. I better head in."

"I'll be here," Jarod answered, knowing the words meant so much more than their context.

CeCe smiled and nodded her head ever so slightly, and walked to her store and let herself in the front.

Jarod watched as she walked away from him, thinking of how great her ass looked from this particular direction, and how they'd had a good connection just then he hoped she wouldn't be able to brush off any time soon, or ever.

Twenty-One

To CeCe's amazement, Kelleigh did come into work, but she remained quite quiet, which was just as well, since Cece wasn't up for chitchat. They worked alongside each other in peaceful silence. Jarod came in about mid afternoon.

"Hey. Is everything alright?" CeCe asked, hating the alarm she felt when she saw him enter the store.

"Yeah, I was wondering, since you don't seem too busy, if I could get back up to that camera."

"Oh, uh yeah, sure." CeCe said, directing him to the back where the ladder was.

Suddenly, Kelleigh became jittery, "CeCe, I'm not really feeling too hot again, I'm going to take my break now, if I can."

CeCe was annoyed at the sudden request, "Go ahead and take your break, but, Kelleigh, I have to say, if this continues, I'm going to have to let you go."

The younger woman said she understood and headed out to her car.

"Everything alright?" Jarod asked as he carried the ladder out.

CeCe watched the sexy man carry the heavy ladder with ease across the store and open it. "Yeah, I'm sure it is your fault that I suddenly don't trust her, but I admit, she has been acting funny."

"Just don't give too much away, or hint that you think she might be connected somehow," Jarod said before he climbed up and went to work on the camera.

CeCe busied herself folding product until Jarod stepped down the ladder, camera in hand. She watched him silently head back to the office. She followed right behind him, concerned with the look on his face. He was at the security system checking the wiring.

"Something wrong?"

"Yeah, a lot of things." Jarod said before he let out a scream of frustration. "Fucker!"

CeCe rushed to his side, "What?"

"Someone hacked into your security feed."

Her eyes went wide at his words. Jarod explained how the box fed the wires to the system and how they ran through the ceiling to where the four cameras were.

"But you see this blue wire?" he asked as he showed her the camera he held in his hand with two black wires, and a much smaller blue wire, coming out of it. "It doesn't belong to your security system, but I can't tell where the feed is going."

Suddenly, she felt completely exposed and violated. Someone was watching her, every day, every moment she was here. Suddenly this went beyond the sick prick wanting a date by sending anonymous flowers, this was worse, much worse than anything she thought beforehand.

She listened as Jarod called Max; her attention returned to his face as he spoke intently into the phone, "No way, this is going to my guy today. Well, I guess you will just have to arrest me, Idarraga." Jarod disconnected the call and returned the phone to his pocket.

Just then, Kelleigh came back in, but she avoided eye contact with CeCe and Jarod.

"Look I need to take this down to my tech guy right now, Max says he has someone en route, but I would rather not wait. Will you be okay?"

Even though she didn't feel it, she answered, "I'll be fine."

Jarod looked over CeCe's head and addressed Kelleigh, "Are you working out the rest of your shift?"

She responded yes, it was going to have to be good enough. He looked back to CeCe and she held his gaze for a moment before saying, "Go."

"I'll be back in one hour." And then he was out the door and in his truck.

The next twenty minutes were tense until CeCe decided she was being ridiculous. The police would be here in a moment, if they weren't already. She squared her shoulders and went back to work. She looked to Kelleigh, who was holding her stomach and grimacing in pain.

"Kel? What is going on?"

"CeCe I just don't feel well." Her friend replied, but the way she was holding herself didn't remind CeCe of a stomachache. But she couldn't disagree; Kelleigh did not look well.

CeCe rushed to her friend, applying a hand of comfort to the younger woman's arm, "Are you okay to drive, or do you want me to call someone?" Being this close to Kelleigh she noticed the heavy makeup on her face. Suddenly, warning bells were going off.

"Kelleigh, is the reason you've been out for days is you needed to let the bruises heal?" CeCe felt like an interloper, but if the roles were reversed she would want someone to care.

Suddenly Kelleigh began to cry, "Oh Cees, I've been so stupid. Talk about textbook case of idiocy and foolishness. I believed him, I believed he cared about me, but the minute I began asking questions he turned on me, so viciously. I was so embarrassed and ashamed. I couldn't face you, or anybody."

CeCe felt horrible, and for second-guessing the sweet girl she knew Kelleigh to be, and allowing doubt to blind her to what she knew; Kelleigh may be a different type of person, but she was still a good person, through and through.

"Is this stomach pain because of him?"

Kelleigh couldn't muster the words, she just nodded her head, and suddenly CeCe wanted to find this poor excuse for a man and give him an introduction to her four-inch heel.

"Okay, this is what you are going to do, you are going to go home and rest. I really would like you to call the police and report him. I will stand by you with whatever comes of your report. Just know I will not allow you to go through this alone." CeCe insisted. Flashes of what she went through, the shame she felt, as well as the loneliness of the situation. CeCe was lucky, Dylan rescued her, in many aspects, and if she could return the favor to Kelleigh, she would.

"But Jarod told me to work out my shift, and I can't afford to lose this job, CeCe."

"Yeah well, Jarod's name isn't painted on the front glass either. And your job will be waiting for you when you are well enough." She gave her friend a kind look.

Once Kelleigh was in her car, CeCe watched her pull out of the plaza parking lot. She then noticed the parked patrol car facing her store.

See all's good, Cees.

The patrolman, Officer Nichols, entered the store next, asking her if everything was all right, and while she was talking to him, Derrick entered.

CeCe was thrilled to see him, but at the same time, disappointed he wasn't Jarod.

Officer Nichols asked if CeCe knew him, and when she assured him she was perfectly safe with Derrick, he moved to leave.

She thanked him for coming by. Tipping his hat to her, he left the store and a moment later, the patrol car pulled away from the curb.

"Did I miss something?" Derrick asked confused at the sight of the police.

"Unfortunately, yes, but I don't want to talk about it. I'm so happy you came in," she answered.

After another few moments of chitchat, Derrick remembered he had forgotten something in his car for her and said he'd be right back. She started using the carpet sweeper while she waited; she had just finished the area in front of the service desk when Derrick returned carrying something behind his back.

"I brought you something." He smiled as he walked towards her.

"Oh, you didn't need to do that." She leaned the carpet sweeper against the counter.

"I wanted to—no, I mean, I needed to. It's been too long," he pulled a floral box from behind his back.

CeCe smiled, knowing if anyone could erase the memory of bad floral boxes, Derrick could. She opened the long white floral box, and her breath seized and her heart stopped. Amongst the green tissue paper lay twelve long stem white roses. Beautiful, perfectly pristine and exquisite, but to CeCe they were poisonous. She dropped the box and the blooms spilled out. Her hands flew to her mouth, muffling the scream that couldn't make it past her throat.

"Cees?" Derrick asked, befuddled.

"Derrick? It was you?"

"What?"

"The roses?" she couldn't believe the words were passing her lips.

She watched as his face went from confusion to astonishment, "Oh my God! No! I would never. You have to believe me. This was a mistake, a huge, colossal mistake on my part. CeCe, I'm an idiot. I've been so busy I didn't even think. Please baby, you can't think I would do such a thing!"

CeCe stepped backwards slowly at first then all she could think to do was run. She ran back to her office, grabbed her cell phone and locked herself in the bathroom. Without thought, her fingers moved across the screen until his deep voice answered.

She screamed, "It's Derrick! He is the one who has been sending the roses!" Not processing anything else, she withdrew the phone from her ear, but held onto it as if it controlled her gravitational pull to the floor.

She could hear Derrick pleading his innocence as his fist pounded on the other side of the sturdy door. The handle jiggled over and over again. CeCe slid down the wall until her bottom rested on the floor, still clutching her phone in her hand.

It seemed like he pounded on the door forever, but finally, all attempts to break down the door stopped and for a moment, there was silence. CeCe was still too scared to move. Then she heard the deep voice coming through the door instead of through her phone. Yelling ensued followed by a thumping sound and then silence. After another few moments, there was a soft knock on the bathroom door.

"Kitten, it's okay, you can come out."

Cece pulled herself up slowly, and with shaking hands undid the surprisingly sturdy lock. She slowly opened the door and was met by the cool blue eyes she would know anywhere.

Without thought, she ran into the open embrace that was waiting for her. She was engulfed in warmth and strength, and it felt wonderful. With bravery she did not feel, she moved her head to the left, peaking past Jarod's strong bicep to where Derrick sat. He was hunched over in one of the extra chairs with his hands behind his back. As if sensing her gaze, Derrick lifted his head and she saw the bruise that began to grow under his right eye, and what looked like a something stuffed in his mouth.

Their eyes connected and suddenly CeCe felt uneasy. But not from being threatened, rather her conscience was trying to tell her something. She chalked it up to her adrenaline and quickly looked elsewhere.

"Ms. Cervetti?" the Latin accented voice trailed in from the storefront.

CeCe walked out and the lieutenant and two uniformed officers greeted her.

"Lieutenant?"

"Gates called me. Where is Mr. Lowell?"

Before CeCe could answer, Max's attention moved past her, over her shoulder, and CeCe heard movement behind her. She turned and found Jarod gruffly pulling Derrick along by his arm. They stopped a good distance away from CeCe. She watched as Jarod pulled whatever was in his mouth out.

The minute he was free of the gag, Derrick looked at CeCe and began pleading for her to listen, "CeCe, I swear I didn't do this. You have to believe me!"

"Get him out of here," Idarraga ordered, before the two uniforms escorted Derrick out. CeCe watched as they placed him in the back of the Appleton police car.

CeCe stared at Derrick's dark eyes that remained connected to hers from the back of the squad car, as the flashing blue lights interrupted the dimming summer sun.

She was numb, her brain was shutting down; suddenly, she was so tired she just wanted to sleep.

"Ms. Cervetti? Did you hear me?"

"What?" CeCe was pulled from what seemed like an odd out of body experience, "I'm sorry?"

Max softened his voice and let his eyes roam over her face before repeating himself, "I said, I need to take your statement."

"Can't it wait? She looks dead on her feet," Jarod barked out.

The Lieutenant eyes never left CeCe as he opened his mouth to argue, but CeCe spoke first, "No it's alright, I can do it now."

She turned to return to her office, when she passed Jarod he began walking backwards to accompany her.

"No. I'll just go with Max." With no other explanation she continued on her route, feeling his eyes bore into her back. She didn't know why she didn't want Jarod with her, but it didn't change the little voice in her head telling her to do this on her own.

The next fifteen minutes felt like hours to Jarod. He sat on the counter in the store, examining his right hand's knuckles. Opening and closing his hand repeatedly, focusing on the pain with each movements.

When he'd gotten her call and heard the fear in CeCe's voice, he'd hopped out of his truck leaving the door wide open. He slid over a car's hood in 70's television fashion doing whatever he needed to do to get to her as quickly as possible. When he entered the store, he could hear Lowell banging on the door she'd barricaded herself behind. The next few moments seemed a blur to him, he needed to get the threat away from her.

He heard Lowell spouting what a mistake this all was, but Jarod honestly didn't care. His fist connected to Lowell's eye and it felt good. It felt good to immobilize the other man. To know he was the alpha, in true Neanderthal thinking, survival of the fittest, and in this sense, the toughest. With a quick application of a zip tie to Derrick's wrist, Jarod's attention returned to the girl. His girl.

When the door cracked open, and her scared beautiful eyes looked back at him, he felt his own soul begin to chip. He would do anything to keep that look from her eyes.

As he sat there, he began to chastise himself for not seeing it was Lowell. He'd run this guy through the investigation wringer and he came up clean, each and every time.

Jarod looked over his shoulder and looked at the dropped floral box. Hopping down, he went over to where it lay, squatted down and examined the mess. The bloom sizes were different than the ones before. These were smaller, daintier than all the others were. The floral tissue paper was pink and there was a handwritten floral note card thrown not far from where the flowers and box lay.

Jarod moved over to read the personal card.

Simple truth. I've missed you. –Derrick.

This was the position he was in when CeCe and Idarraga returned from the office. It was Max who inquired to what he was doing.

"Uh, just looking over the evidence. This is your department, Idarraga." Jarod stood and looked toward CeCe who was successfully avoiding his gaze. "Cees, you ready? I'll take you home."

Finally, she looked at him and he thought she would just collapse, right then and there from exhaustion. All three walked out together, after the store was locked up, Idarraga went to his car while Jarod and CeCe walked to his truck. In the empty parking lot, the beater pickup looked even worse with its driver's door open and faded interior light.

As they walked closer to his vehicle, Jarod grabbed onto her hand, his heart warming when she didn't pull away from his hold, but he hated the fact her hand was cold as ice, confirming her adrenaline crash. They walked hand in hand and he wished their walk was longer, but it came to a quick close. He opened the passenger door and nestled her there before walking around to the drivers. However, when he placed the key in the ignition, the engine would not turn over.

"Yup. Should have seen that coming," he mumbled. "Give me your keys, we'll leave the Beast here and retrieve it in the morning."

Without a word or fight, she pulled her keys out of her bag and exited the car. Once they were in the mustang, Jarod watched as she started to nod off.

When he pulled up to his apartment he couldn't believe how out cold she was. She never even stirred when he carried her out of the car and up the stairs. He had just gotten her into his bed, when she roused enough to say, "Don't leave me," then fell into a deep sleep.

"Not a chance, Kitten." He whispered back.

Jarod sat in the chair watching CeCe sleep for hours. She never moved or made a sound. She looked like one of those slumber princesses little girls go gaga over. Her dark hair hung in a perfect curtain along the pillow. Her full lips looked plump and inviting. Her long lashes cast the smallest of shadows on her soft cheeks, and her chest rose and fell in perfect REM sleep.

It was closing on 3AM when he decided to get some shuteye himself. With the stealthiest of moves, Jarod laid down on the bed, on top of the covers she was snuggled into and gently pulled her towards him. Unconsciously, she nuzzled into his embrace and continued her undisturbed sleep. He nodded off inhaling her wonderful unique scent and continuing his self-serving actions of pushing the doubts that Derrick Lowell was CeCe's stalker out of his mind.

The buzzing of his phone pulled Jarod from his dreams. With a quick look at the bedside clock, he had only fallen asleep three hours ago. With a look to CeCe, she remained unmoved and still asleep, Jarod slid out of bed and grabbed his phone and walked into the bathroom. With the door closed behind him, he answered, "Idarraga?"

"Yeah, Gates, I wanted to let you know, you were right, Lowell isn't our guy."

Shit.

"I said no such thing," Jarod answered for lack of anything else to say.

"Yeah, well, whatever, but when you mentioned looking at the flowers, I took the pictures from my phone and had my guys examine them. After talking to Lowell, all his info checked out. He had receipts and corroboration from the florist. I'll be processing him out of custody within the hour."

Jarod remained mute, suddenly intrigued by the chipped grout on the bathroom floor, when the other man broke the silence only then did he respond, "Yeah, okay."

"I'll be calling Ms. Cervetti after I hang up with you to let her know."

"Don't bother, I'll tell her."

"I think it would be best if I tell her. You know, officially, considering it is a police matter."

Fuck that shit! Jarod didn't want to share anything that occurred between CeCe and him, but he lashed out at the dig, "Well, she isn't in your bed, now, is she?"

His words were met with silence.

Just keep opening your mouth, Asshole!

"I'll call her later this morning and let her know,"

"Yeah, you do that," Jarod disconnected the call.

When he felt himself gain some sort of control over the emotions swirling through him, Jarod padded back to the bed and tried quietly to crawl back in. Just as the mattress dipped down under his weight, CeCe roused. Blinking fast she took in her surroundings and sat up quickly. Her hair fell over her face, and she just as fast flipped it back over her head. She pulled the sheet up covering herself even though she was still in all her clothes.

"Gates!?! What the hell?"

She continued to look around as if the walls would offer an explanation.

"Kitten, calm down. You were dead on your feet, I brought you here to decompress." Even he knew how pathetic that reason sounded.

She looked at him alarmed and annoyed, then, as if something clicked, she threw the covers off her and stood. She looked down and seemed surprised to find herself completely clothed. He got some joy out of that.

"Where are you going?"

"I'm going down to the police station." She answered as she looked around vigorously for her bag and keys.

What? Did she hear his phone call? Did she have ESP? He was seriously missing something, and it pissed him off.

"And why the fuck would you do something like that?" he placed his hands on his hips and stared her down.

"Well, Mr. Nosey, I need to talk to Derrick. He didn't do this. I know that, and I need to apologize to him. And right the wrong." She met his gaze, jutted out her hip and gave the attitude right back.

Okay maybe this was a sick and twisted dream he was having.

"How do you know?" he asked quietly as he searched her face.

"Because I know Derrick. All I can hope is he will forgive me, for everything." She said the last part under her breath, but he heard it loud and clear.

"And what the fuck is that supposed to mean, CeCe?" he yelled at her retreating back.

She had reached the door before he caught her. With his hand on her upper arm, he turned her around so she faced him. Nose to nose he repeated his question.

His blue eyes searched her hazel ones and where he hoped he would see an obvious denial, he saw her pride and what she so desperately clung to. It cut him, deeply. He released her.

"It means I can no longer live in fantasyland. I need to wake up from dreamland. This is life. My life, and I will not have regrets. With each passing day, it seems my dreams are getting further and further away from me. I can't allow it. Like how it was my dream to fill my store with only my designs, but now, considering, they will stay just that, a dream. I will not allow another aspect of my life to be hazed over because of what I feel physically, when I know, emotionally, I couldn't bare it." Her voice cracked, but by God, she never let the water that pooled in her beautiful eyes spill over.

He needed to tell her, he needed to go for broke, but even as his brain was screaming for his tongue to do just that he only said, "Someone once told me, dreams are just desires your heart is too afraid to ask for."

Her lip quivered as his words triggered the memory of a long ago time, when a girl and a no good young man sat on the hood of his Camaro and looked out over the valley on a warm fall night. That was when she first told him about her dream to design clothes, and when he first saw her speak with such passion and hope.

"Sounds like someone who needed something to grasp onto."

"Maybe, but words like that can only be spoken when they are believed. I believed her then because I knew she was completely sincere. She is also the most beautiful girl I know. I've ever known."

"Jarod..."

"Why are you fighting this, and me, so hard? Is it so hard to listen to your heart? To believe in me? If you want to deny your dreams, then go ahead, but I will not deny mine. My dreams then and now, have only ever been about one thing. I'm looking at the object of all those years of dreams."

He watched as she struggled for control, and he focused on that, and the pain radiating from his leg and thigh. Wanting the fire that burned there to consume him because he knew what was coming. He knew his pleas were met with the ultimate of resistance.

CeCe finally broke from their locked gaze and looked at the new day's sunlight beginning to filter through the small window. When she returned her attention his too close face he knew he had lost. "You want the truth why I can't have those dreams become reality? It's because you have the power to destroy me. Do you hear me? I can't let you in any further. I can't not have control. What you are asking me will require me to renege on the one promise I made to myself."

He had no words, nor did he move a muscle when she took two steps backwards and placed her hand on the doorknob, saying in departure, "I'm choosing to leave what you and I had as incredible sex and a dark memory that has been repainted. Your debt is repaid; now, leave me to move on with my life as I want to."

Jarod watched as she walked out of his room, and his life, on her terms. He was unable to do anything about it, either.

Twenty-Two

"Remind me what the hell I am paying you for?" Dylan demanded.

"Fuck you, Cross," Jarod shot out of the seat he occupied opposite Dylan's desk in the S&D office and began to pace.

"I pay you for results, and instead I have CeCe terrified to be in her own store knowing that someone is watching her!" Dylan continued to bark as he got up, and turned to look out the huge window behind him.

Jarod didn't need Dylan telling him he fucked up, but Jarod needed something to focus his aggravation on, and until something better appeared, Dylan would do.

Dylan turned back around and with less gusto said, "So where are we with finding out where the cable IP address is coming from?"

"My guy is working on it now, but as he said, whoever this guy is, he's good at covering his tracks. It is going to take him a couple of days to crack it."

Dylan pressed, "But you think he will be able to."

"I bet my life on it," Jarod countered.

"Let's just make sure it really is *your* life you have on the line, not CeCe's," Dylan clarified when his desk phone buzzed.

Dylan, the guy you were expecting is here.

"Thanks, Josie, send him in." he pressed the intercom button. Dylan looked to Jarod and said, "Our conversation will have to wait."

"I'll head out," Jarod began for the door.

"No, I think you should stay."

The pretense of Dylan's directive left Jarod puzzled, and then suddenly, it was clear when Derrick walked through the office door. He did not notice Jarod right away.

"Hey, Dylan, thanks for taking the time to see me," Derrick said as he extended his hand to the other man. "I will make this quick, I wanted to let you know I plan on asking CeCe to marry me in a couple of weeks when we head to Napa. She considers you her family, and I wanted you to know my intentions."

Suddenly, there was a new target for Jarod's anger.

Jarod saw red. "No fucking way!" he bellowed as he began to charge the newest arrival. However Dylan must of known that would be his move, for he stepped in front of Jarod, holding him in place.

Derrick, caught off guard from the objecting outburst, as well as the unexpected addition to the conversation, took a moment to steady himself. When he was ready, he directed his next statement to Jarod, "Excuse me?"

No way could CeCe marry him. Over Jarod's dead body. "You heard me."

"Gates, you aren't really in a position to have an opinion," Dylan pointed out and Derrick must have found that statement as a point in his column.

"Look, I've had my fill of you. I know all about your weekend in Boston as well as your past with her." Jarod's face betrayed his shock enough for the Fucktard to call him out on it. "Oh, what? You didn't think she would tell me? She told me everything, and I am not going to lie, it hurt, but for us to move forward and for her to accept my proposal, we cannot have secrets. I accept that. She assures me all that happened between the two of you was nothing more than sex, and I believe her."

With ease, Jarod threw off Dylan's block and charged Derrick. He had Lowell's collar before Dylan was able to pull him off the other man. When

Jarod was forced in the opposite direction, he paced away running his hands through his hair trying to find some sort of calm and stop the feeling his house of cards was falling around him, and was failing miserably.

"Shit! Come on guys!" Dylan said from one man to the other before turning his attention to Jarod, "Do you really think this is what she would want, Gates?"

"Him?" Jarod barked, knowing that wasn't what Dylan was asking.

By the look on Dylan's face, he too knew Jarod was grasping at straws. When everyone had taken a breath, Dylan turned his attention back to Derrick, "You don't need my permission, but I appreciate the gesture. I'd be thrilled."

Derrick went to leave the office, but stopped and faced his adversary, "I love her, man."

Jarod didn't know where his calmness came from, but it was as if he was a balloon and all the air was leaving him. He looked Lowell in the eye and spoke clearly and honestly, "I'm sure you think you do. But, I've loved her forever. I'm the better man for her."

"Says you."

"Says CeCe."

"You and I both know that is bullshit. You are oil to her water. Look, I get it. How could a man not fall in love with her, but I'm asking you to back off, this is the last time I will be civil about it."

Jarod folded his arms across his chest and quirked his eyebrow, knowing even Fucktard here couldn't believe that threat would mean anything, "Oh, and what does that mean?"

Derrick swallowed then looked the other man square in the eye, "It means, CeCe's heart only has room for one man, and I'll be damned if that man isn't me. Now, if you'll excuse me, I have a ring to buy."

Jarod watched as the other man exited the office and disappeared from his sight. He turned to Dylan and tried to refocus his anger, "You knew he would be here, and that he'd tell you what he did."

Unabashed, Dylan answered, "I had a feeling. After he was arrested for stalking and harassing CeCe, and then accepted her apology, as well as that of the police, he reached out to me, wanting to talk. I narrowed it down to either his intentions for CeCe, or to tell me how much of an asshole you are."

Jarod looked at Dylan, annoyed with his last remark. Dylan smiled at Jarod's reaction.

"Look, Gates, I am plenty pissed off at you for what you did to CeCe all those years ago. If I had any idea then, you would not have needed the Marines, you would have needed a plastic surgeon. But, as my wife points out to me, it isn't any of my business. However, I will tell you what I would never say to that little woman, I disagree. Whether you like it or not, CeCe is my business, she always will be. You can't gorilla your way through this. Sometimes you have to love her enough to let her go."

"So you're saying you would want her to marry that dickstick, Lowell?"

"I'm saying I support CeCe. Whoever she chooses better take care of her, or they will have me to contend with."

Jarod looked to the man he had considered friend all those years ago, and knew Dylan was right. Without a word, Jarod left Dylan's office, trying to ignore the pain in his leg that was threatening to buckle him. However, the more Jarod thought, perhaps this time the pain wasn't coming from his leg, perhaps it was coming from his heart. When he reached his truck, he chastised himself for being such a pussy. He rubbed his thigh out of habit and punched the steering wheel. Doing the right thing was never his way ever since his mom died, and unless it was concerning CeCe, the right thing didn't seem to hold much salt for him in adulthood, either.

He would fight for her with the last bit of oxygen in his lungs. He can't give up, if he lost her because he didn't try everything he could to keep her, then this was all for nothing and that knowledge he refused to live with. In the end, he may have to live without her, but he'd be damned if it was because he was being noble, or some shit like that. His mind, body, and soul needed to fight until the very end, and by God, that is exactly what he would do.

"Hello?" Jarod answered, out of breath, thanks to the mad dash he made from the shower to his phone.

"Hi Jarod, it's Natalie Cross. I hope you don't mind me calling you. I got your number from Dylan's phone."

"Is everything okay, Mrs. Cross?" Jarod asked, confused as to why she would be calling.

"Come on, I told you not to call me that, the name is Natalie. Any ways, the reason I'm calling is I've decided to have some friends over to the house tonight for an impromptu dinner and drinks."

Jarod was beyond confused, "And?"

Natalie laughed, "And I'd like to invite you to join us."

"I'm sorry ma'am, but I don't understand."

"Hmm, you struck me as a smart guy, but okay, I'll explain, I'm inviting you over to join us for some lasagna and beer. Or wine, if you'd prefer, but you don't strike me as a wine guy. You are kind of like Dylan in that aspect, but I'm flexible."

Confusion continued to overtake Jarod's brain, "Look Mrs. Cross— uh, I mean Natalie—I don't think that would be such a good idea."

"Well, it's a good thing I didn't call you for your opinion. I'll see you at six."

And then, Jarod heard the indication from his phone the call had been disconnected. There was no way he was going there, physically or figuratively.

Twenty-Three

CeCe was confused at Natalie's insistence of her getting the knock at the door, but she did it anyways. When she swung the heavy door open, her breath froze in her throat. The question stuck, unable to come out; thankfully, Jarod answered it for her.

"I don't know why I'm even here."

With perfect timing, Natalie and Mae both came up behind CeCe.

"Because it would have been rude to blow off an invitation," Natalie said as she opened the door farther, Mae took the box of chocolates and six-pack of beer from Jarod's hand.

Once he was ushered in the house, CeCe noticed a couple of things; she suddenly felt very warm, as she looked at his snug fitting jeans and broad shoulders in the white t-shirt he wore. The other was Dylan looked just as surprised as CeCe to see the newest arrival.

After a quick look from his wife, Dylan showed complete class, and walked over and shook Jarod's hand followed by the other males, Seth and Wes.

With quick introductions to all the kids running about, and the teenagers that occupied the couches, Jarod's attention was suddenly diverted to two very eager little bodies wanting a repeat performance of their last encounter.

"Orsy! Orsy!" was yelled before each little girl jumped up and down trying to reach his back.

CeCe found herself chuckling, as Jarod squatted down picking up one, and when her ride was over picking up the other.

"Gibby um orsy, gibby um orsy!" Ria instructed as she kicked with all her might right into his sides, with cheers from her sister to keep going.

Dylan caught CeCe watching Jarod willingly, and happily taking the twins abuse with a gooey look on her face. He said nothing, just lifted his eyebrow in question.

The smile fell from her face, and CeCe rushed out of the room and into the kitchen where Natalie, Mae, and Lola were getting dinner ready.

CeCe turned her head to make sure no one else would hear her before she unleashed on Natalie, the little plotter, "Real cute, Natalie! And just what are you doing inviting him over for dinner?"

Natalie looked from Mae to Lola, Wes' wife, who all suddenly had something to do, but were unable to hide the ear to ear smiles from their faces, before she responded, "I don't know what you mean, we have enough food to feed an army, what's one more? I thought he might be hungry."

Suddenly, the tomato Natalie was slicing for the salad needed all of her attention.

"And what if I'd invited Derrick? Don't you think that would have been awkward?" CeCe hissed, annoyed all her friends were finding humor in this.

Natalie lifted her head, "Oh, and is he coming?"

"No, I told you he had to fly to New York overnight. He will be back tomorrow," CeCe said as she snagged a carrot from the enormous salad bowl.

"Then I guess there is no need to worry about anyone feeling awkward."

With a groan of frustration, CeCe left the kitchen and returned to the living room to find Jarod on the floor brushing a doll's hair with a twin on each leg, instructing him in the proper technique.

CeCe took a seat on the couch closest to where the trio sat and asked, "So which princess do you have Jarod?"

He looked to her with complete and utter terror etched on his face, and CeCe was unable to keep the glee off of hers. Cat, who sat closest to CeCe, looked to her, held up her doll and said, "Pweddy wike ou." Her twin agreed, but went a step further, Ria put her hand on Jarod's face pushing it so he also looked at CeCe when she said "ya pweddy wike ou."

Ria was not willing to move her little hand from his face until he agreed, "Yes, the dolls are pretty like her."

His words made each little girl happy as they turned their attention back to the princess program on the television, completely unaware of the adult gazes that were still glued to each other.

Natalie announced dinner was ready and that the adults would be eating in the dining room, while the kids would be dining picnic style in the living room. By the time Jarod and CeCe reached the dining room, the only two seats still available were across from each other, much to CeCe's delight, at the end of the table where Natalie and Mae sat.

After a course of salad and lasagna, the conversation was dominated by the men discussing the upcoming New England Patriot's team lineup; specifically, their need for improvement on special teams. The woman quickly became bored with the topic.

"Your necklace is stunning, Cees. I first noticed that gorgeous piece when we were in Boston, but I just forgot to mention it. It is fabulous. I have the perfect pair of shoes it would go with." Mae said as she took a sip of her wine.

Natalie shook her head and laughed in mirth, "You and your shoes, Mae. I think you may need an intervention, my friend. But I think you are going to have to dream of borrowing another piece. I happen to know, for a fact, a certain software programmer dropped mega dough in Tiffany's while in Manhattan recently. Besides, I haven't seen it off of her neck since she got it, I'd say it is symbolic that CeCe may be off the market pretty soon." Natalie sipped her own wine, before looking to her husband at the other end of the table.

"Really?" Mae and Lola said in unison as CeCe's face showed anything but joy, as her gaze looked toward Jarod's face of stone.

Abruptly, Jarod stood up, throwing his napkin on the table, "If you'll excuse me," he didn't even wait for a response.

CeCe looked to Natalie, furious, before she too got up and chased after Jarod.

She caught up with him just as he was leaving through the front door.

"Jarod! Jarod! Wait!" she followed him outside and down to the driveway.

He stopped, but didn't turn around to face her.

"Look, I…" but whatever she was going to say died on her lips when he turned to face her.

Jarod's face was cold and void of emotion. He pointed his finger, jabbing it at her throat as he shouted, "What is that?"

CeCe swallowed hard and remained mute.

He repeated the question, with less volume, but somehow with more emotion.

"What is what?" she asked, but she knew what he meant, as she wrapped her fingers around the circle.

"Is it true?" he whispered.

She looked at his eyes and they were no longer the deep vivid color they had been; they were almost gray, as if the color had been drained out of them, reflecting his mood. Her voice quaked as she spoke "Is what true?"

"Did Fucktard give that to you?" Fury ripped the words from his throat, as she was sure the wind carried them down into the valley.

Now it was time to get her own temper up, "Will you stop calling him that? He hasn't done anything to you!"

"No, he only sticks his dick into you! Answer the damn question, CeCe!"

"Yes, Derrick bought this for me." She ran her fingers along the cord suddenly wanting to rip it from her neck.

"When did he give it to you?" he probed with a softer voice again, but he might have well been shouting as her bones rattled with each word.

Nothing. She couldn't speak. Her voice refused to tell him the truth. Or perhaps it was her heart that stopped the words from coming.

"WHEN!?!"

Dylan came out the house, but only got as far as the front porch, before Natalie called him back. He ignored his wife.

"Cees, you okay?"

CeCe turned her attention to Dylan and said, "Yes, D, I'm fine. I'll be in in a moment."

Dylan looked to Jarod, who returned his dangerous gaze, and Dylan must have decided she was safe enough and he returned inside.

CeCe looked back to Jarod and knew he deserved the truth, she released the cord and slipped her hands into her pockets, "The night he took me to Giovanni's."

Jarod remained mute and she thought he actually wouldn't say anything, and when he did, she wished her first thought was correct, "Every time I've fucked you, you've worn it. Why?"

"It's just a necklace, Gates!" she flung the words at him, wondering why she suddenly felt claustrophobic outside.

"Is it? Or is it the reminder that I'll never be the guy for you? The shield you needed to don, to drive that fact home?"

She wanted to deny his accusation, but she couldn't. Tears began to build in her eyes, but before they could make it past her lashes he continued.

"And that is why you will never get it."

"Get what? What is 'it'? If you have something to say, say it." She pleaded for him to do so, but she was terrified what she would hear next.

"If I have to say it, you don't deserve it anyways." He turned his back on her and began to walk to his truck.

Panic built up in her, panic like nothing she has ever felt before; he was leaving. She chased after him, only stopping to speak angry, fear-filled words, "Jarod, I don't know what you are talking about."

He opened the door to his truck, but stopped before turning back to face her, he was calm and quiet and it scared her more than his fury. "I'm talking about love, Kitten. Of all the times I wanted to say those words, to officially say, *I love you*, I chose not to. Not because the moment was wrong, or I was afraid, but because I was sure I didn't have to. I was so fucking sure you already knew I did, you have known for a long time." He stared into her eyes as the tears began to fall down her cheeks, but even this unseen emotion in CeCe was not enough for him to hold his tongue, "I love you more than any man has loved any woman. My heart beats your name. My lungs take in oxygen for the soul purpose of loving you. My brain is wired to love you, and serve only you. But I guess that is my fault. And as sure as I am of my love for you, I'm sure of your love for me. You are just too damn chicken to think it, let alone say it. In order to let the thought to bounce around in your beautiful head means you have to tear down this stupid fucking wall you've built up."

This wasn't a fight she would soon get over, this felt like the battle for her life, "I built that wall because of you! I can't go through that again! You ripped my heart out, Jarod. How can you expect me to let you do it again?"

His fury was back, and if she thought it was tangible before, how wrong she was.

"You are forever going to throw that in my face! No matter what I do, what I show you, you will never get over it, will you?"

"You enlisted!"

"I enlisted because of you, dammit! You could destroy me; I knew it then, just like I know it now. Don't ever think that was the easy thing to do because it wasn't. It was the hardest!" It was Jarod's turn to look away, and when he returned his gaze to hers, CeCe's eyes weren't the only ones with water in them, "You were so much better than me, even then. You had a light about you, and look at you now, I was right. You deserved a decent man, yet you wanted me. I couldn't be selfish. I couldn't think of only my wants, my dreams, I had to think of yours. If that meant leaving you, then that was what I had to do. But don't ever think it was easy for me!"

CeCe wrapped her arms around her middle, suddenly feeling she needed to hold herself together.

"But you know what? What you've been trying to drill into me has finally sunk in, and this was the last nail in my coffin. You want me gone? Well, Kitten, I'm gone. But not because you pushed me away, get that through your thick skull, right now. It's because I love you more than I appreciate and value my own sanity. I was driven mad when I came back from war, and I'm willingly going back to that terrifying and crippling place because of my love for you. So when you are off living the lie that you are trying to tell yourself is your happy wanted life, know that I went to hell, just like I would go to the ends of the Earth for you. Everything is because of you, and will always be."

He hopped in his truck and peeled out backwards. CeCe tried to chase after him, "Jarod! Jarod! Gates! GATES!" But suddenly, she couldn't talk any more; the tears were falling too hard. He was gone, was along with her convictions that she knew what the hell she was doing.

Dylan watched out the open door as CeCe's mustang pulled out of sight, when he turned away, the twins were playing quietly on the living room floor and Natalie was in the kitchen. He walked in the kitchen and she was at the sink doing dishes. He stepped up to his wife, wrapped his hands around her waist, and whispered in her ear, "Well, that kind of blew up in your face, babe."

Natalie turned to face her husband, wrapping her arms around his neck before responding, "I don't think it did at all."

"She only finally dried her tears, Natalie. Whatever he said to her, hurt her like I've only ever seen her once before. Whatever you were trying to prove by inviting him here, didn't happen."

"Yes, it did. You just don't want to admit it. CeCe needed to see with her own eyes what the rest of us have seen every time those two are within a mile of each other."

"Oh yeah, and what is that?"

"They belong together. They are voltaic—they feed off each other. As individuals they are powerful, but put them together and their potential has no limits or bounds, just the ability to make something beautiful, and once in a lifetime. It really is quite romantic."

Dylan looked at his wife, bewildered.

"And besides, CeCe helped me see that the best thing in my life was listening to my heart, and ignoring the fear. The least I can do is return the favor."

"You know, babe, you brought such light to my life," Dylan whispered against his wife's lips.

"Only because you taught me where the switch was." And then Natalie did what she would never get sick of doing: she kissed her husband.

Twenty-Four

By the time CeCe pulled into her apartment complex's lot, her eyes were so puffy they threatened to swell shut. She had tried Jarod's cell so many times, but it went directly to voicemail. She tried one more time, but this time when it went to voicemail she didn't hang up right away, she listened to his deep voice, afraid he was truthful in his threat that he was gone.

When she hit disconnect, new tears welled up in her eyes and spilled over, pooling onto her already wet chest, where all the other tears landed. How could she screw everything up so badly? She replayed their fight, over and over again, in her head. Everything he said was true; every word about her wall was completely accurate. He said he loved her, but she was convinced he hated her more. Could she blame him? This was all her doing. Her entire adult life, every aspect of it she said who, she said what, all for the purpose to shelter herself, and she was okay with the lies she convinced herself were truths. Natalie was right, she chose easy and unattached to protect herself against being hurt, but really what she was doing was hurting herself by denying the biggest truth of all: she didn't want this type of life.

Looking at her phone on the passenger seat, she knew it was futile to call him again, he wouldn't answer, and he wouldn't return the call. Not that she could say anything to him if he did, she didn't know what to say, but at least if he was in front of her he wouldn't be gone. Gone meant time's up. Gone was decisive. Gone was final. She needed a hot shower and as many bottles of wine as she could consume, but this time, when the numbness took over, there would be no blue eyes to bring the feeling back into her.

She let herself into her apartment, locked and chained the door. She walked into the bathroom and began the water. She needed the hottest of hot water and sometimes it took a bit to get it steaming. She walked into her bedroom and began to kick off her shoes, and she noticed the window shade closed. Perplexed, that's when she saw it. The single, long stemmed white rose lay on her bed.

CeCe froze in place, the silence and darkness of the room made the hairs on the back of her neck and arms stand up. Her eyes would not, or could not, drag themselves away from the perfect bloom. *He's been in my house!* She needed to run. She needed to call Jarod!

"Hello, Cees!" the voice came from behind her, she knew it like she knew her own.

CeCe whipped around to face him—her stalker—and scream, but the scream died in her throat as he pressed the Chloroform-soaked rag over her mouth and nose. She fought him, kicking and punching, but the effects took hold of her senses and knocked her out.

Jarod broke the bureau draw when he slammed it shut after pulling all his clothes out.

GREAT! Jarod decided he would just leave Mr. Burns an extra hundred dollars when he dropped the keys threw the mail slot.

He turned and threw the rest of his clothes into the duffle bag. Looking around the small apartment, he wanted to make sure he didn't forget anything. His laptop sat open on the small table, it dinged indicating a new email.

Jarod walked over and punched the key to bring up the newest email.

Turn your phone on, Jackass! I was finally able to break the encryption. I know who the IP belongs to.

Jarod was tempted to give Idarraga's phone number to Ryder, but decided he needed to know the name of the fucktard. He pulled his powered off cell out of his pocket, when it buzzed to life, he was taken aback at how many attempts she made to reach him. But there was no voicemail, or text from her.

She couldn't have wanted to say anything that badly then.

Jarod listened to the voicemail Ryder left and his insides went cold. He knew the surname; Dylan ingrained it in him thirteen years ago.

SHIT!

Jarod drove as if the hounds of hell were chasing him. He broke every traffic law known to man, and it still felt like it took him too long to get to CeCe's apartment. Glancing up to her window, he knew something was drastically wrong; the shade was closed to her bedroom.

He was out of his truck before the parking gear engaged.

"Get out of the way," he screamed to the middle-aged couple coming out the security door. He pushed between them and took the stairs two at a time. When he reached her door, he made quick work of the lock and was inside four seconds later.

Her apartment was eerily empty, but the shower was running. He was in the bathroom a second later, but to his terror, she was not. He went to her bedroom and found the same emptiness. He picked up the rose from where it lay and spoke to it, as if it was a communicator to her, "I'm coming, Kitten, you can count on it."

Jarod left the vacant apartment and rushed to his truck with his phone to his ear, "Ryder, give me everything you got. I want to know the last time he had his teeth cleaned because he isn't going to have them much longer."

CeCe's dream was strange and left her feeling apprehensive, but the finger that caressed her cheek brought her out of it. However, when she opened her eyes her dream became a nightmare.

"Troy?" she squeaked as she squinted at the hazy form in front of her.

"Hello, sweetheart. Did you have a nice nap?"

His voice was so familiar, yet so disturbing, all at the same time. It had been thirteen years since she last laid eyes on him. Despite the small town they lived in, she never ran into him when he was home for visits, or heck, she never ran into anyone that said, "Oh, hey, I just saw Troy at so and so."

Not that CeCe minded at the time, the further she put Troy Mitchell out of her head, the better off she was, until she met Jarod. *Oh Jarod! You are the one I need right now. If only I wasn't so stupid!*

Her vision cleared and she was finally able to look at the man who has haunted her the last six weeks. Time had not been kind to him. His face was bloated and aged twenty years. His hairline receded, and the crown of his head was as bare as a baby's bottom, with the exception of a few long hairs he tried to matte downward. Where his hair did grow on the sides, it was no longer the soft chestnut brown it had been in his youth, but now it was a grayish, wiry looking texture. His once fit body now carried around a belly, resembling a midterm pregnancy on top of skinny legs

"Did you hear me, sweetheart?"

CeCe raised her gaze to his face, cringing as he touched her cheek once more. She went to bat his hand away only to find her hands and legs were immobilized.

She wiggled and strained against the zip ties, but it was useless.

"I picked up the tip of the zip ties from your muscle friend, I suppose of all his faults, that is one thing I should be grateful for: the good idea. If it was good enough for him in his security services, then it would serve my purposes."

She may be bound to the chair but her tongue wasn't, "You want to talk about Jarod's faults, don't you think that is a little hypocritical, Troy?"

"Don't talk to me in that tone!" Troy raised his hand to emphasize his words.

The brazenness of her tongue and the strength of her personality couldn't stop the flinch she made at the sight of his hand drawing backwards.

"No. No, Sweetheart, I know it is going to take some time for you to fall into line, but my temper will not be for bad, it will be only used to help you find your way back. I take medication now. My temper shouldn't be an issue if you follow along, CeCe."

This guy was out of his tree! "I hope those meds are antipsychotics."

Rather than rise to her taunt, Troy just smiled and rubbed his middle finger along her cheek. With a snicker, he turned his back and walked several steps away from her and out the doorway. CeCe used the opportunity to take in her surroundings. She was in some sort of basement. There were small windows, like a home's foundation, and by the looks of the amount of junk and boxes that surrounded her in the small room; it must be a much older home. A creak sounded from above her.

Someone is up there! CeCe screamed, "HELP ME! Troy Mitchell is holding me prisoner!"

Troy reappeared, the smile on his face was one of irony, "You might want to save your breath, she is," indicating with his finger the floor above their heads, "deaf as a doornail."

His words confused her, but she complied when she saw the scissors in his hands.

Come on, CeCe; keep your head in the game. Keep him talking.

"Why are you doing this, Troy? Why me, after all these years?"

"Because I needed beautiful and expensive things to capture your attention. I always spent my money on you, in one form or another, so what better way to show you I'm the same guy you were in love with then, than to remain the same now."

I never liked those things, I was the happiest when you would let me sketch you and we spent time together. Jeez did he even really know her at all then?

"The truth of the matter is I need you, CeCe. I came up with a way to offer surveillance to companies to ensure employee loyalty. It requires very minimal additional hardware to most securities systems, which you and muscle dude know, considering you found the camera feed in your store, but still, even after its brilliance, it's acceptance has not gotten off the ground. I did everything I was supposed to do. I made all the right connections in Los Angeles, yet still nothing. I've sunk every dollar I have into it, as well as most of my Mother's money, and then it dawned on me, I needed something that would get me noticed. *You!* I knew if I called you, and told you my intentions, you would snub me. No one takes me seriously because of my looks. I mean if anyone could relate to that feeling, you should be able to, after all that is what everyone thought when you and I were together."

"Is that a fact?" CeCe asked, but he continued as if she didn't say anything.

"No one can reject me, especially if I have you back on my arm. You see, I figured it all out; I can make something of myself if people know I've kept you in line. They won't even think of rejecting me if they know what I truly am, and that is the most popular guy."

Holy crackpot! "You are insane!"

"Don't call me that!" Troy bellowed, making CeCe jump. She watched as sweat beaded at his temples, and stains began to appear under his shirtsleeves. She watched as he breathed deeply, like in a Lamaze class, he must of thought it had cleansed him enough as he began to speak again, "But regardless, CeCe, you shouldn't speak to me like that. I am your man; you should respect me, always; obedience in its biblical form. You see, I think that is where we went wrong when we broke up."

"Broke up? You pushed me out of a car, Asshole!"

The slap wasn't hard, but just enough to stop the words flowing from her mouth.

"See what you made me do?" Troy became agitated; his extremities shook as he paced the tiny room like a caged animal. He spoke to himself quietly. CeCe couldn't make out the words, but she knew it was the same words he repeated them to himself, over and over again. Just as quickly as he digressed, he stopped and turned back to face her, "Now, as I was saying, once you see that I'm right, we can forego this whole unpleasant, restraining thing; unless, of course, you like that kind of stuff?"

The implications of his last reference had her stomach curdling and threatening to spill out of her mouth. With the thought of being sick, thoughts of Kelleigh rushed into her brain. *Oh my God! Troy is the one that did that to Kelleigh. He used her to get in to connect to the security system.* Suddenly, sympathy for Kelleigh rose tenfold for having been subjected to this asshat.

"Why did you use Kelleigh?" CeCe asked. At the mention of her name, Troy just smirked.

"Figured out that connection, did you?" He raised his hand to his face; using the side of his index finger, he rubbed his chin back and forth. The sound of the five o'clock shadow being scraped by his dry skin sounded like nails on a chalkboard to her. "Once I decided I needed to put my plan into action, I needed a way into your store. It wasn't hard to watch her and know she was the key to my entrance, a swamp donkey trolling for a carrot. Showed her some interest and she was eating right out of the palm of my hand. I played the part perfectly, if I do say so myself."

"I know what you did to her! You really are a sick fuck! How could you?"

Her accusation didn't seem to phase Troy; he just shrugged his shoulder and answered, "Collateral damage. For such a fugly girl, you think she would be just happy to have a man, but no, all she did was want to talk and shit. When she questioned my disappearance for those days I followed you to Boston, I just snapped."

I want to snap YOU!

CeCe's heart broke for the pain Kelleigh had yet to go through when she found out his identity and his true reason for courting her.

"But don't fret, Cees, don't feel sorry for her. Oh well, maybe you should, you are stealing her man after all."

"Like I said, you're a sick fuck! What makes you think I'm going to go along with any of this, Troy?" His face showed the strain her resistance caused. He actually thought she would just hop up and agree? *Fat chance!* "As crazy as you are, there is no way you actually think I would even consider this."

"Well, then I guess we go with plan B," he said simply.

"And that would be what?"

"That would be, I hope you are comfortable, you're going to remain down here until you do agree. I've worked too hard in life to be back in this God-awful town. You're the clean slate I need for my plan to work; for my life to go forward."

Selfish then, self-centered always, he just upgraded to kidnapping now.

"Okay, I think that is enough for now, I need to go check on Mother, make sure she takes her medication. I can't have that pain in the ass meddling in what I'm doing. Dosing her is much easier."

Such cruelty to his own mother, he truly was a sociopath. CeCe was rendered speechless at his off-handed explanation of how he could condone such a sin. As she processed his inability to think like a decent human being, Troy walked out of the room he was keeping her in, closed the door, and CeCe listened as the lock turned.

CeCe's wrists were raw from all the attempts she made of getting free. She was parched from the heat in the tiny room, and she really needed to use the bathroom. She didn't know how long Troy had left her down here, but considering it was night when she was taken from her apartment, and the light outside was becoming dimmer, it must have been closing in on twenty hours.

The locked clicked then, and she held her breath.

"Miss me, Sweetheart?"

"Yeah, like a root canal." CeCe said clearly.

"You really are making this much harder on yourself." He chastised, as he maliciously took a sip of water without even offering her some.

FUCKER!

"Why the white roses, Troy?"

He nursed the drink for another few moments before draining the glass and wiping the condensation from the cool glass against his forehead, he smiled at her before he answered. "I wanted the perfect equivalent. The white rose represents your pristine appearance, and your virtuous state." He looked at her as he answered, and of all he has said to her so far, these were honest words. His eyes changed, it almost looked as if he had a regret.

"You do know I'm not a virgin, Troy!"

Troy walked to the door a few feet away, turned and leaned back against it and spoke solemnly, "I know, and I am not happy about it, but I'm willing to forgive you for that, as long as you are mine now. See, CeCe, I can be reasonable."

The door was shoved open, Troy flew into the pile of boxes in front of him, hitting his head and landing on all fours.

"Reasonable? Don't know where you learned the definition of the word, but your Mama needs a refund for that screwed up piece of education, Fucktard!"

Jarod!

He stepped over Troy's huddled form; retrieving a knife from his pocket, he leaned around CeCe cutting the zip ties and freeing her arms.

"You okay, Kitten?" Jarod lifted her so she stood, as he examined her from head to toe.

"Yeah, I'm good…just…WATCH OUT!" CeCe yelled as she tried to warn Jarod, but she wasn't fast enough, and Troy stabbed the scissors through his left shoulder.

Jarod let out a howl, but remained on his feet, "Seriously, Dude?" Jarod kicked out his leg backwards, connecting with Troy's groin. He grumbled as he slid to the floor, holding his package, lying in the fetal position.

CeCe stared at the scissors sticking out of Jarod, "Oh my God!"

"Close your eyes, Kitten," Jarod clenched his teeth together, and with a groan he pulled the scissors up and out. CeCe watched, wide-eyed. "When are you ever going to listen?"

CeCe moved her eyes from his shoulder to his eyes and just stared at him. She knew the question was meant for her watching, but it reminded her of their last conversation, and all the things he told her.

"Come on, let's get out of here." Jarod ushered CeCe out through the cellar door he had successfully picked.

By the time they reached the front yard, Max and four cruisers pulled up, along with Dylan and Natalie.

Once Dylan and Natalie hugged her, and ensured she was all right, Max needed to take hers and Jarod's statements. Wrapped up in the retelling of what occurred CeCe was unaware Jarod removed himself from her side, while Natalie held her hand the entire time. Commotion came from behind them and they watched as three officers carried Troy out of the basement, as he claimed he couldn't walk.

CeCe was in the middle of arguing with the EMT who arrived that she didn't need to be checked out, when Derrick pulled up. Given all the cars, he had to park a bit away, but she heard him call to her as he ran toward her. CeCe looked to Dylan, who had never ventured far from her, and silently questioned him.

"I didn't call him," Dylan said, looking just as bewildered.

When Derrick reached CeCe, he immediately embraced her. He then lifted his hands to her face as he kissed her lips and said, "I died three times over when Gates called me."

At the mention of Jarod, CeCe turned and noticed Jarod was no longer there. She craned her head looking this way and that way, but coming up with no sign of him. Her eyes continued to search through the commotion and chaos of the scene and then she saw him walking away—from the scene and from her. With a cry trapped in her throat she watched as he climbed into his truck. Their eyes met for a moment, but then he looked away. She watched as he pulled away and all the while until his truck vanished from sight.

Suddenly, the floodgates opened, and tears poured down her face.

It was Derrick that caught them, "Oh baby, let them fall, you must have been so scared," he crooned as he held her.

But as CeCe buried her face in his chest she knew this wasn't the chest she wanted to be leaning into, nor would tears be falling if she were touching that chest.

Twenty-Five

"Thanks for meeting me, Gates, you are a hard man to track down," Max said as he indicated the seat opposite him in the small diner where he was having lunch.

"Jesus, man you are worse than a teenage girl, you blew up my voicemail with all your messages." Jarod complained as he sat down and waved off the waitress that tried to take his order.

"Be that as it may, I just wanted to take this opportunity to thank you for all your help. Mitchell has been arrested for kidnapping and aggravated harassment. The judge insisted on holding him without bail for a psych eval, should not be hard to get a conviction. I received all the documentation from your guy, Ryder, on the IP address and dummy companies Mitchell worked under. How dumb can one man be to link everything, including his system passwords, to his Mother's address? Then, the kicker is that's where he took Ms. Cervetti, what a dumbass."

Jarod's face remained unchanged, "Yeah, tied up nice and neat for you with a perfect bow, congrats, Lieutenant. Is that all?"

Max took a sip of his coffee before responding, "Not exactly, there is one more thing," Max pointed to the counter.

Jarod turned his attention to his right, and Natalie Cross smiled back at him. She hopped down and thanked Max, who got up and walked right out the door. Natalie slid in Max's vacated seat.

"Hi, Jarod. I'm sorry I had Max lure you here, but you would not return mine, or Dylan's calls."

Jarod didn't deny her claim.

Natalie slid her hand into her bag and pulled out a somewhat thick letter sized manila envelope, "Dylan wanted me to give this to you; it's your fee for your services."

Jarod's eyes never wavered from hers, letting Natalie just hold out the envelope until she placed it on the table between them.

"You've earned it, Jarod, please take it."

"Look, Natalie, I appreciate it, but put it away for Cat and Ria. Dylan did something for me way back when, this was me just repaying the debt."

Jarod placed his hands on the table, and pushed upward starting to stand, but Natalie's plea halted him, "Please don't go, Jarod, I promise I won't take much more of your time." Whether it was the sweet look Natalie perfected, or her small voice, Jarod didn't know, but he found himself sitting back down. "How's your shoulder?"

"It's fine, Natalie, nothing I can't handle."

Natalie nodded her head and then finished, "The last thing I wanted to tell you was their plane left this morning for Napa. I'm sorry, Jarod."

It felt like he had been punched square in the throat.

"Good for her, Lowell should give her a good life."

"Don't do that!"

"I don't know what you mean, Natalie," he spoke knowing she saw right through his boldfaced lie.

"I mean, don't lay down like a dog. This isn't what CeCe wants!"

"Did she tell you that?

"No, but…"

"But nothing, she chose. Now, I really must be going."

Jarod stood, ignoring the pain from his leg and shoulder as he walked out of the diner into the August sun. He put his aviator glasses on to block out the brilliant sunlight, but he knew it was really to hide the tears that threatened to spill over.

Four Weeks Later...

"This better be good!" Jarod shouted as he made his way to whoever was pounding on his front door. He opened the door, ready to unleash his fury on the inconsiderate asshole that would pound on someone's door at 2AM, but when he saw CeCe, all he wanted to say floated away.

"Kitten?"

"Can I come in?" CeCe asked with a quivering voice.

Jarod pushed the door open allowing her to enter before closing it behind her. Wondering for a moment if he was in a dream, but she passed him and her delicious scent surrounded him and he knew this was no dream. It was weird having her here in his home. Suddenly, he was self-conscience of the clutter and dirty dishes left about. He watched as she took in his private space. The classic farmhouse didn't scream masculinity, but Jarod prided himself on all the work he had done. He knew there was still a lot to do, but when Jarod wasn't working, he found satisfaction in bringing back the charm from the past with his own hands. The concentration of working with his hands, and bringing this home back to its glory, helped him deal with the demons that had returned with vengeance. Especially since his walking talisman was no longer near.

As she studied his home, he chose to study how her legs looked amazing in the skintight jeans she wore, and how odd it was to see her in sneakers, but he liked it. The simple black v-neck t-shirt she wore was feminine and simple, not that CeCe ever looked bad in anything, but right now she looked like a walking wet dream to him, the problem was she belonged to Lowell, her soon-to-be husband. That thought had him clearing his throat, bringing her out of her exaggerated perusal of his home.

And then CeCe did the last thing Jarod thought was possible, she launched herself at him, jumping up holding onto him by the neck as she wrapped her legs around his waist. His leg buckled under her weight and the unexpected movement, but he recovered quickly. She touched his lips with her own and kissed him with everything she had.

Jarod was unable to fight her, not because of strength or dignity, but because this was what he wanted, what he needed, her taste one last time. It would never be enough, but it would have to be. In the moment, he could pretend she was his, but that was all it could be—a false tale for him to justify his pathetic lack of willpower.

"I can't do this!" Jarod pulled away from her delectable mouth, and put her back down on the ground. He spun in place, trying to gain control and considered himself the biggest idiot on the planet for stopping CeCe's kiss. He turned back to her, placing his hands on her shoulders, holding her in place so she would have to hear his words, "I promised you I would leave you alone, but I can't. I have to say this; don't marry Lowell. You can't marry him; I can't lose you again. I can't!" He didn't care that he was begging. If getting down on his knees would put any favor in his corner, he would do it without a seconded thought. "You belong to me. You belong *with* me. I will spend every minute, of every day, showing you this. I fucked up badly, I know, but I just can't live without you. Please don't take my reason for getting up in the morning away from me. Until he puts a wedding band on your finger, I can't lose hope." He didn't care that the water pooling in his eyes began to run down his cheeks. This was his life. If this wasn't worth fighting for, nothing was. His voice cracked and he was unable to speak above a whisper, "It's all I have left! It's all I've had for thirteen years. It was the only thing that has given me the strength to want to open my eyes every morning of these thirteen years."

CeCe began to cry, but her smile confused him. She stuck her left hand up so he could see her third finger was bare.

Jarod didn't dare say what raced through his mind.

Now it was time for CeCe's smile to fade, "I'm a horrible person.

Horrible for what I've done to you, but also for what I did to Derrick. I got on the plane with him, knowing why he was bringing me there, and I still went. He made every effort to impress me and it was a beautiful proposal, but I just couldn't accept. I never thought I would want to be asked the question, but then, recently, I decided I did want to hear those words. I wanted someone to ask me to make them whole, to take his name and wear it proudly. I wanted that, but then, when I saw him down on one knee, I knew…"

"You've changed your mind," Jarod whispered the excruciating hit to his hopes knowing this meant it was over. She would never belong to him.

"The wrong man was asking me," CeCe whispered back, waiting for her words to register.

When he finally realized what she said, he lifted her off the floor and into the most wonderful hug. It was filled with promises and of emotion. The ultimate embrace of two lovers, but also of a man and his wife; nothing compared.

"I love you, Jarod. It has always been you, it will always only ever be you."

Those words would forever be tattooed in his memory and across his heart. She was his. Jarod claimed her lips and kissed her with everything he possessed. He had years to make up for, and there was no time like the present to do just that.

Jarod made quick work of her clothes; soon she was bared to him and lying on his couch, the closest soft horizontal surfaces. With the biggest smiled spread across his face, he brushed the hair off her face and looked at the woman that meant everything to him, "I guess we need to go ring shopping."

"No need to rush that, Jarod, I can wait."

"No way you're waiting, no other man, Cees, I'm not joking. That means I need my ring on your finger as soon as possible. Trust me, Kitten, I'm more than enough for you, and I'll prove it." Jarod leaned down and once again took possession of her mouth. His hands began to play her like a fine tuned instrument. Her moans answered each of his finger's movements, she panted his name and he loved every moment of it. Just when he knew her to be close to purring like her pet name, he pulled away

"What's the matter," she asked breathless.

"Wait, what took you so long to come to me?" His eyes searched hers, needing to hear why she kept him in agony.

A faint blush overtook her cheeks as she looked downward, but then just as quickly she looked into his eyes holding them with her own, "I needed to be sure this was right."

"I hate that you were doubtful. I love you CeCe. Always. I'll spend every day proving it to you. I want to show you I am worthy of your love and of you."

Would she ever believe the amount of love he had for her?

Just as he thought it, she answered it, "You are not only worthy of me, you deserve better. I had to do some deep soul-searching to confirm I was worthy of you."

Oh my Kitten, how I love you. His smile spread across his face and knew life with this woman would be nothing short of amazing. He leaned down and kissed her communicating without words. Just as she clung to him and ground herself against him, he once again pulled away. He stood up and held his hand out to her.

With the smile she loved shining down on her, she accepted her clothes back as he handed them to her. When she was dressed again, she raised her eyebrow expecting an explanation before she voiced her confusion, "I thought you were going to prove something to me?"

"I will, but we have a drive to take first."

"A drive? Where are we going?"

Holding her hand, he led her to the front door, and before he pulled it open, he kissed her lips, "There is a stretch of secluded woods I haven't been to in thirteen years. It was where I made love to the only woman I've ever loved. I'd like to do it again, but this time, I'll take my time, and appreciate every moment, every moan, and every touch because there is no way this will be the end, it is just the beginning of the rest of our lives."

"Then what are we waiting for?"

Epilogue

Fourteen Months Later…

"So you have everything? You only get one shot at this." Dylan asked for the umpteenth time.

"Yes! I have everything! Do you really think CeCe would've let me get this far without having everything?" Jarod chastised, but secretly ran through the mental list again.

"Good point!" Dylan agreed, knowing his honorary sister would never not have everything planned on such a special day.

Each man grabbed a door handle as they swung the venue's double doors open. Beyond those doors was complete pandemonium. People everywhere, clothes racks here and there, models in chairs being plucked, tweezed, primped, and God only knew what else, by the look of them. Jarod felt his face redden at the proud and unabashed women that walked around, pretty damn close to nude.

"Damn!" Dylan mumbled behind him.

Jarod turned on his friend; unable to believe a man so in love with his spouse would enjoy the view so much "You know, your wife is around here, somewhere."

Dylan smacked Jarod upside the head, "Who the hell do you think I'm looking at? It took CeCe a lot to talk Natalie into being one of the models, but once she explained to my wife she wanted her to wear the dress that meant so much in our relationship, Natalie couldn't say no. But, damn! I'll never get used to my wife's beauty. Excuse me."

Jarod chuckled at himself for his stupid assumption as he watched Dylan walk over to where a very beautiful Natalie sat, nervous, but lovely in some sort of classy yet very sexy dress. But she wasn't who Jarod was desperate to see.

Just then he heard her voice, dictating instructions, and he saw her head going a mile-a-minute. He started to make his way to her, but he was snagged on the arm by a warm hand.

"Oh no! She is busy and has given me strict instructions to usher you out to your seat. She knew you would not listen and stay out there, letting me come and retrieve the items she wanted." the redhead motioned for him to go out the way he came in.

"Kelleigh, let me just talk to her for a moment, then I will be the abiding husband and take my seat."

Kelleigh laughed, "You will have to try that smoldering look on someone else, I'm immune to it by now. Out!"

Jarod knew he wouldn't get any farther if guard-dog Kelleigh was onto his scent. He went to out to his seat and accepted the congratulations by all the people around him. He wasn't used to being congratulated for something he had nothing to do with, but he only could tell someone what an amazing designer his wife was so many times.

Forty-five minutes later, all the models returned to the stage as the room erupted with cheers. After everyone was on their feet, CeCe emerged from behind the curtain, glowing, as she stood amongst all the beautiful models, all wearing Cecille Gates Designs.

"How come I didn't look like that when I was eight months pregnant?" Mae said to Seth from their seats behind Jarod. He didn't wait around to hear Seth's response.

Jarod reached down and grabbed the two things he brought that his wife didn't tell him to have, and made his way to the side stairs leading to the runway. With the room still filled with applause and wolf whistles, Jarod climbed the stairs and took his place next to his wife.

He spoke loud to ensure she would hear him, "Feeling okay, Kitten? Our little Butterball is okay, too?" he asked indicating their unborn child.

"I'm perfect. We are both perfect. I did it. My first show!"

"You did, Kitten!" Jarod kissed her cheek, before pulling the long stemmed calla lily from its hiding spot behind his back. He bowed to her as he presented it to her. More cheers erupted from the crowd. Tears welled in his wife's beautiful eyes. It didn't take her long to see the necklace that was tied to the green ribbon.

CeCe's eyes met Jarod's and, as if there weren't three hundred people in the audience, he took the chain from its ribbon and stood behind his wife, draping the three hearts pendant onto her neck where he clasped it closed. CeCe fingered the yellow and white gold hearts that wrapped around each other, infinitely connected before dipping down into a smaller, third heart made of diamonds, signifying their yet to be born son. He then kissed his wife with all that he had, knowing this was exactly how his life was supposed to be.

Out of the broken pieces of one's life comes a stronger and impenetrable hold on one's respect and gratitude for every day you're allowed to live your dream, wide awake.

The End

Turn the page for a preview of
Shelter You
By
Alice Montalvo-Tribue

Shelter You

by

Alice Montalvo-Tribue

"I can only give you thirty minutes to get out of here before I have to report it to my supervisors that you're gone. The clothes I brought for you are in the closet over there," she says, pointing to a long closet built into the wall.

It reminds me of a high school locker, long and narrow. At the age of 17, I've become very familiar with those lockers, having used them all throughout my years in school and they were great years, happy years, right up until the end. It's hard to believe that just a few months ago I was graduating high school, Miss Popular, top of my class, my pick of universities. To everyone on the outside looking in, it appeared that I had my whole future ahead of me. The perfect life, great grades, an amazing family, the world was my oyster. Little did they know that my future had already been decided, mapped out and planned for me. None of which I had any say in, none of which I was comfortable with.

I turn my attention back to the tall gangly woman in front of me. She's unnaturally thin, but I can almost see the attractiveness there, that she might have been beautiful once upon a time. Her blond hair is coarse, straw like and brittle, and her glasses are too big for her face, but I don't care about any of that. To me, right now she's an angel. A real live angel sent down to help me get out of an impossible situation.

"Besides clothes I was able to get you all of the basic supplies you'll need. It's not much, but it'll get you by until you can afford to buy more," she says, as I nod.

"When I leave this room, pick up the phone and call the operator. Ask for a volunteer to bring a wheelchair up to your room because you are being discharged. Once she comes up, tell her that your car is already waiting and that you need her to wheel you to the east entrance. Show her your hospital bracelet. It matches Lily's so you'll be fine; she won't know any better. She'll ask if you have a car seat, so just tell her that it's already in the car."

My heart starts to beat faster as I listen to her directions. Am I really doing this? Am I strong enough, brave enough to defy my parents, go against their wishes?

"The taxi driver will be waiting for you. His name is Seth, he's a friend of my husband's. He'll take you to the bank first. Take out every single penny that is in your savings account and then have him take you to the bus station. Take the first bus out of here, Mia. Leave your cell phone behind and get a pre paid one the first chance you get. You'll be eighteen in one month, and at that time you can call and request a copy of Lily's birth certificate. This way, even if they can track you, they can't legally force you to come back.

It takes me a minute, but I finally find my voice. "I don't know how I can ever repay you for this."

"No one should be forced to give up their child; it's wrong. Just promise me you'll be a good mom and that you'll call me if you need anything at all."

I look up at her with tears in my eyes. If not for this kind woman I'd be handing Lily over to her adoptive parents in a matter of hours. It may seem cruel of me to have promised to give my baby away to a couple who desperately wants one and then to just pick up and run away but none of this was my choice. Four months before my high school graduation I found out that I was pregnant. As you can probably imagine for a seventeen year old to hear that she's going to become a mother is shocking and scary. So I did what I thought would be the right thing, I went to my parents and asked for their help. Their solution? Hide my pregnancy until after graduation and then keep me a virtual prisoner in my own home until I gave birth. When I expressed to them my desire to keep my child they gave me an ultimatum: Give the baby up for adoption, or keep the baby but leave their house with absolutely no financial help from them. What else could I have done? I had no choice but to agree to their demands and I thought I could do it. I thought I could go through with it until I held her, my Lily, and I knew that giving her away would literally kill me—would make it difficult to go on with the knowledge that she was out there in the world somewhere, living a life apart from mine. And because of this I made her a promise and I'll die before I break that promise. I'll die before I ever let her go.

Nurse Kelly's plan went down exactly the way she said it would. The volunteer that came up to take Lily and I out to the car barely checked that our bracelets matched before she helped me into the wheelchair and took me down to the exit where the cab was waiting for me. Seth, the driver helped get Lily in the car seat and then got us the hell out of there as fast as he could. He took me to my house and after verifying that my parents weren't there, I ran inside. After packing some more clothes, all of my important documents and some cash that I had stored in my desk, I took one last look at my childhood bedroom and left.

Seth quickly took me to the bank where I was able to liquidate my entire savings account, a little over ten thousand dollars that I had been saving ever since I could remember. Every single dollar I'd ever been given from birthday and Christmas presents and from working at the local ice cream shop every summer was now in my backpack. Seth thought it would be a good idea to take me to a bus station a couple towns over. I wasn't about to let anyone find me now that I had come this far, so I hopped on the first available bus out of state heading to Savannah Georgia, and told myself that once I got there I could stop for the night and make a decision on where to go next.

I've been traveling for about five hours now. We stopped earlier in Jacksonville, Florida, for about an hour—giving me just enough time to hide in a large bathroom stall to feed Lily in private and grab a bite to eat for myself. I'm terrified that she might start crying and disturb the other passengers on the bus, but the continuous motion seems to help her sleep. I close my eyes and wonder how I'm going to make this work, how I'm going to be able to take care of Lily without any help. The truth behind my situation is daunting. How will I know what she needs, why she's crying, how to get her on a sleeping and feeding schedule? Will I know what to do and how to take care of her when she gets sick? What will I do for childcare when I find a job? The thoughts overwhelm me but I try not to panic. I have to keep it together for Lily, because I have to believe that a life with me is better for her than any life she could have had without me.

It's a little after ten at night when we finally arrive in Savannah. I gather Lily and my belongings and grab a taxi cab. I tell the driver to take us to the most affordable hotel in the area and a little while later he drops us off at an inn right on Bay Street. It's much too dark to explore outdoors but from what I can tell, it's gorgeous here, someplace I'd love to come back and visit one day. When I reach the front desk the clerk eyes me suspiciously as she checks me in but mercifully doesn't ask me any questions. I pay for my room in cash, grab my room key, and hop on the elevator. I get to my room as quickly as I can.

I can't help but to feel exposed when I'm out in the open, as if by some off chance someone might recognize me.

I change Lily's diaper and put her in a pink one piece pajama, turn down the bed and crawl in with her. I lie on my side with her snuggled close and offer her my breast. Kelly showed me what to do that first night after my parents had left for the evening. I remember being grossed out initially but I wanted to be able to feed her even if it was only one time. To be able to give her even just a small piece of me was important, it felt right. I'm thankful that I did it now because given my limited resources nursing her seems to be the most cost effective way to keep her fed. It doesn't take long for me to give into the exhaustion, my eyes start to get heavy and before I know it I'm asleep.

I was looking forward to at least taking in a few of the sites in Savannah but fear of being found or recognized kept me a virtual prisoner in my hotel room. We stayed for two days and then hopped the midnight bus to Richmond, Virginia. We stopped a few hours into the trip in North Carolina and then drove straight through the remainder of the night; thankfully Lily slept most of the way but I sat in the back of the bus and when she woke up for her feeding I was able to cover her up with a blanket and nurse her privately. It helped that almost everyone on the bus was asleep.

The hotel in Virginia is not quite as nice as the one in Georgia but it's safe, clean and affordable. I allow myself to wander around Richmond a bit more than I did in Savannah, but I keep to myself and keep my head down most of the time. I find a small pharmacy near the hotel where I pick up diapers, baby wipes, infant Tylenol just in case of an unexpected emergency, a pair of scissors and two boxes of brown hair dye. If anyone is looking for Lily and me we'll be a lot harder to recognize if I alter my appearance and making my hair darker seems like the easiest way.

"Well isn't this a beautiful baby." I look up and see an elderly woman standing behind me in the line to pay.

I instantly tense up, and go on alert. Maybe I'm paranoid. I mean, it's only a little old lady but I can't be too careful. I'm not sure if there's anyone out there looking for me. I don't know if the police were called, if the media was alerted, or if a reward was offered, but I certainly wouldn't put anything past my parents.

"Thank you," I respond quietly, never actually looking at her and hoping that she'll just leave me alone.

"Is she yours dear?" She questions, just as the person ahead of me is done paying for his items. I ignore her and quickly move up, putting my things on the counter and paying for my purchases as fast as possible. I get the hell out of there and back to the hotel in record time.

Lily begins to cry and I know that she must be hungry because she's just woken up so she can't be sleepy and her diaper is dry. I lie down in the king size bed with her and feed her until she falls asleep again. Strange as it may seem these moments with her calm me down, they give me the reassurance I need that running away was worth it. I'm beginning to feel more and more confident with her, like maybe I can do this, make this work with her and be a good mom. I think about the things I'll have to give up, the things that I have already given up—my friends, enjoying my youth. I know I should be out doing the things that normal kids my age do, partying, dating, living the college life but all of those things were taken away from me and replaced with this life instead and the thing of it is, I'm okay with that. Yes, I'm young, inexperienced and I know that making the decision to keep Lily will never be the easy choice. But when it came down to it, when I was given the option, it was the only choice.

I look different as a brunette, I barely recognize myself when I look in the mirror. I feel better to a certain degree now that I've changed my hair, coloring and cutting it shoulder length, my long blond locks were always my signature look so it will take some getting used to for me but it's what I need to do to keep my anonymity. After weighing out my options, I decided that I prefer traveling at night when there aren't many people out and about. Lily and I left the hotel in Virginia and hopped on our next bus at three o' clock in the morning driving through the night and stopping at eight the next morning in Baltimore Maryland. I decide to stop here for the night and let myself get some rest before catching my final bus into Pennsylvania. I'm not sure why I'm drawn there of all places, it was just a random choice plus it's a big enough state that I can hopefully just blend into.

By the time Lily and I finally reach our final destination, a small Pennsylvania town about forty five minutes outside of New York City, I'm exhausted but grateful that we made it here without getting caught. It's early fall and the colors of the trees here are stunning. I've never seen anything quite like it; the brilliant orange and red leaves fill the streets and it makes me glad that I chose this as the place for Lily and I to start our new lives together. I get us settled into a hotel and snuggle up close to her after feeding and changing her surprised at how connected I feel to her. Yes, she's my daughter and instinctively there should be a bond there, but I was so prepared to let her go, give her up to make my life less complicated. Looking at her now, I know that she's the kind of complication I wouldn't trade for the world. No matter how unexpectedly she was created. I close my eyes and rest. I know that I'll be up at least two times tonight to feed her and I need to be up early, I'm planning on beginning my search for an apartment first thing in the morning. Before long both Lily and I are fast asleep.

I don't know why I thought that finding an apartment would be easy. We don't need much room for now, a studio or a one bedroom apartment will work. I've been searching for days but the places I've seen within my budget dangle on the disgusting and unsafe side.

I'm running out of hope by the time I go to see the last apartment on my list. It's on a busier street but the building is clean and well maintained. A tall and slender middle aged woman meets me out front. She looks at me as if though she's surprised someone as young as me is here alone with a baby and looking for an apartment. I can tell she's not judging me, I think she's probably more concerned than anything else. She stares at me for a second with her kind eyes.

"Are you Kelly?" She questions.

I didn't want to give anyone my real name in case my family really is looking for me. When I called to set up appointments I used the first name that popped into my head, Kelly, the name of the nurse who helped me get myself and Lily out of the hospital. "Yes, I'm Kelly. You must be Janet."

She extends her hand and I reach out and take it. "Yes, I'm Janet."

She shakes my hand and quickly releases it. "Thank you for meeting me today."

"Of course. Come on in and I'll show you the apartment." She opens the front door and allows me to walk in ahead of her. "It's just down the hall and to your left."

When we reach the door she puts the key in the door, turning the knob but stopping just before she opens. "I'm sorry Kelly, I don't mean to pry but what is a young girl like you doing looking for an apartment? Shouldn't you be at home with your family?"

I know she means well but I'm not prepared to answer this question. I answer the best way I can on the spot and what I come up with is not a complete lie, just an altered version of the truth. "My family kicked me out when I got pregnant. I was staying with a friends family but it's time for me to find a place of my own."

"Oh honey, I'm so sorry to hear that. Forgive me for asking." She pushes the door open and allows me to walk through.

"It's alright. I understand what it must look like, an eighteen year old and a baby." I give her a small smile and quickly walk away from her, moving to stand in the middle of a small living room. I look around at the bare white walls and though it's small, it's by far the nicest place I've seen. It's sparsely furnished with a worn old blue couch and chair.

"The bedroom is through that door over there," she says pointing to my left. "It's pretty spacious…big enough to fit a full size bed and a crib for the little one."

I try not to read into it but her words give me hope. "Does that mean you'll rent it to me?"

"We normally require a credit check but I'm assuming since you're so young you haven't built up much of a credit rating?"

"Yes ma'am."

"And you have no furniture?"

"Not yet, no ma'am."

"And can you afford the security deposit and first months rent?"

"Yes I can."

"Alright then, I have the lease with me, if you want the apartment it's yours. You can use the furniture that's here too if you'd like and I'm pretty sure I have some old baby things that you can use. I don't live too far away. I can have my husband drop it off and set it up this weekend."

I look up at her wide eyed, stunned and seriously trying not to cry. "I don't know how to thank you. I promise you I won't be any trouble."

She simply smiles and nods at me.

By the time I leave the building, I have a lease, a set of keys, and permission to move in right away. I grab my belongings, and check out of the hotel. By nightfall Lily and I are all moved into our new apartment.

It's been almost a month since Lily and I ran away from the hospital in Florida. I remember how scared I was when I took my baby and hopped on that first bus. I remember thinking that I would never be able to take care of her on my own. I have to admit that being a mom and taking care of an infant is hard work. There are times when I feel lost and alone, there are days when I'm exhausted and wish I could take just a few hours away for myself but that isn't possible right now and being able to raise Lily makes it worth it. I'm merely a few days away from my eighteenth birthday and I'm certain that our life will be so much easier when that happens. For starters, I can stop lying about my name, about my story. I'll be able to get a job and find childcare and use my real name. No one will be able to come and take Lily away from me once that happens. In the meantime, I came across a free clinic where I was able to take Lily to get her first vaccinations. Sticking to a budget hasn't been too difficult. The apartment's utilities are included in the rent, I have basic cable which consists of about twenty channels, and that's enough for me for now. Since I'm still breastfeeding and I've never been a heavy eater, I've only had to go to the grocery store a couple of times.

The day after I moved in, Janet's husband dropped off an infant swing, highchair, play yard and a simple stroller for Lily. I honestly couldn't believe it but he explained that the items had been sitting unused and collecting dust in the basement. He actually thanked me for taking it off of their hands. I'm almost positive that he was just trying to make me feel better about having to take the handout but I'm grateful nonetheless. These are the things that I didn't think about when I left, taking Lily and virtually disappearing into thin air and even though I still have the majority of my money I know that it won't last forever. I need to find my way and take care of Lily at the same time.

At this time last year life was so different, the biggest decision I had to make was choosing which universities to apply to. My dream had always been to go to NYU and live in the city, finally free to live and experience everything that life had to offer. I never imagined that I'd end up pregnant and alone, without my family or any of my friends to lean on for support. I try not to get sad when I think about the dreams and the goals that I had set for myself, I try to look on the bright side but life has dealt me an unfair hand and I can't help but to feel sorry for myself at times.

Lily's screeching cry pulls me out of my head, I get up off of the couch that I've been lounging on for most of the afternoon and pad over to the play yard. I scoop her up into my arms and gently rock her back and forth. I fed her less than an hour ago and her diaper is dry. I continue rocking her for awhile with no luck. Her cries get progressively worse and before long I'm genuinely worried that there's something wrong with her. I try feeding her again but she's having none of it. I reach for my phone, thinking for a split second that I can call my mom and ask her what to do. If anyone would know what I should do it would be her, but then I realize that I can't do that. She didn't want anything to do with my child and because of it forced me to take matters into my own hands. The truth of my life is that there's no one that I can call for advice at a time like this, and normally that would make me sad, but right now all I can focus on is Lily. I quickly call a cab, pack up her diaper bag, and bundle her up. When the driver arrives, I instruct him to take us to the nearest hospital.

I check us in at the emergency room, telling the girl at the front desk that I was so nervous I'd forgotten my identification. I know enough about the law to know that a hospital can't refuse emergency treatment so I feel confident with my excuse.

We're sitting in the waiting room for what seems like an eternity. Lily is still crying and my nerves are now frayed. I'm barely holding it together.

The emergency room doors open and a couple of paramedics are wheeling in a young man on a stretcher. He looks as if he's been beaten badly. They take him to the back immediately, which only serves to further frustrate me about my long wait. I walk over to the front desk again and question the receptionist.

"Can you please tell me how much longer it's going to be before we're seen? We've been here for over an hour."

"There's a few patients in front of you. You'll just have to wait," she answers me shortly.

I go to speak, but before I can she plasters a fake smile on her face and bats her eyelashes. "Oh, hi Officer Tate," she says. "How are you?"

I turn my head to where her comment is directed and I'm pretty sure my heart stops momentarily and I'm not sure if it's caused by fear or a totally different emotion. A police officer is walking in our direction and these days I try to avoid them at all costs but one look at this particular cop and my feet are rooted firmly to their spot. I can vaguely hear Lily crying as I take in the sight of him. I know that men of any kind are the last thing I should be thinking about, but his piercing blue eyes draw me in. He looks to be around six feet tall with a tan complexion and hair that's cut low in a military style buzz cut. His full lips are all kinds of sexy and when he looks me dead in the eye it takes every ounce of strength I have to look away.

"Hi, Jennifer. Assault victim brought in a few minutes ago?"

I didn't think it was possible for her smile to get any faker but it does. "Of course," she says, leaning over giving him the maximum view of her boobs and touching his arm in a blatantly obvious attempt to get near him. "They took him back already. He's in bed number ten."

"Thanks." He turns away from her and suddenly he's in my space. "Is she alright?" He questions, motioning to Lily.

His acknowledgement of me makes me both nervous and excited. Yes he's beautiful, sexy and he seems kind but he's still a cop and technically

I'm still a runaway. As much as I'd love to have a conversation with Officer Tate, it's in mine and Lily's best interest if I extrapolate myself from this situation as quickly as possible. "She won't stop crying and I'm worried, but we've been here for a while and still haven't been seen."

He gives me a slow nod and turns back to fake Jennifer. "Isn't there anything you can do to get her seen? Poor thing looks miserable and I'm sure the rest of the people in the waiting room would appreciate a reprieve from a crying baby." He looks back at me. "No offense," he says with a slight grin.

"None taken." I return.

We both turn to face fake Jennifer again. She looks like she's just swallowed a sour pill but quickly plasters on her smile that she clearly reserves only for Officer Tate's benefit. "Well, since you asked so nicely I'm sure I can make an exception for this cute little one." She walks over to the bin of patient files, moves mine to the front and then gives him a wink.

He gives her an equally fake smile and in that moment I can tell that he sees right through her syrupy sweet routine. "I really appreciate it." He pats Lily on the back and then looks back up at me. "I'll check in on you a little later okay?" he asks, and quickly walks away. (Although it sounded more like a statement of fact than anything else.) He wants to check back in on me and Lily? But why? Why would he care whether Lily gets seen by a doctor or not? If she's alright or not? He doesn't know us, has no emotional ties to us, and he doesn't even know our names so why should he care about our well being?

The sound of the privacy curtain being opened startles me. I turn to see Officer Tate standing there. He stares at me for a moment and gives me a timid smile.

"Hey, how's she doing?" He questions quietly.

I look down at Lily, sleeping in the hospital bed and I smile. "She's okay. We're just waiting on the discharge paperwork. The doctor says it was probably just gas." I respond. I look up and our gazes meet.

"Well that's good," he says with a nod.

"Yeah," I say with a light chuckle, shrugging my shoulders. "I guess I should have known that huh?"

He shrugs his shoulders too. "I don't know. You're a new mom, so I think it's understandable."

"I guess," I say, turning away from him.

"Hey," he calls out. There's a strength to his voice, a resolve that I can't help but respond to.

I turn, giving him my full attention again. "You did the right thing. She wasn't acting like her normal self and you made sure you got her checked out. That doesn't make you stupid or naïve it makes you a good mom."

"You don't have to say that. You don't even know me."

"In my line of work I see a lot of things. I know the difference between good and bad, and I promise you, just from what I've seen tonight I know that you're doing a good job."

I sigh, taking his words in, letting them wash over me and sink in. He's right, I may be young and unsure but I'm doing my best and I am a good mom. "Thank you. I appreciate you saying that."

"You're welcome." He walks further into the room and stands at the foot of the bed, looking down at Lily. He opens his mouth to speak but then hesitates, maybe thinking better of saying or asking whatever it is that he wants to say and then just like that he blurts it out. "Where's her dad?" he asks, his eyes never leaving Lily.

I'm silent for some time because really I don't want to talk about this, not with him, not with anyone. Talking about it won't change the facts, won't rewrite history. "He's not around, it's just me."

"I see," he says with a nod.

"But we're fine. We're doing fine on our own," I reply quickly, making myself sound a little bit too defensive.

He crosses his arms across his chest, a move I'm sure he uses to intimidate people. It makes him look like a no nonsense badass cop and it honestly terrifies the shit out of me. "What's your name?"

"Kelly."

He tilts his head to side and his eyes pierce through me. "How old are you, Kelly?"

"I'm eighteen. I recently turned eighteen alright, but like I just told you a second ago, we're fine."

"Are you working?"

"No." I mentally kick myself for being honest. What the hell is wrong with me? I need to be more careful about what information I divulge, especially to him.

"What are you doing for money?"

"I'm using my savings right now. I'm looking for a job but without a babysitter, it's kind of hard." My heart is racing again and I hold onto the railing on the bed because I think I might just faint if I'm not careful. I knew it was a bad idea for me to tell this man anything. A man who's a cop nonetheless. "Look, please don't call child protective services." I'm practically begging him now. "I know I'm young, okay? I get it. And ideally I'd like to have an amazing family by my side, helping me take care of her, but that's not how it worked out for me. My family didn't want anything to do with us so I had to grow up and do the best I can. You said it yourself, I'm a good mom. I'll be fine, I'll make sure that she's fine, and I'll be damned if I'm going to let you or anybody else take Lily away from me."

He looks at me for a minute, probably processing my outburst but he says nothing. He looks unsure of himself which is very different from the confident demeanor he displayed earlier in the evening. He pulls out a notepad and begins to write something down. When he's done he rips the paper out of the pad and hands it to me. "I have a friend who owns a daycare. She may be able to help you, maybe give you a job. I can't make you any promises but this is her number. Tell her I told you to call."

"Oh. Thank you. I…I'm sorry, I just thought…"

"I understand but you have to relax, alright? No one can take Lily away from you if she's not abused or neglected and clearly she's none of those things." He reaches behind him and pulls a card out of his back pocket and hands it to me. Our fingers graze and my body grows warm at his touch. "This is my card. You call me day or night if you need anything Kelly, alright?"

I nod my response, unable to say another word to him. He gives me a slight smile, and as quickly as he appeared he leaves. Yet, he leaves behind just a little bit of hope that maybe I can make a life for myself and Lily here.

www.ingramcontent.com/pod-product-compliance
Lightning Source LLC
Chambersburg PA
CBHW050026180626
46810CB00002B/596